"Do you know something you're not telling me?"

Sure enough, that got her attention.

"Back off," she said, narrowing her eyes.

Marc didn't move. "I'd be a fool not to consider your behavior suspicious."

She was breathing heavily. But what he saw in her smoky gray eyes wasn't just guilt or fear. It was desire.

As her chest rose again, his gaze dropped to her breasts and the hard points of her nipples jutting against the soft cloth.

In that moment, he felt very masculine and powerful.

Dear Reader,

June brings you four high-octane reads from Silhouette Romantic Suspense, just in time for summer. Steaming up your sunglasses is Nina Bruhns's hot romance, *Killer Temptation* (#1516), which is the first of a thrilling new trilogy, SEDUCTION SUMMER. In this series, a serial killer is murdering amorous couples on the beach and no lover is safe. You won't want to miss this sexy roller coaster ride! Stay tuned in July and August for Sheri WhiteFeather's and Cindy Dees's heart-thumping contributions, *Killer Passion* and *Killer Affair.*

USA TODAY bestselling author Marie Ferrarella enthralls readers with *Protecting His Witness* (#1515), the latest in her family saga, CAVANAUGH JUSTICE. Here, an undercover cop crosses paths with a secretive beauty who winds up being a witness to a mob killing. And then, can a single mother escape her vengeful ex *and* fall in love with her protector? Find out in Linda Conrad's *Safe with a Stranger* (#1517), the first book in her miniseries, THE SAFEKEEPERS, which weaves family, witchcraft and danger into an exciting read. Finally, crank up your air-conditioning as brand-new author Jill Sorenson raises temperatures with *Dangerous to Touch* (#1518), featuring a psychic heroine and lawman, who work on a murder case and uncover a wild attraction.

This month is all about finding love against the odds and those adventures lurking around every corner. So as you lounge on the beach or in your favorite chair, lose yourself in one of these gems from Silhouette Romantic Suspense!

Sincerely,

Patience Smith
Senior Editor

JILL SORENSON

Dangerous to Touch

ISBN-13: 978-0-373-27588-5
ISBN-10: 0-373-27588-9

DANGEROUS TO TOUCH

This edition published by arrangement with Harlequin Books S.A.

Visit Silhouette Books at www.eHarlequin.com

Printed in U.S.A.

Books by Jill Sorenson

Silhouette Romantic Suspense

Dangerous to Touch #1518

JILL SORENSON

has been an avid reader for as long as she can remember. In the small Kansas town where she was born, there wasn't much else to do. She picked up her first young adult romance at age eleven and fell in love with the genre at first sight. When she discovered Silhouette Intimate Moments, she didn't leave her room for a month.

Jill moved to San Diego and fell in love all over again, with awesome weather and year-round sunshine. She met her third great love, her husband Chris, in high school, and they married after only eight years of dating. Before becoming a full-time mom and a part-time romance novelist, Jill held down a number of odd jobs, most of which involved children and/or animals, but none of these jobs were as rewarding as writing.

Jill earned a degree in English literature and a bilingual teaching credential from California State University. Upon graduating, she promptly decided to stay home with her new baby. She started writing one day while her daughter was taking a nap and hasn't stopped since. She is delighted to be working with Silhouette Romantic Suspense, formerly Silhouette Intimate Moments, her first crush.

To my agent, Laurie McLean, who finally agreed to represent me after reading the first three chapters of this book.

To my editor, Stacy Boyd, who writes brilliant editorial comments and draws cute little hearts in the margins.

To my daughters, without whom I never would have started writing this book.

To my mom, without whose incredible generosity and superior babysitting skills I never would have finished writing this book.

And to my husband, who will have to wait for another book (he knows which one) to get his rightful dedication.

Chapter 1

Sidney woke to the sound of a dog barking.

For a moment, she thought she'd fallen asleep in the office at the kennel again, but when she opened her eyes she saw the pale yellow paint and outdated light fixture gracing the ceiling of her own bedroom. Her cat, Marley, was curled up into a soft tortoiseshell ball at the foot of the bed, unperturbed.

She threw back the rumpled sheet and climbed out of bed, wondering who had gotten a dog. In this neighborhood, just steps away from Oceanside City Beach, everyone owned or rented tiny two-story houses, like hers, each with the same nonexistent yard space. Dogs weren't allowed on the beach, either, so most area residents didn't own them.

Especially not large, menacing dogs with deep, resounding barks, which was most assuredly what she'd heard.

Yawning, Sidney strode over to the open window in her underwear and pushed aside the gauzy curtains to catch a glimpse of heaven. She inhaled the salty ocean scent, studied the play of the early morning light off the rippled water, listened to the rhythmic crash of waves breaking against the shoreline.

There was no dog barking.

Rubbing the sleep out of her eyes, she stepped away from the window, dismissing the noise as a remnant of a particularly vivid dream. Visual illusions, unfortunately, were not an infrequent occurrence for her. Now she was going to have to add auditory hallucinations to her list of oddities.

With a wistful glance at her comfy wrought-iron bed, Sidney grabbed a pair of jeans off the floor and pulled them up her slender hips. Shoving her feet into old sneakers, she performed a hasty morning toilette that consisted of washing her face and brushing her teeth.

As she left the bedroom, Marley let out a staccato farewell meow, indicating that she was sleeping in.

Downstairs, while Sidney waited for a bagel to toast, she turned the knob on the ancient ten-inch television atop her kitchen counter, more to distract than entertain herself. She only had three channels, and all of them were broadcasting news, the Sunday morning variety, high-fluff, low-violence. As she sipped hot coffee, enjoying the jolt of caffeine to her system, Crystal Dunn—a petite blond reporter whose sweet countenance and angelic blue eyes couldn't mask a cutthroat nature—broke in with an important newsbreak.

"Hal and Sandra, I'm on location in a quiet residential neighborhood known as Sunshine Estates. Candace Hegel, who lives in the area, was last seen walking her dog here early yesterday morning. Her sudden disappearance has caused a local panic. Friends and family fear Miss Hegel may have fallen into the hands of a serial killer."

At the news desk, even the coanchors appeared skeptical. "Crystal, has law enforcement given any indications of foul play?"

Crystal batted her dark lashes engagingly. "No, Hal, they have no comment, but if you remember Anika Groene, the killer's first victim, you'll note the similarities. Anika was presumed to have been taken while walking her dog, a dog which was never found. Miss Hegel's dog is also missing."

Sidney's half-eaten bagel transformed into a hard lump in the pit of her stomach. Photos of Anika Groene, a fresh-faced college student, and Candace Hegel, an attractive woman in her thirties, flashed across the screen, along with home-taken snapshots of both dogs.

"Anyone with information should contact the Oceanside Police Department..." Crystal continued, reciting a hotline number.

Anika Groene's dog was a goofy-looking Doberman with a poorly done ear crop. Sidney felt a rush of sympathy at the sight of his sweet, lopsided mug, sure the dog had met the same fate as his owner.

Candace Hegel's dog elicited a very different reaction. He was an Australian Shepherd mix, by the look of him, although he didn't appear to have the friendly personality typical of the breed. With his mottled blue-gray coat, mangy appearance, and fierce, colorless eyes, he was the kind of dog you crossed the street to avoid.

He also looked perfectly capable of making a loud, insidious bark—just like the one she'd heard that morning.

"Ridiculous," she said, switching the television off abruptly and promising not to turn it on again for another six months.

At Pacific Pet Hotel, the business she'd been scraping a living off of for the past five years, Sidney found something far more unsettling than the Sunday morning news: Candace Hegel's hellhound, stalking the fence line.

"Why me?" she whispered, slowing to a stop in front of the gate and resting her head against the steering wheel. It made no sense. The kennel was miles from Sidney's house, but she knew with one hundred percent accuracy that this dog's barking had disturbed her slumber.

Grumbling, she got out of her truck to unlock the gate and roll it open. As she drove into the small parking lot, the dog made no move to follow. He merely watched as she exited the vehicle again. By the time she called the police department, he could very well bolt.

She knew enough about dogs to understand that this one would need careful handling and a lot of finesse, two attributes she didn't associate with most officers of the law.

Keeping her truck door open, she whistled engagingly. "Go for a ride?"

He sat on his haunches.

On impulse, she lowered the tailgate and sat, thumping the space next to her. "Go for a walk?" she tried.

He didn't move an inch.

She sighed, feeling a reluctant respect for a dog that couldn't be bought so cheaply.

After disengaging the kennel's rinky-dink security alarm and entering through the side door, she wrenched open a can of puppy food and dumped it into a stainless steel bowl. Grabbing another bowl, she filled it with water from the sink and walked back out.

He was still sitting there, watching her.

She placed the bowls just inside the fence line. His jet-black nose quivered with interest, but he didn't move. Intending to trap him in once he came, Sidney rolled the gate until it was almost closed, leaving him just enough space to get through. As she waited for hunger to overcome good sense, she studied him.

It had to be the same dog. He was tall and rangy, more German Shepherd than Australian, now that she saw him in person. He probably weighed at least ninety pounds, and he didn't have that energetic, innocuous expression Aussies wore. His ears were straight up, not floppy, alert rather than playful, and his coat was more wiry than soft.

If not for his coloring, he'd look purebred, but that thick, charcoal-gray fur, liberally spotted with black, was a dead giveaway for his mixed heritage. Blue roan, they called it.

"So what'll it be, Blue?"

He cocked his head to one side.

"Is that your name?" she asked softly, not surprised she got it on the first try. She had a gift—or a curse, to be honest—for guessing right.

The dog entered the space warily, his hind legs shaking, ready to run. Instead of going for the food, he came right to her, sat down and put his head against her jeans-clad thigh in a move that was positively heartbreaking.

"Oh, honey," she said, securing the fence behind him and placing her hand on his trembling head.

In an instant, she was swept away into a maelstrom of images.

Blue was running, running. His teeth were numb from chewing and his head hurt. Fuzzy. Everything was fuzzy.

He was running in shallow water, through fields and over gravel roads, running. Running away from the bad man, the pain, the sound of gunshots and the acrid odor.

He had to follow the river.

He had to get back home.

The last thing he remembered was walking with his mistress, like any other day, before everything went fuzzy. He woke up in a strange car, chewed and clawed and broke his way out. He searched for his mistress, knowing she was hurting.

He smelled her blood.

Then gunshots and the bad man and now he was running.

He had to get home, find his mistress. So he was running. Running along the river that flowed into the ocean, running home...

Sidney lifted her hand, returning slowly to reality as the stream of consciousness ended, feeling drained. She hadn't experienced such a strong outpouring of emotion in a long time, maybe never, and she was far out of practice. Her touch didn't always produce a vision, which made her particularly unprepared for the strong ones.

Normally she took precautions against physical contact, even with animals, but the dog had been so forlorn, so needy. She couldn't deny him the simple comfort of her touch.

"Damn," she whispered, hating herself for being so careless. Keeping this information from the police would be like failing to report a heinous crime. Whether they believed her or not, she led the risk of ridicule, humiliation and exposure. "Damn," she repeated, trying to think of a way to share what she knew without sacrificing her anonymity or revealing how she'd discovered the information.

She clenched her hands into fists, and felt a hot sting cut into her palm. Opening her hand, she saw that a chunk of safety glass had embedded itself in her skin. Scowling, she yanked the glass out and threw it aside before she realized it might be evidence.

Examining Blue critically, she saw burrs, stickers and a few more shards of safety glass. Perhaps he was carrying enough clues in his mottled gray coat as to make divulging her secret unnecessary.

After all, what did she know? Dogs weren't exactly a fountain of specific information, any more than humans were. Brain waves weren't as easy to read as storybooks, and visions didn't provide foolproof information.

She rested her elbows on the top of the fence, a more practical problem occurring to her. The police would have to open the gate to get in, or to get Blue out. If he ran away, and she figured he was wily enough to do just that, so would the evidence.

She'd have to take this troublesome mutt to the station herself.

Lieutenant Marc Cruz had seen better days.

Deputy Chief Stokes had sentenced him to two Sundays of desk duty as punishment for failing to use his allotted vacation time. He couldn't, in good conscience, take off in the middle of a case, and it seemed he was always in that unenviable position. Worse, she was making him catch up on paperwork, his least favorite activity.

He hated sitting at his desk almost as much as he hated idle time, but for every minute of actual police work it seemed like he had to complete an hour of computer-generated logs.

"I've got a lead on a missing person," Stokes said to the mostly empty room.

Marc straightened immediately.

"Some woman outside says she's got Candace Hegel's dog."

Dog? He hunched down at his desk, trying to make himself invisible.

No such luck. "Cruz, you and Lacy take it," she said, narrowing her shrewd eyes on him. "After Crystal Dunn yapped her fat mouth all over the news about the connection to Groene, we can't afford to treat this like anything but a possible homicide."

He arched a glance at his partner, Detective Meredith Lacy, who was hiding her smile behind a manila folder. She was here on Sunday because she was new, barely out of beat, and didn't have any choice in the matter.

"Yes, ma'am," he said under his breath.

"What was that?"

"I said we're on it," he replied, and Lacy strangled a laugh.

Stokes waved a hand in the air, indicating that his presence was annoying and superfluous. She'd been especially testy since the trail for Anika Groene's killer had grown cold, but she couldn't seem to stay home, or let it go.

"Your favorite," Lacy said as they walked down the hall.

"What's that?" he said, his mind still swimming with computerized forms.

"Dogs."

"Don't get smart, Lacy," he muttered, striding into the lobby. The last time Stokes had taken out her petty revenge on him, she'd made him stand in as a training dummy for patrol's attack dogs. He had all of the protective gear on, but one of the ferocious beasts had knocked him down and dislodged his face mask. The handler called off the dog, but not before Marc humiliated himself by fainting. That was two years ago, well before Lacy joined homicide, but he still hadn't lived it down. Apparently stories like that never got old.

When the woman standing alone in the lobby turned toward him, all thoughts of dogs and deskwork vanished.

At first glance, she wasn't his type. She was dark-haired, for one thing, and short-haired, for another. Nothing about her clothes or manner was designed to attract a man's attention, either. Maybe he was shallow, but he liked women who weren't afraid to show a little skin. She looked like she might jump out of hers.

Her faded green T-shirt was several sizes too big, and her battered blue jeans were two inches too short, exposing a pair of trim, nicely tanned ankles. She was wearing dingy white sneakers with Velcro straps, no socks.

The clothes were atrocious, but the body underneath warranted further examination. She was tall and slim, almost to the point of being skinny, except for her breasts, which looked soft and malleable. If she had a bra on, it was one of those no-frills types that molded to her shape as well as the worn cotton T-shirt.

Her face was even better than her breasts. Her features were finely drawn and angular, her eyes a misty, ethereal gray, framed by lush black lashes. With her close-cropped black hair, unisex style, and no makeup, she resembled an exceptionally beautiful teenage boy. He dismissed her as one of those women who couldn't be bothered with men. She already had one, she wasn't looking for one, or she'd given up on finding one.

"Miss Morrow?" he inquired, introducing himself politely.

She looked down at his outstretched hand with undisguised distaste. Puzzled, Marc dropped his arm. Taking the hint, Lacy didn't even attempt a handshake.

"I have the dog in the back of my truck," she said quickly, pointing outside. She was wearing latex gloves. "If you can just tell me where to take him, I'll be out of your way."

He looked out at a sturdy red pickup in the parking lot. Sure enough, an ugly mongrel just like Candace Hegel's was in an extra-large dog cage in the back. "Any chance of him getting out?"

"Not unless he grows human hands."

He waited for her to claim that was in the realm of possibility. When she didn't, he shoved his own hands in his pants pockets, for they seemed to make her uncomfortable. It was as if she feared he was going to reach out and *touch* her, of all horrors.

"Let's talk," he said. "Do you have time for a short interview?"

"Can't we do it here?"

"This is a sensitive case. We have to keep the information confidential, if possible."

She looked around the empty lobby in confusion.

"Witnesses tend to remember more in a place free of distractions," he added.

"Oh, I didn't witness anything—"

"Do you have something more pressing to take care of?" he interrupted.

"It will only take a few minutes," Lacy said with a reassuring smile, probably because he was being rude. "A woman is missing. Anything you could tell us would be greatly appreciated."

"Of course," she said, resigned.

Marc's curiosity was piqued further. Most people couldn't wait to share everything they knew, to contribute, to feel important. Most innocent people, anyway.

He followed Lacy and the mysterious Miss Morrow, employing the age-old "ladies first" excuse men used to ogle women behind their backs. There was nothing boyish about the way she filled out her jeans, he noted.

As he and Lacy took seats opposite her at the table in the interrogation room, it occurred to him that there was another reason women opted to downplay their femininity, one that had nothing to do with men. His partner, Meredith Lacy, was living proof of that.

He gave himself an illicit thrill, wondering if she was Lacy's type. "Where did you find the dog?" he asked, dragging his mind out of the gutter.

When she met his eyes, her own darkened slightly, an almost imperceptible expansion of pupils signaling her awareness of him as a man.

Not indifferent to the opposite sex, he decided. Too bad, Lacy.

"He was outside the fence this morning," she said, staring down at her gloved hands. "At Pacific Pet Hotel."

A kennel worker, he thought with mild distaste. "You're an employee?"

"I own it."

He raised his eyebrows. She didn't look old enough to own a business. "How'd you get him in that dog carrier?"

"I offered him some food and water. He wasn't interested, but he seemed to trust me after that. Enough to go in the carrier, anyway."

"Did he bite you?"

She followed his gaze to her left hand. Under the latex, in the middle of her palm, there was a bandage. "No. He had glass in his fur. And quite a few burrs and foxtails."

"Did you take them out? Clean him up?"

"No. I just reached down to pet him and…the glass cut into my hand."

Marc read a lot into that short pause. She wasn't telling the whole story. "Anything else we need to know?"

"I think he'd traveled for miles," she hedged. "He was panting, and his feet were wet. Smelly wet, like river. The San Luis Rey is nearby."

He'd never before felt as though a person were lying and telling the truth at the same time. He leaned back in his chair, paradoxically pleased. It wasn't every day that plausible suspects walked in off the street.

"Would you like some water?" Detective Lacy asked after an uncomfortable silence. "A soda?"

"No, thanks," Sidney said, tucking her gloved hands under the table, annoyed with Lieutenant Cruz for scrutinizing her so blatantly. He was one of those effortlessly handsome men who made her feel sloppy, awkward and unkempt.

He was taller than she was, and his clothes fit him perfectly, hinting at a nicely formed physique. Even motionless, he managed to convey grace and power. His features were well-arranged but unyielding, showing no trace of softness or compassion. He might have appeared cold if not for his coloring. His skin was dark, his hair a rich, warm brown and his eyes a shade lighter, like smooth Kentucky whiskey or strong iced tea.

With brown hair, skin and eyes, and a tobacco-brown suit, he should have looked average, even drab. He didn't. There was an elusive quality about him that probably intrigued women, a dangerous edge that excited them, and an overall appeal she couldn't describe but responded to nevertheless. He was also quite young, in his early thirties at the most, although he appeared worldly rather than naive.

Staring back at him, Sidney was uncomfortably aware of how long it had been since she'd hazarded the perils of a man's touch.

Lieutenant Cruz must have decided the interview was over, because he stood abruptly. Lacy followed suit, so Sidney rose to her feet as well.

"If you think of anything else," he said, holding out a card with his name and number on it, "feel free to call."

She took it from him gingerly, not allowing his fingers to brush over hers, and shoved it in her pocket. "What are you going to do with him?"

"The dog? Process him for trace."

"And then?"

He shrugged. "Turn him over to the pound, unless his owner or another family member comes to claim him."

"If they don't, will you call me?" Sidney posed this question to Detective Lacy, deciding she was the more amenable officer. "I'd hate to see him put down." Large, mean-looking dogs were rarely placed in good homes.

"Absolutely," she promised as they walked out together.

"Is Gina working today?" Lieutenant Cruz asked Detective Lacy.

"Yep."

"Why don't you go sweet-talk her into meeting us over there?"

"You don't want help with the dog?" she asked with a slight smile.

"Why would I?" he returned.

"Whatever you say, Marcos," she said, punching him lightly on the shoulder before she ambled away. Sidney watched her go, feeling a spark of envy for the basic human ability to touch another person in kindness, humor or affection.

Detective Lacy's tone was teasing, but something about what she said bothered him. "Marcos? Is that your real name?"

"Just Marc," he replied as he held open the door for her. Ever-cognizant of his proximity, she moved by him carefully, resisting the urge to tell him to call her by her first name, as well. She didn't want to remind him of her embarrassing refusal to shake his hand upon their initial introduction.

As they approached the back of her truck, he didn't make direct eye contact with the dog or do anything else cornered animals considered threatening, but Blue let out a series of rapid barks, gnashing at the grate.

Lieutenant Cruz didn't even flinch. "Friendly, isn't he?"

She smiled at his dry humor. "Don't you like dogs?"

"They don't like me," he corrected.

When she laughed, he turned his head to study her face. He was attracted to her, she realized in a flash of intuition that was more feminine than supernatural. Something must be wrong with him. Men were always put off by her aversion to physical contact.

"As much as I'd like to wrestle him out of there and into my own vehicle—" he gestured to a champagne-colored Audi with all-leather interior "—I think he's more comfortable with you. If you don't mind."

"Not at all," she said. "Where to?"

"Vincent Veterinary Clinic. You can follow me."

"I know where it is," she said, finding the situation highly ironic.

She was accompanying Lieutenant Cruz, the first man she wanted to touch her in ages, to see Dr. Vincent, the last man who had.

Chapter 2

Vincent Veterinary Clinic was less than a mile from Pacific Pet Hotel. Sidney often took dogs and cats there if they became sick while boarding. In turn, Dr. Vincent recommended her facility to clients, so the business relationship between them was mutually beneficial.

If only the personal relationship had been.

Lieutenant Cruz and Detective Lacy met her there, along with another young woman in a white van that said LabTech on the side. While Lacy helped her unload some kind of specialized equipment, Sidney studied the easy interactions between the two women.

Detective Lacy was petite and compact, with shoulder-length strawberry-blond hair and a smattering of freckles across her nose. The lab tech was taller, but curvy. Her dark hair was pulled back into a sleek ponytail and her uniform neatly pressed.

Both of them were pretty, smart-looking and confident. Sidney didn't need to glance in her rearview mirror to know that she didn't match up.

She got out of her dusty pickup, a flustered breath ruffling her bangs, and climbed into the back to get Blue. Lieutenant Cruz watched her from a safe distance, and the dog came out readily, allowing her to slip a nylon leash over his head. When he saw Lieutenant Cruz, he growled.

"Easy, Blue," she chided, hopping off the tailgate.

"How did you know his name?" he asked.

Sidney fumbled for an explanation. "I must have heard it on the news."

His gaze caressed her face, reading the lie more easily than she'd told it.

"Sidney!" Bill exclaimed from the open doorway, saving her from any more awkward questions. "What are you doing here?"

Bill Vincent was tall and handsome, about ten years older than Sidney, with thinning blond hair and a whipcord build he kept in shape by bicycling on the weekends. He looked casual in a short-sleeved shirt and tan slacks, and he smiled, as if pleased to see her.

Blue lunged at him, barking.

"Whoa," he said with a jittery laugh. "You've got a live one there."

"Hush," Sidney ordered.

Blue sat.

"We'll have to sedate him," Bill remarked to Lieutenant Cruz. Because no introductions were made, Sidney surmised that the two men were already acquainted. Judging by the way they were staring each other down, they weren't friendly.

Sidney was surprised. Bill was an easygoing, sociable kind of guy, especially with people he considered influential. He went out of his way to ingratiate himself to others.

"I'd like to get a blood sample first," Lieutenant Cruz said. "In case he's already been drugged."

Bill's lips thinned. "Are you volunteering to hold him for me, Lieutenant?"

"I'll hold him," Sidney offered, knowing it was the only way to get the job done. "He *was* acting sluggish when I first found him."

"Sluggish?" Bill eyed the dog warily. "He's certainly up and at 'em right now." Seeing the stubborn tilt of her chin, he said, "Come on in," making a show of checking the time on his watch. Either he billed the police department for emergency hours, or he was implying that he had better things to do.

"I'm Gina, by the way," the lab tech offered.

"Sidney," she replied, using Blue as a convenient excuse not to offer her hand. Bending down beside him, she hooked her left arm around his neck, securing his head against her chest. With her right thumb, she held off the vein in his forearm. It was the basic position for drawing blood, and she had a good grip on him, but as soon as Bill came close, the dog exploded.

"That's it," he said, backing away. "I'd like to keep my face intact, if you don't mind."

Sidney fought the urge to smile. Bill's face was a matter of great importance to him.

"Let Gina try," Lacy suggested. "The dog doesn't seem to like men."

Bill handed off the syringe. "It's your funeral."

"He won't bite you," Sidney said to Gina reassuringly.

"How do you know?"

"She just does," Bill said, rolling his eyes heavenward. "She always does."

Sidney ignored him in favor of rearranging her hold on Blue, murmuring words to comfort him. When Gina kneeled to get the sample, he was docile as a lamb.

"Good dog," she praised, patting him on the head.

Gina gave the dog his sedative as well, a quick injection to the flank. Blue tensed at the sharp sting, but took the pain with neither a whimper nor complaint. In moments, he was weaving on his feet. Soon, he laid his head down and slept.

"That went well," Gina said, smiling at her.

When Sidney smiled back, Lacy stepped between them. "Thanks for the help," she said, indicating her presence was no longer necessary.

Feeling rebuffed, Sidney glanced at Lieutenant Cruz. Again, he was watching her. "If you don't mind, I'd like to follow you. To check out...your place."

"Okay," she mumbled, unable to think of a reason to refuse.

"Doing investigative work now, Sidney?" Bill asked, looking back and forth between them. "What an accommodating little citizen you've become."

Sidney felt the blood drain from her face.

Lieutenant Cruz noted the exchange with interest. "If not for her, I doubt we'd have been able to get near that dog," he defended.

Bill didn't care for the mild reprimand, or the reminder that he'd been intimidated by Blue. "I'll call you later," he said to Sidney, as if they were still involved. She would have laughed at his ridiculous posturing if the situation weren't so tense.

"Ladies," Lieutenant Cruz said, leaving Detective Lacy and Gina to their work. He didn't bother to say goodbye to Bill, but neither did Sidney.

"You dated that guy?" he asked as soon as they were out of earshot.

"Is that pertinent to the case, Lieutenant?"

"Marc. And probably not."

Annoyed with all men in general, she turned to glare at him. Then she sucked in a breath, because he was standing very close.

His eyes trailed down her body. "Did he hurt you?"

She pressed her back against the side of her truck, anxious to put space between them. "No. I was like this before."

He must have accepted her answer, because he stepped back. "Meet you over there," he said over his shoulder as he walked away.

Pacific Pet Hotel was a small white stucco building on Oceanside Boulevard, in an industrial area populated with offices, warehouses and construction supply companies. It was a convenient location for dropping the pooch off on the way to work, or while heading out of town.

Marc let Sidney attend her duties while he cased the perimeter of the building. Other than a few glass shards, and the stainless steel bowls she'd used to offer the dog food, he didn't find anything noteworthy.

Standing on the blacktop parking lot with the hot sun beating down on his head, staring out at the desolate landscape, he began to sweat. He'd already discarded his jacket and loosened his tie. Beads of perspiration dried on the back of his neck before they could trickle.

Studying the area, he analyzed her description of the dog's

physical condition. His paws were wet, she'd said. The San Luis Rey River was at least a mile to the north, through a thicket of weeds, sagebrush and eucalyptus trees.

Wet paws after that journey? Not bloody likely.

Another detail of her account bothered him. He knew damned well she hadn't heard the dog's name on the news. He'd watched the only televised segment himself, with his usual disdain for Crystal Dunn's salacious reporting style. Crystal would sell her soul for a story, and she wasn't above making one up, so it wouldn't have surprised him if she'd let the dog's name slip. But she hadn't. He was sure of it.

Whistling a vague tune, he wandered out back to see what the strangely sexy Miss Morrow was up to.

She was hosing down outdoor kennels. Dogs of various breeds and sizes were barking happily, pacing in runs, leaping up and down, or putting their faces in full bowls of food or water. Her short black hair clung to her forehead, and a damp spot was visible between her shoulder blades. This was not a woman afraid of hard work, he thought with reluctant admiration.

Definitely not his type.

Neither did she seem a likely murder suspect. As she worked, she chatted with the dogs around her, taking the time to give each one a piece of her undivided attention. She was unusual, no doubt about that, but she was also kind.

The kennel area was small, well-maintained and clean. The dogs didn't appear to be wasting away or suffering unduly, not that he was any expert in the care of animals. When she turned to wheel a loaded cart of empty dishes back inside, she startled, noticed him standing there for the first time.

The precariously loaded tray wobbled, and several stainless steel bowls came crashing down. As he bent to help her pick them up, his fingertips grazed across hers when they reached for the same bowl.

She froze. Having taken off her gloves, for reasons unknown, the contact with her bare skin seemed to jolt her.

To be honest, he wasn't immune to it, either. The quick flash of heat, and matching spark in her eyes, made sensual awareness sizzle down his spine. Never had he experienced such a strong reaction to a fleeting, purely innocent touch.

Maybe that was why she wore latex—the slightest brush against her flesh had the power to bring a man to his knees. He'd figured her for an extreme germaphobe, an obsessive-compulsive, or just a kooky, off-center chick.

"Sorry," he said, because she seemed affronted. She thought he'd done it on purpose, he realized. Straightening, he set the bowl atop the cart.

Without a word, she pushed the cart into the back door of the facility and dumped the dishes into an industrial-size sink. Grabbing a pair of yellow rubber gloves from a drawer, she shoved her trembling hands into them and hit the faucet handle.

"Do you know Candace Hegel?"

"No," she said, adding a stingy amount of dish soap to the rising water.

"What about the dog? Did he come here for boarding?"

"No."

"How can you be so sure?"

"I know my clients."

"You remember every dog who's ever come in here?"

"I'd remember that one," she said, shutting off the faucet.

He conceded her point. "The news report didn't give his name."

She began scrubbing furiously, drawing his attention to the way her breasts moved beneath the soft cotton T-shirt. "That dog is a blue roan. It's an obvious choice."

With some effort, he lifted his eyes to her face. "What's a blue roan?"

"The color of his coat. It's like calling a black dog 'Blackie.' An easy guess."

Marc was annoyed with himself for asking an important question while he was distracted. He couldn't tell if she was lying. "Do you know something you're not telling me?" he asked, crowding her a little. Sure enough, that got her attention.

"Back off," she said, narrowing her eyes.

He didn't move. "I'd be a fool not to consider your behavior suspicious."

She was breathing heavily, from the exertion of her duties, which she performed with brisk efficiency, and the implied threat in his words. But what he saw in her smoky-gray eyes wasn't just guilt or fear. It was desire.

As her chest rose again, his gaze dropped to her breasts, and the hard points of her nipples, jutting against the soft cloth.

In that moment, he felt very masculine and very powerful.

"Oh, get over yourself, Lieutenant," she said, disgusted, shoving away from the sink. "Just because I look like—" she gestured to herself "—this, and you look like—" she waved her hand at him "—that, you think I'm going to fall all over you?"

He opened his mouth to protest then closed it.

"Go dominate one of your dumb blondes," she added, leaving him standing there.

Marc couldn't decide what astounded him more: her low assessment of her own attributes, or her scathingly accurate critique of his.

Following her, he started to ask how she knew him before he realized it was an admission. Shaking his head, he tried to get back on track. "Why do you wear those gloves?"

"Because I work with animals," she said. "It's very unsanitary not to." Proving it, she removed a litter box from a roomy cat cage.

"You weren't wearing them outside."

"I don't wear them when I hose down kennels. Water is clean enough."

"Maybe I'll ask Dr. Vincent," he said softly.

"Go ahead," she said, the panic in her expression belying her bravado. "I'm eccentric. It's not a crime."

"We'll see," he promised, pleased to have regained the upper hand.

After parking in the covered garage all the units on the block shared, Sidney trudged down the sidewalk to her house, feeling defeated, confused and exhilarated.

Her life must have been getting particularly monotonous lately for her to enjoy any part of being a witness and suspect in a kidnapping-murder case.

Guilt was a major factor in her unease. If she'd been completely honest, she might have been able to help the investigation. To do so would have made Marc Cruz even more suspicious. He had disbeliever written all over him.

Throwing herself down on her green futon couch, she considered the handsome detective. When he'd touched her, she hadn't been swept away by a tidal wave of psychic impressions; she'd been completely distracted by physical sensation. His hand on her bare skin was like a match striking flame.

Then she'd noticed him studying her clinically, assessing her reaction, and she was taken back into her own memory, to a time when boys at school had poked and prodded at her just to watch her squirm.

Reaching into her back pocket, she found his card. It was a simple, cream-colored rectangle with black lettering, offering only his name, rank, department and phone number. Tracing her fingertips over the surface, she couldn't get more of a read on him than she had before, a vague feeling that she wasn't his type. The insulting remark she'd made about him preferring biddable blondes was an educated guess.

And a direct hit, judging by his expression.

She never knew when a psychic flash would hit her. Every time she reached out to touch someone, or something, she did so with trepidation. Usually the insights revealed to her were as mundane as a mental grocery list, and often she saw nothing at all, but every once in a while she was assaulted by ugly thoughts, dark musings people hid from others and words better left unsaid. The experience was discomforting, to say the least.

It was kind of like shaking hands with a clown and getting zapped by one of those gag buzzers. The anticipation of the shock left her on pins and needles.

Sidney tossed the card on the coffee table, rested her cheek on a throw pillow and wondered what to do with the rest of the afternoon. She kept the kennel closed on Sunday, and although she went in twice to feed and clean, it was her lightest day. Sometimes the free hours loomed rather than beckoned.

Marley jumped on her back and began a vigorous kneading,

cheering her. At the same time, she became aware of a strange sound emanating from the kitchen.

"What's that?" she asked, lifting her head.

Marley kept digging her soft paws into her back.

Sidney clambered off the couch, sending the cat sprawling. It was the answering machine. She pushed the blinking button with relish.

"Sid? Are you there? The kids are driving me crazy about going to the beach. Call my cell when you get this. Bye."

Her sister hardly ever brought her daughters over to visit. It was one of the great sorrows of Sidney's life. Picking up the phone, she dialed Samantha's number from memory.

"Hello?" her sister answered in a low-pitched voice.

"It's me."

"Sidney?" The sultry tone disappeared. "Are you home?"

"Yes."

"Thank God. We're parking right now. The girls are wild today."

Sidney couldn't hear any background noise to corroborate that statement. Taylor and Dakota were the most sedate children imaginable.

With no further explanation, Samantha hung up.

Sidney raced upstairs to change, giddy at the prospect of spending time with her nieces, the last of her close relatives who didn't cringe away from her touch. On impulse, she rummaged through her bedroom closet until she found the bikini her sister had given her as a birthday gift last summer.

Tearing off the tags, she shimmied into it, checking her reflection in the mirror to make sure the fabric covered all of the required parts. The bikini showed a lot more skin than the serviceable black Speedo she usually wore, in a way that was far more flattering.

It was a perfect fit, actually. Stylish and sexy, like the clothes Samantha favored. So why had Sidney never worn it before?

When the doorbell rang, she ran downstairs to greet the girls with open arms. They hugged her dutifully, with a lack of enthusiasm that was more a product of their raising than a reflection of their true feelings for her. She hoped.

"Hey, sis," Samantha said, gracing her with an air kiss and a wooden smile.

Sidney tried to ignore the painful twist in the middle of her chest. Her sister's rejections weren't personal, but they hurt all the same.

The girls fawned over Marley for a few moments before returning to their mother. "Can we go to the beach now, Mommy?" Dakota asked, tugging on the edge of Samantha's gauzy skirt. "Please?"

"You see how they are?" Samantha said, taking off her designer sunglasses. Beneath the lenses, her vivid blue eyes were bloodshot. "Sometimes I can hardly catch my breath."

At seven and eight, the girls required a lot of attention, no matter how quiet and well-behaved they were. Samantha relied heavily on the help of a live-in nanny, as her husband, Greg, was almost never home. She was still recovering from the ordeal of having two babies in rapid succession.

Sidney winked at Taylor, who giggled. "Why don't you girls grab a drink from the fridge before we go? I have lemonade."

Dakota blinked up at Samantha. "Can we, Mommy?"

When she waved them away, they both squealed, more excited by the prospect of refined sugar than an outing with their Aunt Sidney.

"I'm off to the loo," Samantha said, sashaying toward the bathroom, a sleek leather clutch clasped in her expertly manicured, expensively jeweled hand. Sidney didn't need any special abilities to predict her sister was going in there to pop another pill.

On the beach, Sidney made sandcastles and frolicked in the waves with her nieces for an hour before joining her sister to sunbathe on the sand.

"You're good with them," Samantha said with a drowsy smile.

Sidney warmed at the unexpected praise. "They're angels. You're incredibly lucky."

"Where did you get that suit?"

She glanced down at the blue and white bikini. Under the relentless sun, her tan lines were embarrassingly apparent. "You gave it to me."

"I have excellent taste," she murmured.

"Yes," Sidney agreed. Samantha looked marvelous in a tiny black two-piece, her subtle, sculpted curves displayed to perfection.

"I forget you have a great body," she said. "You're always covered up."

Sidney was surprised by her sister's faintly envious tone. She often felt like a lurching shadow next to Samantha, who was petite and feminine. Fashionably thin, achingly beautiful and gorgeously blond, men stared at her sister wherever she went. And she stared right back.

"So what have you been up to?" Samantha asked, rolling over onto her flat stomach.

She hesitated. "I met someone today."

Samantha looked over the rims of her sunglasses. "Oh really?"

Pushing aside her misgivings, Sidney told her sister about this morning's strange events. True to character, Samantha was more interested in the man than the fact that her little sister's life had been turned upside down. She'd always been boy-crazy.

"A cop, huh? Is he hot?"

"Yes," Sidney admitted.

"Mmm. What does he look like?"

"Dark. Hard. Well-built."

"Hard? How delicious."

"Not like that," she said, her cheeks heating. "Tough, kind of. You know."

Samantha smiled wickedly. "Was he in uniform?"

"A suit."

"Did he have a gun?"

"Probably."

"And cuffs?"

"I didn't frisk him, Sam."

"Oh, well. Did he frisk you?"

"No," she said, smiling back at her.

"Ah, but you wanted him to. Right?"

When she shrugged, Samantha ran with it. "I always wanted to do a cop," she mused. "Something about being overpowered. Or maybe it's just the handcuff thing."

Sidney didn't doubt that Lieutenant Cruz would be willing to oblige her sister on that front. Samantha's bored, sophisticate attitude and golden girl good looks were probably right up his alley.

She wasn't a bimbo, but she played the part well. And she played men, her favorite game, like a pro.

"He considers me a suspect," she reminded her sister, and herself.

Samantha was silent for a moment. "Greg and I are getting divorced."

Sidney laid her head back on the towel, annoyed with Samantha for changing the subject and always putting her own problems first. She and Greg had been getting divorced for years. Sidney hoped they would stop torturing the kids and get on with it.

"It's for real this time, Sid. I think he's cheating again."

Sidney shifted uncomfortably, wishing she could make herself scarce.

Samantha straightened. "You already knew? How could you? I haven't even touched you today." She looked down the beach, where her daughters were playing in the sand. "Son of a bitch," she said between clenched teeth, her blue eyes hard as ice. "He brings that slut around my kids? What does he do, bribe them not to tell?"

"I don't think they understand. So he doesn't have to."

"Son of a bitch," she repeated. "If I wasn't sleeping with his business partner, I'd take his ass to the cleaners."

Chapter 3

The next morning, it wasn't the sound of a dog barking that rose with Sidney from the depths of her dream to the cold surface of reality. It was a woman's scream.

She struggled to break free from the cloak of darkness that surrounded her, but her arms were bound behind her back. Thrashing her head from side to side, she fought against the restraints.

A plastic shroud covered her face.

When she opened her mouth to scream, the plastic drew closer, cutting off her airway completely.

She was sinking, drowning, suffocating.

A dark, dank cold invaded her body, seeping beneath the plastic. At first, it was a relief to gain a precious inch of space, a single breath. Then a pungent, earthy smell engulfed her, the scent of decay and sea and wet blood. The cold pressed in, crawling up her spine and around her neck, rushing into her mouth, her eyes, her nostrils...

Sidney clawed the sheet away from her face, gasping for air. Her heart was pounding, her lungs pumping hard and fast, her pulse racing.

Marley was sitting at the foot of the bed, tail twitching, highly annoyed with Sidney for disturbing her slumber.

"Oh God," she groaned, laying her head back down on the pillow. "This has got to stop." Her whole life, she'd been fighting against this strangeness inside herself. Now it was fighting back, mutating, stronger than ever. She could wear gloves, shun society and deny touch, but how could she chase away dreams?

The blankets got wrapped around her head while she was sleeping, she rationalized. She'd been tossing and turning all night, bothered by the uncharacteristically high temperatures outside and a deeper, more invasive heat within.

It was no more than she deserved for entertaining lustful fantasies involving Marc Cruz, tangled sheets and handcuffs.

Now she was cold. Chilled to the bone, in fact.

A gentle morning breeze from a balmy onshore flow ruffled the curtains. The oscillating fan in the corner rumbled lazily, barely causing a stir. Shivering, she climbed out of bed to switch it off, rubbing at the gooseflesh on her arms. She closed the window, too, noticing that her nipples were tightly puckered and painfully hard.

Resisting the urge to rub herself there, as well, she hurried into the bathroom and turned the shower faucet all the way to "Hot."

Marc pulled at the collar of his shirt. It was a sticky day, hazy and warm, almost ninety degrees before 9:00 a.m.

In other parts of the country, where temperature and humidity levels soared, this kind of weather would be a nonissue. For a city whose residents were spoiled by high seventies most of the year, it was damn near intolerable.

Deputy Chief Stokes and a handful of homicide officers were milling around the gravel pull-out on Pacific Coast Highway near Agua Hedionda Lagoon. Literally translated as "stinking water," the lagoon separated downtown Oceanside from uptown Carlsbad, educated from underprivileged, rich from poor.

Driving along PCH through O'side, one could encounter almost any kind of vice, from prostitution and drugs to adult bookstores and sleazy strip joints. Camp Pendleton Marine Corps Base, on the northern border of town, supplied plenty of young male clients for the burgeoning sex industry. It could also be responsible, in a roundabout way, for the number of homeless vets on the city streets.

For all its shortcomings, Oceanside was still a nice place to live. The inland hills were speckled with single family homes and quiet communities. The beaches attracted hundreds of thousands of tourists every year, so they were clean and well-maintained. Stretches of flat white sand weren't the best venue for illicit activities, so most of the dregs of society stuck to the heavy brush near the San Luis Rey River, which offered less interference and more cover.

Carlsbad, on the other hand, didn't have a seedy area. Or a middle-class area, for that matter. The rivalry between the two cities was pronounced, from high school sports to police divisions. With better funding at their disposal, Carlsbad usually came out on top.

Behind a police line at the edge of the water, a suited representative from Carlsbad PD was arguing with Deputy Chief Stokes over turf. The lagoon belonged to them, so they laid claim to the body floating in its murky depths. Stokes was adamant that whoever tossed the tarp-wrapped package into the lagoon had been standing on the gravel pull-out along the highway, clearly Oceanside's territory. The Coast Guard was obliged to oversee the handling of any human remains found in coastal waters, so they were also on site, and the lagoon was part of a wilderness preserve, so State Parks was there, too.

They could debate all morning over recovery issues, but the body was under the county medical examiner's jurisdiction until after the autopsy. Stokes talked the good doctor into working with Oceanside's homicide unit instead of Carlsbad's, citing the distinct possibility that the victim was local resident Candace Hegel.

The killer's first victim, Anika Groene, had been found in water as well.

Finally the M.E. ordered the retrieval, after a consultation with an E.P.A. affiliate about algae levels and possible impact to the endangered water fowl.

Stokes leveled her evil eye on him. "Get in there, Cruz."

Marc looked down at the opaque surface with trepidation. First dogs, now stinking water. He wasn't queasy about dead bodies, having seen more than his fair share, but water-logged flesh was particularly gruesome, and Agua Hedionda was dark and stagnant.

No telling what was down there.

Stokes shoved white Tyvek coveralls at his chest, indicating the issue wasn't open for discussion, and he walked to his car to change. No way was he ruining a perfectly good suit with marsh muck. Grabbing a pair of basketball shorts from the trunk, he stripped right there on the side of the road while Lacy watched.

"What are you looking at?" he asked, feeling surly.

"Nothing interesting," she said, smothering a laugh.

Lacy had never been on the scene for a floater, he recalled, wondering if she'd lose her breakfast when they unwrapped the soggy package.

He pulled the jumpsuit over his shorts and covered his hands with gloves to protect the scene from being compromised with trace. As he lowered himself into the lagoon, he winced at the temperature. It might be hot as hell outside, but Agua Hedionda was as cold as the Pacific, a chilly sixty-five degrees.

"Make sure it's what we think it is," Stokes ordered.

The oblong shape, wrapped up like a mummy in a green plastic tarp, lurked just below the surface. Grimacing, he wrapped his arms around it in a macabre embrace. When he squeezed experimentally, he felt the give of flesh and slender, feminine curves.

"It's a woman."

"Well, don't yank on it," Stokes said, as if he would. "Reach under there and see if something's weighing it down."

Bodies did sink on their own, and came up several days later, depending on the temperature. This one had either been dumped recently, weighed down, or both. Following the rope tied around the body's midsection, he pulled gently, feeling tension.

He was going to have to duck under to investigate. Holding his breath, he followed the rope to its anchor.

"Cinder block," he said when he resurfaced, trying not to smell or taste the water. "And half-inch rope. Hemp, maybe."

"Cut it," she said, giving him a razor knife.

He did, but the body didn't rise.

"Fresh," she said, nodding with satisfaction.

It was awkward, but he managed to heft the body onto the shore without doing too much damage to it, himself, or the crime scene. Even covered in dark plastic, it was plain to see that the corpse was a slight woman, about the size of Candace Hegel.

When the M.E. cut the tarp away from her face, befouled water gushed out.

Because she hadn't been there long, and the lagoon was cold, the effects of decomposition were minimal. Enough to discolor her complexion, but not so much that her body was bloated or her skin sloughing off, which would have made sight identification difficult.

In life, Candace Hegel had been a pretty woman. In death, with a greenish tinge to her face, particles of brown algae clinging to her skin and tiny surfperch burrowing into the delicate tissues, she was hideous.

Marc's stomach clenched, and he felt an unmanageable hatred for whoever would defile a woman this way.

Stokes narrowed her shrewd eyes at him, so he quickly blanked his expression. She'd dealt with his overenthusiastic pursuits of justice before, and didn't consider it sound police work. Officers were not supposed to get emotionally involved.

Detective Lacy, on the other side of Stokes, was doing an admirable job of suppressing her nausea.

"Wrap it all up," the M.E. said. "I'll cut the rest of the tarp away on the table."

"I want that cinder block," Stokes said as they loaded the body into the van.

"Of course you do," he muttered.

"What was that?"

"Right away, I said."

It was no easy task. He could only lift the block a few feet at a time, drop it a little closer to shore and come back to surface for air. By the time he passed it off to CSI, he'd inhaled, swallowed and sputtered about a pint of Agua Hedionda.

"You'll need a hepatitis vaccine," Stokes said as he climbed out.

Lying on his back on the dusty gravel bank, shuddering with cold and panting from exertion, Marc prayed he wouldn't be the one to lose his breakfast instead of Lacy.

* * *

After a hot shower and a hotter cup of coffee, Sidney was feeling warm and toasty. It was a muggy day, cloudy and warm, the thick marine layer overhead trapping the earth's heat like a thermal blanket. By the time she reached the kennel she was sweating.

Mondays were always busy, so work kept her body, if not her mind, occupied most of the morning. She had several pickups scheduled for later that afternoon, and any dog that stayed more than three days got a complimentary bath. Time spent in close confinement tended to emphasize the "doggy" smell, and she didn't like to send home stinky pets.

She'd just finished her last bath when the phone rang. "Pacific Pet Hotel," she answered crisply.

"Sidney." It was Bill. "You've got to come get this dog."

"What's he doing?"

"Trying to rip everyone's face off."

"What about the family?"

"They want him boarded until the owner is…found. Candace Hegel lived alone, and the dog isn't used to men, obviously. None of her friends or relatives have female-only households."

She glanced up at the clock. Almost lunchtime. "I'll be there in a few minutes."

At Vincent Veterinary Clinic, Sidney parked next to the employee's entrance and let herself in. Standing on the other side of the door were Bill, Detective Lacy and Lieutenant Cruz.

She froze dead in her tracks.

"Miss Morrow," Lieutenant Cruz said in greeting, an avaricious gleam in his brown eyes.

Her gaze darted to Bill, who had assumed a defensive posture. "You told," she accused.

"They have a warrant for your arrest, Sid. I had no other choice."

Feeling cornered and betrayed, she began to back away.

Lieutenant Cruz reached out and clamped his hand around her wrist. "Do you see bars in your future?"

She struggled against him, but he held tight. A woman's ravaged face flashed before her, slimy things squirming in the soft tissues. Just like in her dream, a brackish taste filled her mouth and the smell of blood flooded her nostrils, strangling her, drowning her.

Examining her strange expression, he released her arm.

"I'm going to be sick," she said, rushing to the nearest bathroom. She fell to her knees as the contents of her stomach came up, not swamp water or blood, as she almost expected, but the pulpy remnants of an orange she'd eaten for lunch in her truck on the way over.

With nothing more to purge, she dry heaved quietly, tears burning in her eyes, citric acid stinging her throat. When she was finished, Lieutenant Cruz handed her some wet paper towels.

"Thanks," she said in a hoarse whisper, wiping her face.

"Do you have a weak stomach, or a guilty conscience?"

"Neither," she muttered. "I have a sensitive nose, and you smell."

He turned to Detective Lacy, frowning. "Do I?"

"A little bit," she admitted.

"I thought maybe you'd had a 'psychic vision.'" He sneered around the words, showing not only disbelief, but utter contempt.

Sidney flushed the toilet angrily.

"We're going to need you to come back down to the station," he said, not offering to help her to her feet.

"What for?"

"To take your statement."

"Look, I'm not psychic. I don't have visions. I don't know anything more than I've already told you, and I'm not interested in being jerked around."

His jaw tightened with displeasure. "Vincent wasn't bluffing about that arrest warrant, you know. I have it right here," he said, patting his suit pocket. Today's was dark blue, with a crisp white shirt underneath. He looked immaculate, but she hadn't been lying about the odor. A vaguely swampy, fishy scent clung to him. "You can come willingly, or unwillingly, it's all the same to us." Letting his eyes sweep down her trembling form, he added, "But I don't think you'd like the booking process. There's a lot of…manhandling."

"I have a business to run," she said, hearing desperation edge into her voice. "I'm the only employee."

"You get a lunch break, right? This shouldn't take much more than an hour."

Sidney looked to Bill, who offered no support. "Can you come back here afterward?" he whined. "I'm serious about you taking that dog. He's vicious."

Given no alternative, she allowed them to escort her back to the station. Sitting in the back seat of Lieutenant Cruz's Audi, she noticed a grocery bag with a pair of wet blue shorts inside. The unpleasant smell and sensation rushed her once again, and she hit the button to lower the window, needing fresh air.

"You're not going to throw up again, are you?"

Putting her face to the lukewarm breeze, she shook her head dumbly.

"I'll pull over," he offered, probably more for his leather interior's sake than her own.

She waved him on, because she didn't have anything left in her stomach anyway.

In front of Oceanside Police Department, a crowd of reporters had congregated. Lieutenant Cruz let out an inventive combination of expletives. "What do they want?"

Lacy shrugged. "Go around back."

He maneuvered his car into the rear parking lot and jumped out. To Sidney's surprise, he opened the door for her. As she exited the vehicle, a tiny blonde strode toward them with a purpose, cameraman in tow.

It was Crystal Dunn, Sidney realized, mildly starstruck.

"No comment," Lieutenant Cruz said before the pretty reporter could ask a question.

"Are you a witness in the investigation of Candace Hegel's death?" Crystal asked anyway, shoving the microphone in Sidney's face.

"Death?" Sidney repeated dully.

"She has no comment," Lieutenant Cruz grated, clamping his hand around Sidney's bare upper arm. Even in public, on camera, no less, his touch elicited a shiver of excitement. And a startling secret: He'd been romantically involved with Crystal Dunn, at one time or another.

Her pleasure fizzled. No wonder Sidney wasn't his type, if he chased after doll-sized blondes with rapacious personalities. As he strode across the parking lot, practically dragging her along, she could hear Crystal Dunn's no-nonsense voice as she shared the details of the latest homicide:

"Miss Hegel was found dead early this morning in Agua Hedionda Lagoon. Police officials have no comment—"

"You're hurting me."

He looked down at his hand, wrapped around her arm. "Sorry," he said, loosening his grip. Sidney could tell he was furious, although he hid it well. He probably didn't care for Crystal Dunn leaking details of a homicide to a possible suspect.

It had been petty and unprofessional of her, actually. With so much animosity between them, it was hard to guess who dumped whom.

"Detective Lacy, would you show Miss Morrow to one of the interview rooms, please?" he asked, looking down an empty hallway. "I'll be there in a minute."

Lacy kept her face bland and authoritative. "Right this way, ma'am."

The women's locker room was clear. Marc breathed a sigh of relief, knowing he'd catch hell from Deputy Chief Stokes if she found him snooping around in here.

He located Lacy's locker and began rifling through its contents. She had some girl stuff, makeup and deodorant, but no perfume or jewelry. A clean, pressed patrol uniform hung on a wooden hanger.

He grabbed a mesh bag from the bottom. Towels, shampoo. Damn.

Frustrated, he grabbed her oversize brown leather purse, preparing to dump out its contents and use it as his prop. Inside, however, there was a flimsy purple scarf, folded into a tiny square. Perfect.

He shoved it in his pocket, hoping to discredit Sidney Morrow for good. The look on her face, right before she got sick, had been damned convincing. He was still pissed off at himself for getting caught up in her ruse, even for a second.

Lots of women could vomit on cue. It was called bulimia, not ESP.

When he opened the door to the interview room, he was all

business. Lacy was intimidating the subject with a cold, hard stare, arms folded over her chest. On the other side of the table, Sidney was fidgeting.

As he took his seat next to Lacy, he studied his quarry, confused by her appeal. He liked confident women. Bold, aggressive women who knew how to please a man. Women who were well aware of their own allure.

Sidney Morrow was as timid as a rabbit. If he touched her, she'd jump. If he kept touching her, she'd squirm. She was like a bundle of raw nerve endings. Against his better judgment, he speculated on what it would be like to go to bed with her.

"Dr. Vincent says you…know things," he began. "Sense them."

"I don't."

"Come on," he said. "You knew the dog had been drugged. You knew his name and that he'd come along the river—"

"All perfectly reasonable assumptions."

"Either you're a psychic or a suspect, Miss Morrow. Which do you prefer?"

When she remained silent, he slid a picture across the table, an autopsy photo of Anika Groene, her bare skin riddled with red marks. "See those bites? Whoever killed her tied her up and let rats crawl over her. They feasted on her naked body while she was still alive."

"Please," she whispered, looking away, her eyes watery and tortured.

Marc steeled himself against the sight. "What was he doing to Candace Hegel yesterday, while you were insisting you didn't know anything? What was he doing while you were pretending 'Blue' was just a good guess?"

"I don't know," she moaned, twisting her hands in her lap.

Marc felt a surge of triumph, sensing her upcoming capitulation. "Tell us what you *do* know," he urged.

"I had a dream," she said finally. "Or something. I heard a dog barking, yesterday morning, as I was waking up. When I got to the kennel, there he was."

It didn't make any sense, but nothing about her did. "And?"

"And I did guess his name, okay? I called him Blue, and he came right to me, so I knew I was right. When I reached down to pet him—" She broke off, searching for the words to explain. "I just knew stuff."

"Like what?"

"That he'd broken out of a vehicle, and he was groggy. I don't know where he'd been, but I think he heard gunshots, and he spooked."

"Gunshots? What kind?"

"A shotgun, maybe."

"Would you know the difference by sound?"

"No. It's just an impression."

"Go on."

"He ran through the river, trying to get back to his owner. That's it."

Mark's eyes narrowed. She hadn't told him anything specific, or anything that could be disproved. By keeping it vague, she was covering her bases. Tapping the tips of his fingers on the surface of the desk, he asked, "Anything else?"

"I had another dream this morning," she admitted. "Of suffocating, drowning. Being restrained."

"By what?"

She rubbed her wrists. "I don't know. My face was covered with some sort of dark, thick plastic. I couldn't breathe."

Marc nodded thoughtfully, as if taking her at her word. There was no way she could know Candace Hegel had been alive when the killer had thrown her in the lagoon, or that the victim had been wrapped in a plastic tarp.

He reached into his pocket. "If we had an article of clothing belonging to the deceased, could you get an 'impression' from it?"

"Probably not. It doesn't work on command. I can't always—"

"Would you try?" he asked, pinning her with a look. "It would mean a great deal to her family."

Her stormy-gray eyes were black-rimmed, thickly lashed and startlingly beautiful. "All right," she said softly.

He handed her the gauzy purple scarf, noting Lacy's sudden tension beside him.

Puzzled, Sidney focused her concentration on the swatch of fabric, letting it slide through her fingers, caress her skin. Marc watched her in utter fascination, mesmerized by the performance. She was very, very good. To look at her, eyes closed, moist lips slightly parted, breath coming in short, soft pants, one would think she was lost in sensation, completely unaware of their presence.

And sexually aroused.

As her chest rose and fell, her nipples pushed impudently against the cloth of her sleeveless cotton top, hardening before his eyes.

Damn, she was good. Marc didn't have to look at Lacy to know she was equally riveted. He couldn't imagine a more provocative display.

Unless she actually started touching herself.

To his disappointment, her eyes flew open and she pushed the scarf away from her, cheeks tinged pink.

"Very nice," Marc murmured when he was capable of speech. "What do you do for an encore? Strip naked?"

Her eyes darkened. "Why don't you two play your twisted sex games with someone else?" she retorted, looking back and forth between them.

"*Our* twisted sex games? That was a one-woman show you just gave us, Miss Morrow. Delightful, but all you."

"Well, that game—" she pointed at the slinky, purple scarf "—involved two women. And neither of them was Candace Hegel."

"Oh really?" he drawled. "My mistake." He glanced sideways at Lacy. "I assure you I wasn't a participant. What were these lovely ladies doing, by the way?"

"Drop it," Lacy warned under her breath.

"Never mind," he sighed, training an appreciative eye on Sidney Morrow. He'd underestimated her. She was frighteningly intuitive, a consummate actress and the best damned charlatan he'd ever seen.

Her distract and dazzle technique was wickedly effective, he had to admit. He couldn't have been more turned on. "Let's go," he decided, stifling his lust. "No more games."

"I can leave now?"

"After a brief stop, yes, you'll be free to go."

Lacy gave him an incredulous stare, which he ignored. Yes, it was foolhardy to let her walk; she might be an accomplice to murder. If physical evidence didn't point to a male perpetrator, he'd consider her the prime suspect.

Whatever her role, he'd be watching her like a hawk until he figured out what she was up to, and before he let her off the hook, he couldn't pass on the chance to shake her up again.

With grim determination, he led her down to the morgue.

Chapter 4

Sidney shot daggers into Lieutenant Cruz's well-formed back with her eyes as she followed him down a dark staircase. He'd set her up on purpose by giving her an article of clothing that belonged to Detective Lacy, not Candace Hegel. The attempt to prove her false had backfired, yet Sidney was the one wallowing in humiliation.

When she'd held the slippery fabric in her hands, a thrill had raced through her, as undeniable as any of the emotions she channeled secondhand. She'd felt the scarf trailing over her naked body, followed by a woman's eager mouth, and she'd responded.

She couldn't believe how she'd responded. Intensely aware of his presence, even while under the sensual spell, she had mistakenly assumed she was witnessing a *ménage à trois* between Lieutenant Cruz, Detective Lacy, and another woman.

The very idea of it heated her cheeks.

Equally embarrassed, Detective Lacy had made her excuses, leaving Sidney to complete whatever sinister task Lieutenant Cruz had in store for her. They stopped in front of a heavy door marked Morgue.

"Oh, no," she said, shaking her head.

"Oh, yes," he countered. "You're going to use that psychic touch on Candace Hegel."

"No," she repeated, shivering. This morning's chill was back with reinforcements.

"I still have that arrest warrant, if all else fails," he warned. "Have you ever heard of a body cavity search, Miss Morrow? It's very invasive, I assure you. Especially for someone as sensitive as you."

Fury washed over her. "You are such a bastard," she said.

A muscle in his jaw ticked, but he made no reply as he unlocked the door. Leading her into the depths of the cavernous interior, he located a metal locker and pulled out the horizontal drawer. Before she could turn away, he unzipped the body bag.

Sidney felt the color drain from her face.

"What do you want? Her hand?" With callous indifference, he opened the bag further, exposing a woman's head and upper torso.

It was Sidney's first glimpse of death.

Candace Hegel's attractive features were slack, robbed of beauty, devoid of expression. Her naked chest was bisected with a hideous, Y-shaped incision, and with no oxygenated blood pumping through her body, her skin was strangely discolored. Her lips were dark and her areolae an odd purplish-gray. She looked…cold.

Taking the corpse's pale, limp hand away from her side, Marc held it out toward Sidney, his expression inscrutable.

Her eyes filled with tears as she pressed the dead flesh between her two palms.

With no warning, cold enveloped her, encompassed her, consumed her. She couldn't breathe, couldn't move, couldn't think. Pain exploded inside her head, a quick flash, and she sank heavily into the darkness.

Marc caught her as she fell.

He couldn't believe she'd actually held her breath until she passed out—what kind of grown woman would resort to such extreme measures? Laying her out on the floor carefully, he reevaluated her motives. Maybe she was just a sad, lonely basket case, one who truly believed she had special powers.

However she'd come by her information, he couldn't imagine her hurting anyone, and she didn't deserve to be treated this way. He rarely used cruelty as an investigative technique, and had to admit his motivations for doing so now were more about his personal bias than about her.

In his opinion, psychics were little better than vultures, picking on the bones of the bereaved. Because of people like her, his mother was still trying to communicate with his father via the spirit world. She couldn't let go of him, a man who hadn't been worthy of her affection while he'd been alive.

It drove Marc crazy, thinking about all the time she spent chasing ghosts. Walking down dark alleyways and being ushered into back rooms. Paying money in exchange for lies.

Clenching his jaw in annoyance, he stared down at Sidney's chalk-white face, waiting for her to resume breathing. She didn't. After falling unconscious, the body's natural inclination was to kick up the oxygen, yet she lay there, as quiet as Candace Hegel's corpse.

What the hell?

Her pulse was visible, throbbing delicately in her slender neck. While he watched, it slowed, then stopped altogether.

Muttering a curse, he leaned over her prone form to give her two quick breaths. Her lips were soft and cool, completely slack. If this was a trick, he was buying it hook, line and sinker. He checked her pulse, couldn't find it, panicked and gave her two more breaths.

Gasping, she lurched forward, clutching her chest.

Weak with relief and stunned to the core, he lay stretched out on the ground beside her, placing a hand over his own heart, which was knocking hard against his ribs.

"What happened?" she wheezed.

"You died."

"Oh my God."

"He didn't save you," Marc asserted. "I did."

She leaned to one side and wretched pitifully, her shoulders shaking.

Marc put Candace Hegel back in place, folding her arms across her chest with careful reverence and zipping up the body bag. His hands were trembling as he grabbed some paper towels for Sidney and a plastic cup of water.

She accepted his tepid peace offering in silence, dabbing at her damp mouth. "Why did you do that?" she asked after a moment, her huge gray eyes swimming with tears.

He looked away, hating the reflection of himself he imagined there. "Because I'm a bastard, just like you said."

"I'm sorry. I didn't mean it that way."

His gaze jerked back to her face. He'd just forced her to hold hands with a dead woman, and she was apologizing to him? "Don't worry about it. It's true across the board." He watched her take a small sip of water. "So what did you see?"

"Nothing. It was just…black."

Bleakly he wondered what she'd see in his soul. "I'll take you home," he offered.

"I have to get back to work," she argued.

"You just died, woman! Take the afternoon off."

She chuckled weakly. "I don't have anyone to cover for me."

Marc stared down at her in disbelief, frustrated with the entire situation. He couldn't decide what he thought about her, and that was a complication he didn't need. No way she was legit. So what the hell was she?

"Don't worry, Lieutenant. You'll find the real killer."

"Are you a prophet, too?"

"No," she said with a rueful smile. "I was just trying to be supportive."

Although he was wary of misplaced kindness, he couldn't resist smiling back at her. "Don't you think you can call me Marc now? After all we've been through?"

"Okay," she said, taking his proffered hand. "And I'm Sidney."

Ignoring the burst of warmth in her eyes, and the matching sensation in the middle of his chest, he helped her to her feet.

At Vincent Veterinary Clinic, Marc attached a GPS tracking device to the chassis of Sidney's pickup truck while she went inside to get Blue. When she came out, mangy-looking hound in tow, both dog and woman regarded him with mistrust.

"Can you take some time off tomorrow?" he asked, shoving his hands into his pockets.

"Why?"

"I thought we could drive him around. Walk him along the river, maybe. See if he…smells anything."

She released the tailgate. "Why would you waste your time? You don't believe me." When he made no reply, she gave the dog a brisk order in a foreign language. Blue jumped up and went inside the carrier.

"You speak German?"

"No." Realizing she just had, she said, "I've picked up a few commands. A lot of people train their dogs that way, and he's part shepherd."

"Really? I thought he was half wolf, half hyena."

She shot him a dirty look as she shut the kennel door.

"What did you say to him?"

"Get in," she decided.

She'd said "up," but he didn't bother to correct her. "So how about tomorrow?"

"We could go early, before the kennel opens," she offered with a tense shrug. "It would be cooler."

"Five-thirty?"

"I guess," she said in a resigned voice.

"I'll come by your house," he tossed over his shoulder as he walked away.

"Don't you need my address?" she called after him.

He shook his head, because he already had it. By late afternoon, he'd not only located her small, two-story residence, he'd familiarized himself with every square inch of it. The covert-entry search warrant he'd obtained allowed him to rifle through her personal belongings at his leisure. Sidney would be notified of the "sneak and peek" search when she was no longer under investigation.

Unfortunately there was nothing incriminating inside.

Nothing interesting, either. All of her clothes were well-worn, casual and inexpensive, from her pocket T-shirts to her simple cotton bikini briefs.

The place was quaint and spotless, with mismatched furniture, unusual knickknacks and colorful accents. She saved things like birthday cards and photos in a disorganized drawer, as if she meant to go through them later. Flipping through the photos, he saw a great-looking blonde with two dark-haired girls and a middle-aged couple who must have been Sidney's parents.

There was no indication of a man in her life, but she had a smush-faced little cat, sitting proprietarily atop her wrought-iron bed. The powder-blue chenille bedspread looked as soft as a cloud, the hardwood flooring was polished to a dull shine and the pale yellow paint was warm and unassuming.

It was…cozy.

On impulse, he reached out to place his palm on the pillow where he imagined she put her head. His hand stood out against the white pillowcase, obscenely dark and masculine in the feminine space, and the hairs on the back of his neck prickled with awareness.

It was just like his mother's house, he realized with horror. Nothing new, nothing matching, nothing expensive and a sense of complacent loneliness that tugged at the heartstrings.

He jerked his hand away from the pillow, unsettled by the revelation. Sidney's cat startled at the sudden movement, flying off the bed and losing her footing on the slippery floor as she rounded the corner. Berating himself for the moment of sentimentality, he went downstairs and attached a listening device to the cordless phone on his way out.

In addition to the search warrant, a judge had signed his request to run video and audio surveillance. If the killer was in contact with Sidney, feeding her specific details about the murders, that made her an accessory after the fact.

If she was telling the truth…

Marc shook his head, because he couldn't fathom it. Maybe he was a cynic, but at least he wasn't a sucker. There was one born every day, his father had always said, and he'd been a master at spotting them. He claimed there was nothing more rewarding than pulling off the perfect con. Marc respectfully disagreed. Catching the player at his game was far sweeter.

So why did the thought of arresting Sidney leave a bitter taste in his mouth?

Deputy Chief Stokes had given him the authority to run full surveillance, if not the budget. He'd booked a cheap hotel room less than a block away, but he couldn't get a visual on her back door from there. They couldn't afford to have undercover officers parked on the street in front of her house or hanging around the beach behind it.

He grabbed the white hard hat he kept in the trunk of his car for assuming alternative identities and climbed the telephone pole closest to her house, hoping anyone who saw him would think he was a well-dressed phone company employee.

Near the top, he saw the angle gave him a bird's-eye view into her backyard. It was a miniscule space with an array of potted plants and a large outdoor shower, probably for washing off sand from the beach. He set up a small, nondescript video camera, similar to the ones that come with your basic home computer nowadays, but of marginally better quality, and made sure it was pointed toward her back door.

With that done, he returned to the hotel room, engaged the feed for the bugs and the video camera and waited.

Detective Lacy arrived after he'd done all the work, but she brought excellent takeout so he didn't fault her.

"I was thinking," she said around a mouthful of mu shu pork, "maybe she's not faking."

Marc gave her an expression that meant she was incredibly naïve, and kept eating his beef and broccoli.

"I mean, how did she know about the scarf?"

"Your face is an open book," he said, because he didn't know, either.

She grunted in disbelief. "Next time you're going to pull a stunt like that, could you let me in on it? I almost died of embarrassment."

"How was I supposed to know you had kinky stuff in your locker? It was the only article of clothing I could find in there besides a uniform."

"Well, I don't see how she could have known—unless she talked to Gina." She narrowed her eyes. "They did smile at each other."

Marc laughed at her display of jealousy. "I don't think so."

"Why not?"

"She's straight."

"How do you know?"

"I just do," he said, aware that he sounded very arrogant.

Lacy crossed her arms over her chest. "Not every woman is after your schlong, Marcos."

"Well, if I stick with the ones who are," he said lightly, taking no offense, "I still have a variety to choose from."

"Don't you ever get tired of it?"

"What?"

"Fulfilling a badge-and-holster fantasy for jaded bimbos?"

"No. Why would I?"

"Because it's degrading."

"Not to me."

"To them, then."

He shrugged, because he didn't care.

"Sidney Morrow is not your type," she announced, coming around to the point she really wanted to make.

"She's not yours, either," he retorted, starting to get pissed off.

"I don't know," she said thoughtfully. "She might go for it. A bottle of wine, a couple of scarves…"

Over my dead body, he almost said before he realized she was teasing. Then he scowled at his reaction. Since when had he been possessive over a woman—a suspect no less—one who was unequivocally hands-off?

Lacy was right, anyway. She wasn't his type.

When Sidney came home, Marc and Lacy settled in for a brain-numbing evening. Stakeouts were always tedious.

From their vantage point inside the hotel room they could see Sidney's front doorstep and the south side of her house, complete with one bedroom window, blinds closed. The street she lived on was moderately busy, as was the enticing stretch of sand beyond.

After opening the windows to let in a hint of breeze, she walked out the back door in a demure black Speedo and bare feet.

"That's the ugliest swimsuit I've ever seen," Lacy said.

He grunted in agreement.

On the beach, Sidney didn't sunbathe or stroll along the shore but swam straight out into the Pacific and started doing vigorous laps.

After thirty minutes she came out of the waves like a wet seal, sluicing water off her arms, black bathing suit clinging to her. The Speedo was a crime against nature. It flattened her breasts and covered everything from neck to upper thigh, thoroughly disguising her shape.

As she approached the house, they switched their attention to the video monitor, which gave a view of the side yard. She turned on the outdoor shower, her back to them, and he noticed the sleek muscles in her shoulders.

Especially when she peeled down the upper half of her suit.

The shower had block walls on both sides and a pair of shuttered wooden doors in front that parted, saloon-style. It was a perfectly modest setup, except that the angle of the camera allowed them to see down into it.

"You put the camera there on purpose," Lacy accused.

"No," he said, his throat dry. This scenario really hadn't occurred to him. Videotaping a subject without their knowledge, in a place where they had the reasonable assurance of privacy, was illegal. Bathrooms, locker rooms and bedrooms were off-limits. An outdoor shower was kind of a gray area.

Until now.

"I wouldn't have…" Whatever he was about to say was lost, because she pushed the swimsuit off her hips and turned around.

"Oh my God," Lacy murmured. "Who would've thought she was hiding a body like that underneath those horrible clothes?"

Marc had to admit his wild speculations hadn't done her justice. Her rose-tipped breasts were lush and natural, a sight he could appreciate in this age of implants. Her belly was sleek and flat, her hips flared out sensually from a slim waist and her legs…they went on forever.

"We shouldn't be watching this," he said hoarsely. There was a protocol for surveillance, and ogling naked women in the shower didn't follow it.

"Definitely not," Lacy agreed, making no move to turn off the monitor.

Hugging her arms around herself, Sidney felt the hot press of tears against her eyelids as the cool shower spray pelted her back.

She couldn't stop the barrage of images assaulting her senses.

Anika Groene's red-marked body. Candace Hegel's sea-ravaged face.

Yesterday, Candace had been alive. Last night, she'd been fighting for her last breath.

Sidney should have done something.

She *could* have done something.

Shutting off the water, she grabbed the towel hanging on the shower wall and wrapped it around her dripping body. In the kitchen, Marley was waiting expectantly for her dinner, reminding Sidney that she hadn't eaten, either.

While her cat munched on dry food, Sidney munched on cold cereal and milk at the kitchen countertop, staring mutely at the blank television screen. When the phone rang, she almost jumped out of her skin. Hands trembling, she picked up the receiver. "Hello?"

"Sidney? Is that you, dear?"

Who else would it be? "Yes, Mama."

"Thank goodness. I've been trying to get through to you all afternoon."

"Really?" Her message machine showed no calls. "I was at work."

"Oh. Yes, of course."

Her mother had a selective memory. She often "forgot" about the kennel, and any other detail of Sidney's life she didn't approve of.

"I was so worried," she continued. "Samantha called yesterday."

Sidney was torn between annoyance with her sister and annoyance with her mother. "It's really not a problem," she lied.

"Not a problem? I beg to differ! Contemplating divorce is the biggest problem a married woman can have."

Sidney sank into a chair, kicking herself for thinking her mother had been worried about her, not Samantha, or that her egotistical older sister would have bothered to call home and talk about anyone besides herself.

"You've got to do something," her mother was saying.

"Like what?"

"Talk her out of it."

Sidney laughed softly, so she wouldn't cry. "Samantha does what she pleases. She'll get a divorce if she wants one, no matter what you or I say."

Her mother was silent for a moment. "I just don't understand you girls sometimes. In my day, a woman gave her husband some leeway."

"He's cheating on her," she said shortly.

"Yes, well, men are more susceptible to sins of the flesh. A true lady is forgiving, not vindictive."

Sidney smiled. Not only was her mother old-fashioned, but she had no idea what Samantha was capable of. "Not everybody has a marriage like you and Daddy," she said. "He's devoted to you." Hen-pecked, too. "Greg is…not the same."

Her mind drifted to an awful scene at Samantha and Greg's wedding. Sidney had been a sweet nineteen, a reluctant bridesmaid in the frothy lavender dress her sister had forced her to wear. It pushed her breasts up to her chin and cinched in her waist, so it must have been partially to blame for Greg's clumsy, roving hands when he found her alone in a dark hallway.

That was a secret she'd never told. Samantha was already pregnant and Sidney couldn't bear to hurt her. By the time her sister's second baby came along the point was moot. Samantha had already caught Greg cheating and blamed her postpartum body for his indiscretions.

In the years since, her savagely achieved perfection hadn't kept him faithful.

"I'm really tired, Mama," Sidney said, rubbing her aching forehead. "I think I'll go to bed early. Tell Daddy I love him, 'kay?"

"Okay, dear. Take care of yourself."

"You, too."

Sidney pushed the button on the receiver, feeling tears flood her eyes. "You're pathetic," she told herself, brushing them off her cheeks. Before she realized her mother had been calling about Samantha, a ray of hope had spread through her chest, filling an empty part of her.

Now it was hollow once again.

She'd never been able to talk to her mother about her feelings, supernatural or otherwise. Aurelia Morrow had "spells," too, ones that required days of bed rest and absolute quiet. Sidney's "feelings" had always given Mama "spells."

"Whatever," she said dismally, trying to convince herself she didn't care. So what if she didn't have a best friend or close relative to confide in? So what if she didn't have that special someone who understood her and believed in her and supported her?

In her experience, few people did. Her mother's illness, real or imaginary, baffled her father. He'd been walking on pins and needles around her for the past twenty years. Greg and Samantha certainly weren't soul mates.

So why did Sidney feel so cheated by circumstance?

This was all Marc Cruz's fault, she decided, trudging upstairs to her room. He stirred up latent desires. Placing her cordless phone on the nightstand, she stretched out on the bed in her damp towel and buried her face in the pillows.

She gasped, feeling his touch.

Scrambling to a sitting position, she searched the dark room with wide eyes, clutching the towel to her breasts.

He wasn't there.

She lay back down experimentally, her head making a soft indentation in the pillow. She felt his presence, like a ghost hand cradling the back of her head. In response, her nipples peaked against the soft terry cloth, and a tingling warmth throbbed between her thighs.

Ashamed of her body's reaction, she squeezed her legs together, trying to will her arousal away. Instead the tension built, slowly becoming unbearable.

With no one else to touch her, she surrendered to temptation and touched herself.

Chapter 5

When Marc showed up on her doorstep at 5:25 the next morning, he looked tired.

In deference to the heat, or the occasion, he was wearing lightweight trousers and a short-sleeved shirt, not tucked in. His eyes were guarded, devoid of warmth, but his chocolate-brown hair appeared invitingly thick and lustrous. It was the kind of hair a woman liked to run her fingers through, and perhaps one just had, considering its tousled appearance.

Half as polished as usual, he was twice as handsome.

"Ready?"

"Yes." She didn't know proper etiquette for greeting a police officer at the door. "Do you want a cup of coffee…or anything?"

His dark gaze flicked over her. "No." He took a pair of sunglasses out of his front pocket and covered his eyes, although it was barely light out.

Frowning at his brusque treatment, she stepped through the door and locked it behind her. She had to hurry to keep up with him on the way to the parking garage.

"We're taking your truck."

"Fine," she replied. It made sense that he wouldn't want Blue in his fancy car, growling and breathing down his neck.

"I'll drive," he offered. Shrugging, she tossed him the keys and climbed in the passenger side. Obviously he didn't want to be here with her. So why had he suggested this outing? Deciding two could play at being unfriendly, she let the silence stretch between them.

They picked up Blue at the kennel, where Sidney did a quick feed and clean while Marc acted bored and looked impatient. By the time she was finished, the sun was burning through the early morning clouds, promising another hot, hazy day. Wiping sweat from her forehead, she moved to put Blue in the bed of the truck.

"I want him up front with us."

"Why?"

"How else are you going to know if he reacts to something? You've got to pick up on his…vibe, right?"

It would be a tight squeeze with the three of them in the cab. Blue would have to sit next to the window, leaving her sandwiched beside Marc. She squinted at him over the hood of the truck. "Are you just trying to get close to me?"

She couldn't see his eyes behind the lenses of his sunglasses, but she could feel his tension. "Why would I do that?" he asked in an even voice.

"To crowd me in. Intimidate me. You know."

"Oh. Right." He nodded, acknowledging that he'd done that before. "I make it a rule not to crowd a woman with an aggressive dog at her disposal," he said with a sardonic smile. His teeth were strong and white against his dark skin.

Her stomach jumped at the sight.

Smiling back at him, a little uncertainly, she scooted across the bench seat and coaxed Blue in after her. When Marc got behind the wheel, she held herself stiff, careful to keep her body from touching his. Out of the corner of her eye, she studied his hands, manipulating the gearshift, noting the thickness of his wrists and the veins running down the length of his forearms. Remembering how she'd imagined those hands on her last night, she felt her entire body flush.

With a hundred pounds of panting, drooling, fur-covered mutt beside her, Sidney wondered how she could be so intensely aware of Marc's presence. Blue had been bathed and brushed yesterday, but he still smelled like a dog.

Marc, on the other hand, smelled like a man. A clean, warm-skinned man. The faint scent of Old Spice clung to him. Deodorant, she realized, suppressing the urge to bury her face in his armpit and inhale.

They drove around the inland hills of Oceanside, through the neighborhoods near the San Luis Rey River for the better part of an hour, during which they hardly spoke. Blue sniffed and hung his head out the window, but didn't seem to sense anything.

"Does he know what we're doing?"

"I doubt it," she admitted.

"Can't you read his mind?"

She didn't turn to look at him, because he was too close for comfort. "No. I don't read minds, I just sort of get flashes. Feelings. Images."

"What's the difference?"

She shrugged. "You were implying that I know what everyone around me is thinking every moment."

"Even if you touch someone, you don't always know?"

"No. I usually don't."

That seemed to relax him a little, although she was sure he didn't believe anything she said. "I guess I could have brought something of the owner's for him to smell. Most dogs that haven't been trained for search and rescue don't know what to do with it, though."

Abandoning the effort, he executed a three-point turnaround. As he shifted into Reverse, the side of his palm grazed the length of her bare thigh. The accidental touch sent another shiver of awareness down her spine. She felt his shoulders stiffen, and knew he wasn't as unaffected by her proximity as he pretended to be. When he stopped at one of the many small parking lots along the San Luis Rey, she practically leaped out of the truck, relieved to be free of the sensual trap circumstance had created.

There was a wide sidewalk pathway running east alongside the river from the beach all the way to Camp Pendleton. It was used by nature enthusiasts at their own peril, for the area was known as a homeless hideout. Thick copses of eucalyptus tress and wild brush gave would-be robbers plenty of ambush spots.

"Do lots of people get mugged here?" she asked.

"Not really. Walkers and bicyclists don't typically carry a lot of cash on them. Besides, most homeless are opportunistic criminals, not violent ones."

She eyed the bushes with trepidation.

"Are you afraid?" He seemed amused. "I have my gun."

"Do you?" She searched his body. "Where?"

"Here." He lifted the side of his shirt, showing her his brown leather shoulder holster. Although he wore a ribbed cotton T-shirt underneath, the glimpse of hard torso was still exciting. "We're perfectly safe. No one would think twice about accosting you with that savage-looking beast, anyway."

"Someone assaulted Candace Hegel," she pointed out.

He looked away from her, toward the river. "We'll have better luck along the shore," he said, stepping through the thick brush. She followed, careful not to slip over the pebble-strewn bank. Thorny branches scratched at her bare legs, making her wish she'd worn long pants, but she didn't complain.

They hiked around for another hour, crossing the shallow river several times. Her shoes became wet and squishy, her footing precarious on the uneven ground. Sidney was feeling sorry for those down on their luck enough to live here when they came upon a group of rough-looking young men smoking marijuana in the shade of a California pepper tree.

Marc put his hand on her waist casually, keeping his body between the men and her as they continued along the shore.

"Aren't you obligated to arrest people like that?" she asked.

"For what?"

"Smoking pot."

"If I shook down everyone with a joint I'd never get any real work done. Besides, I can't take on a whole gang. They'd have torn me apart."

"What's your gun for? Show?"

Rather than taking offense, he laughed. "I don't pull my gun unless I intend to use it."

"And have you?"

"No. I've never fired it on-duty." He arched a glance at her. "My job isn't as exciting as what you see on TV. I battle more paperwork than bad guys."

No sooner had he said that than Blue took off like a shot, almost yanking her arm out of the socket. He tore through the underbrush, barking ferociously and dragging her along until they came upon a startling scene.

Under the cover of the trees, a man was on top of a woman, holding one hand over her mouth. His pants were pushed down his heavy thighs; her skirt was shoved up to her waist. As Sidney stood there, stock-still, a trickle of blood coursed over the woman's ruddy cheek.

Blue went wild. It was all she could do to keep him from attacking.

"Oceanside Police Department," Marc said, stepping around Sidney and flashing his badge. She could feel fury pouring off him in waves. "Move back toward me, with your knees on the ground and your hands over your head."

Ignoring the order, the guy hobbled to his feet, pulled up his pants and fled.

He didn't get far. The fugitive was built like a linebacker, but Marc took him down easily. He also punched him in the back of the neck a few times to subdue him. It was police brutality at its finest, and she couldn't tear her eyes away.

She didn't see the fallen woman launch herself at Marc until too late.

"Let him go!" the wild avenger screeched, clawing at his shoulders. Too practical to release his grip on the guy underneath him, Marc had no choice but to take the abuse.

Sidney couldn't understand why any woman would defend someone who'd just been raping and beating her. Upon closer inspection, she had the coarse complexion of an addict and the hard look of a streetwalker.

Stepping forward, Sidney urged Blue along until his intimidating mug was just inches from the woman's crazed face. "This dog is trained to protect police officers to the death, ma'am," she said quietly. "I suggest you move away, real slow and easy."

The woman wasn't so hysterical that she failed to comply.

Thankfully the guy on the ground had been too stunned to retaliate during his victim's effort to defend him. "Look, man, it's not what you think," he panted. "She likes it that way."

"Right," Marc muttered, patting him down. "Assault and battery is illegal, whether she presses charges or not."

The man groaned.

"You're both going to jail," Marc decided. "Can you control him without the leash?" he asked Sidney, glancing down at Blue.

"Yes," she said, releasing the leash and handing it to him. Putting her arms around Blue's neck, she narrowed her eyes on the woman, daring her to feel lucky. Marc tied the strange couple together, back-to-back, and jerked them to their feet.

"Take the cell phone out of my pocket and call dispatch," he ordered. She did, holding the phone to his ear as he requested a patrol car. Within five minutes, both assailants were on their way downtown.

"Boring desk job, huh?" she teased.

"It has its moments," he allowed, casting an admiring glance her way. "I should deputize you. That was pretty fast thinking."

She smiled at the praise. "I couldn't let you have all the fun."

His grunted response told her wrestling with lowlifes wasn't his idea of fun. "I'll have to go to the station now to write up a report. You want to take a rain check on this, or have you had your fill of police work?"

Looking down at Blue, sitting stoic and regal, she found she couldn't say no. "Maybe you should deputize him," she murmured, wondering if the dog's reaction to men and violence was a reflection of what happened to his owner, or something he'd learned long ago.

Marc arranged for Lacy to pick him up at Pacific Pet Hotel, where Sidney invited him in to clean up his scratched neck.

He didn't want her touching him, but he couldn't politely refuse, and he needed an infection from a homeless prostitute's fingernails about as badly as he needed hepatitis from Agua Hedionda Lagoon.

When she sat him down and pressed a cool washcloth to the back of his neck, he corrected himself. He *did* want her touching him. He just didn't want to want it.

It didn't matter that she wasn't his type. It didn't matter that she was probably a liar. It didn't matter that she was a suspect. All he could think about when he looked at her was having her naked body underneath his, making the same soft panting sounds she'd made by herself last night. Listening to her, he'd wanted to order Lacy out of the room so he could finish himself off the same way. Instead he'd spent a miserable night contemplating his own perversity. With plenty of other women at his disposal, why was he lusting after this one?

She sprayed something that felt like stinging nettle on his neck, and he hissed out a breath, welcoming the distraction. "What's that?"

"Antibacterial spray."

She rubbed salve on the raw scratches, soothing the pain but inflaming his desire. If he didn't get away from her soon, she wouldn't need to read his mind to know what he was thinking. She'd only have to glance down at the front of his pants.

"Your arm needs some attention, too."

He cranked his head over his shoulder to see what she was talking about, noticing the dull throb in his elbow for the first time. Blood was crusted in a large circle, the makings of a nasty scab, and dried rivulets snaked down his forearm. Again, it was in an awkward place, difficult to clean on his own.

"Go ahead," he muttered. While he stood over the stainless steel sink, she washed bits of debris out of the wound. It was uncomfortable enough to keep his thoughts pure. "You aren't wearing gloves," he noted.

"Yeah. I should be."

Damn right she should. He'd never touch a stranger's blood with his bare hands. She rubbed triple antibiotic ointment on his elbow then wrapped it up with gauze and tape. "Thanks," he said, curling his arm up to test the bandage. Tight, but not too tight.

"I wanted to be a vet," she said wistfully.

"What happened?"

She shrugged, looking away from him, and he thought she was much too young to be giving up a dream.

"You've got some battle wounds yourself, Deputy," he said, indicating the scratches on her long, lovely legs, using concern as an excuse to keep his eyes on them.

"Are you going to take care of them for me?" she teased.

His gaze jerked to her face. Was she toying with him? Perhaps today's display of bravery, and even last night's...episode...had been calculated. It didn't make sense, because she couldn't have known about the surveillance, and nothing about her was overtly seductive. Her ragged cutoffs were short but baggy, her face was smudged with dirt and her brown T-shirt had a dorky gecko on the front.

Then again, if she was trying to use her understated sexuality to manipulate him, it was working. "I'll take care of anything you need me to," he said in a low voice, just to see her reaction.

"Don't," she said, her eyes flashing with hurt.

"Don't what?"

"Come on to me as an investigative technique."

He'd unsettled her, and he liked that, so he smiled. "If not for this case, I'd come on to you for real."

She laughed without humor. "Please."

He longed to hear her say that in a more intimate context. "Whatever you wish to believe," he said simply, because the conversation had gone way beyond inappropriate. What the hell was the matter with him? Not trusting himself to be alone with her another minute, he walked outside to wait for Detective Lacy, trying to refocus his energy on work.

Stokes was going to rake him over the coals for involving a civilian in a dangerous foot pursuit. He could hear her now, reminding him of protocol, common sense and the inadvisability of taking down an assailant by force with no cuffs or backup. He had no self-control when it came to violence against women, and blah, blah, blah.

Sighing, Marc climbed into Lacy's Jeep, not looking forward to the remainder of the day.

"Check it out," she said, handing him a computer printout.

It was an Internet archive from the *San Diego Explorer,* dated fifteen years in the past. "Local Girl Saves the Day," the article read.

"Sidney Anne Morrow, age twelve, daughter of Bonsall residents Aurelia and Frank Morrow, helped local police officers find a missing girl who'd fallen into a well. The girl, Lisa Jane Pettigrew, also twelve, disappeared several days ago and was feared dead. Miss

Morrow approached two officers claiming she had a 'hunch' that the missing girl was in a long-forgotten well on the outskirts of a rural property.

"She wasn't able to lead rescuers to the exact location, so a public records survey from 1902 was consulted. Sure enough, Lisa Pettigrew was found at the bottom of the well, malnourished and dehydrated, but in fair condition.

"Lisa's parents offered a monetary reward to the Morrow family to show their heartfelt appreciation for the safe return of their only child…"

"So what's this supposed to prove?" he asked, unwilling to give up his initial position. He didn't believe in supernatural nonsense and he was never going to. "That she's been working people since puberty?"

"I'm just keeping an open mind," she said, implying he wasn't.

In curt response, he crumpled up the printout and tossed it into the back seat.

On the way to the station, he muddled through the details of the case. Anika Groene and Candace Hegel had been slim, petite blondes, easy for a good-size man to overpower. Both had been taken in the morning. Both had been raped, beaten, tied up and tortured. Both had been dumped in water while still alive.

And both had large, intimidating watchdogs.

Marc felt as though this clue was key. The killer was targeting single women who walked their dogs in the early morning. Why not grab a woman alone, or one with a smaller, less dangerous dog? Either the assailant knew the women, and their dogs, or Marc was missing something important.

Of course, there were ways to immobilize even the most vigilant canine companion.

Sidney said Blue had been groggy when she found him. She'd been right about him breaking out of a vehicle; lab results on the safety glass indicated nothing more specific than a newer model car or truck. She'd been right about the river; the dog's paws tested positive for elements unique to the San Luis Rey.

And yet, the dog's toxicology report had been clear. No poisons, barbiturates, tranquilizers, or chemical depressants were present in his bloodstream.

"You know what you could do," Lacy ventured after a pause.

"What?"

"Take her to the sites."

Marc scowled, remembering what Sidney had gone through after coming in contact with Candace Hegel's dead hand. How would she react to a crime scene? "The department has regulations against consulting psychics."

"Like you've never strayed from protocol," she chided.

He said nothing. Although he knew of other cops who had gone that route, he would never do so. In his opinion, so-called psychics victimized the weak and vulnerable, lost souls desperate to communicate with dearly departed loved ones. Taking advantage of—and taking money from—grieving lonely-hearts was despicable.

The intense dislike he carried for otherworldly con artists went as deep as his hatred for men who abused women.

After all, his mother had fallen prey to both.

Chapter 6

Sidney was dozing off on her futon couch, dreaming about playing doctor with Marc Cruz, when her sister barged through her front door, Dakota and Taylor in tow.

Sidney rubbed her tired eyes, wondering what tragedy had befallen Samantha this time.

"There's ice cream in the freezer," she said to the girls when she saw the frantic expression on her sister's face. "Go on and serve yourselves some."

"I left Greg," Samantha said when her daughters were out of earshot.

"When?"

"This morning. Do you have any money?"

Sidney gaped at her incredulously.

"He knows about Richard, Sid. He's frozen all the accounts and he says he's going to get custody." Her eyes darted around the room. "What am I going to do?" she whispered.

"He won't get full custody," Sidney assured her sister with more certainty than she felt. "Everything's going to be fine."

"It could be months before the divorce goes through. What am I going to do until then? How am I going to live?"

"You can stay with me."

Samantha's smooth brow crumpled at the indignity of being brought so low. "Can you watch the girls for a few hours? I really need to, um, decompress."

With a sigh, Sidney nodded her assent. Maybe it was better that Dakota and Taylor not see their mother looking so…crazed.

"You're a doll," Samantha gushed, scuttling out the door on high-heeled sandals before Sidney could change her mind.

By the time the girls were fed, bathed, brushed, and in bed, it was almost ten o'clock. Sidney had been on her feet almost eighteen hours and she was completely drained. Samantha was right. Taking care of two energetic children was exhausting.

Because Dakota and Taylor were sleeping upstairs, in the only bedroom, Sidney took a quick shower outside so as not to disturb their slumber. She grabbed a tank top and underwear straight out of the dryer, pulled them on and collapsed in a boneless heap on the couch next to Marley. She was asleep as soon as her head hit the moon-shaped pillow, only to be rudely awakened less than five minutes later.

Cursing all sisters, she stumbled to the door and wrenched it open. Samantha's husband, Greg, was there, his handsome face flushed, dark eyes unfocused. "Where is she?" he asked, slurring the words together.

"Not here," she said, crinkling her nose at his odor and appearance. His clothes were expensively tailored, his watch diamond encrusted, and his shoes Italian leather, but he reeked of bourgeoisie. And booze.

Sidney let him in, mentally calculating the time it would take a cab to arrive.

"That bitch took my kids," he muttered. "Can you believe that? I'm calling the cops."

As he fumbled in his pocket for a cell phone, his bloodshot eyes perused the length of her body, making her uncomfortably aware of her own dishabille.

"Greg, don't," she said, wrapping the sheet around her. "The girls are here."

"Where?" He glanced toward the stairs. "I'm taking them home."

"No," she said, standing in front of him. "You're not."

"The hell I'm not," he replied, stumbling around her.

Sidney reached out to put her hand on his shoulder, then thought better of it and dropped her arm. She didn't want to know where he'd been. "Please," she whispered. "They're asleep. Let them rest."

"I'm their father," he asserted. "They belong with me."

"Fine," she said, pointing at the couch. "Hang out here and sober up for a few hours. Then you can take them."

His mouth twisted bitterly, but he sat. "She's going to pay for this," he said in a grumble. "She drives them around, high as a kite—"

"You were about to do the same," she felt compelled to point out.

He blinked up at her. "Oh God," he moaned, covering his face with his hands. "How did everything get so messed up?" To Sidney's acute discomfort, he began to cry in loud, wrenching sobs, his broad shoulders shaking with emotion.

The display was so pitiful she couldn't help but feel sorry for him. "There, there," she murmured, patting the top of his head. Instantly she was aware of her mistake. Although his thoughts were muddled by drink, they were easy enough to read.

"You're so nice," he breathed, throwing his heavy arms around her waist.

"Um," she replied, trying to pry his hands away.

Groaning, he brought her down to the couch beside him and rolled on top of her, pinning her beneath the weight of his body.

"Greg, stop—"

With an impressive show of strength and determination, considering his blood alcohol level, he locked his hands around her wrists, trapping her arms above her head and trying to force his mouth over hers.

Gagging, she turned her face away, only to have him land a wet, sloppy kiss on her neck. When his teeth closed around the strap of her tank top, she saw red. "Get off me," she grated, yanking her wrists free from his grip.

The spaghetti strap snapped, baring her left breast. His liquor-glazed eyes widened with inspiration as he lowered his mouth.

Sidney's knee connected with his groin before he got there. His face contorted into a comical grimace and he fell away from her, onto the floor. She had an almost irrepressible urge to kick him while he was down.

As she stood over him, seriously contemplating it, another knock sounded at the front door. Samantha, she thought with relief. Holding her top up with one hand, she answered it.

Marc Cruz was standing there, looking more rumpled than he had this morning, wearing the same clothes. His eyes flicked over her, pausing only briefly on her bikini panties before coming to rest at the torn strap hanging off her shoulder.

"What are you doing here?"

"I was in the neighborhood," he claimed, trying to see around her. "Can I come in?"

She hesitated. Greg was a schmuck, but he was her nieces' father, and from what she'd seen this morning, Marc didn't play nice with guys like him.

He didn't wait for her permission. Walking past her, he asked, "Who the hell is this?" gesturing to the miserable heap curled up in the fetal position on the floor.

"None of your business," she replied, wondering when he'd gone crazy.

"You're entertaining some guy in your underwear, and it's none of my business?"

"Who're you?" Greg wheezed.

"I'm her boyfriend."

"He's a cop," she said at the same time.

"I'm her boyfriend, the cop," he clarified. "Want to explain why her shirt is ripped and you're holding your balls?"

"No," Greg decided, lumbering to his feet. "I'm leaving."

"He's too drunk to drive," Sidney protested. "I'll call a cab."

"Don't bother," Greg snarled.

Marc crossed his arms over his chest, his legs braced wide. "I haven't handled a DUI in a while. This should be fun."

"I can drive him," Sidney said in a rush. "I'll find someone to watch the kids." The last thing she wanted was a fistfight on her front doorstep. Especially between a deranged cop and a drunk brother-in-law.

"You look tired," Marc said, studying her face. "I'll take him."

"You and what army?" Greg slurred, having trouble standing in place.

Ignoring him, Marc reached out to take her hand. "Get some rest," he said. "I'm picking you up early again tomorrow." In a casual, boyfriendlike manner, he leaned in and brushed his lips across hers. The kiss could have been called perfunctory if he hadn't used his tongue.

It was the barest touch, so light she might have thought she'd imagined it if not for the rush of cool night air coming in through the open doorway, caressing the moist spot his mouth had made on her trembling lips.

"Are you okay?" he asked, very close to her ear.

Too confused to speak, she merely nodded. Rather than taking her word for it, he ran his fingertips up the side of her neck and along the line of her jaw, checking for injuries. Finding none, he smiled, rubbing his thumb across her cheekbone.

"Tomorrow," he promised, following Greg out the door.

She stared after them, raising a hand to her mouth and tracing the outline of her lips. Why had he done that? If the kiss had been for Greg's benefit, to convince him they were involved, it needed only look real, not feel real.

Sidney shook her head, chiding herself for getting weak-kneed over an empty gesture. It hadn't meant anything to him. He probably tongue-kissed grandmothers.

But why had he charged down her door and posed as her boyfriend in the first place?

Ignoring the tingling warmth spreading over her skin, she changed shirts and curled up on the couch with Marley. "Men," she muttered. "Who needs them?"

Marley mewed her agreement.

"What do you know?" Sidney grumbled, feeling contrary. "You're spayed."

Marc drove Greg's silver Porsche instead of his own Audi under the pretext of generosity. Once inside, he scanned the floors for dog hair, the windows for recent repairs and the gray leather interior for damage.

Any male acquaintance of Sidney's was a suspect of his. Especially one who couldn't control himself around women.

He'd slammed out of the hotel room as soon as he'd heard distress in Sidney's voice. At the sight of her anxious face and torn clothing, he felt an incredible fury rise up inside him, so powerful he wasn't sure he could hold it in check. True, he was sensitive where abused women were concerned, but he'd never been sent over the edge by a hanging tank top strap.

Even now, his muscles were tense and his pulse pounding. He clenched his hands around the steering wheel, still tempted to drive his fists into Greg's liquor-slackened mouth.

"Listen, I'm really sorry about Sidney," Greg said. "I didn't know she was with someone."

"If she were single, you'd have a right to force yourself on her?"

"No." Greg frowned. "I wouldn't do that. My wife and I are going through a hard time, and Sidney was…comforting me. I guess I got the wrong idea."

Marc grunted his agreement.

"I'm really pissed off at Samantha, so maybe I took it out on Sidney. But I would never hurt her. She's like a little sister to me."

"A little sister you want to screw?"

Greg's expression grew belligerent, but he remained silent.

"Your wife," Marc mused, remembering the photo he'd seen in Sidney's drawer, "is blond and slim. Do you ever pick up women that look like her? Take out your frustrations on them, instead?"

His brow crumpled. "What kind of cop are you?"

"Homicide."

"Oh. Oh, no. You don't think that I—"

"Let me tell you what I think, pal," he interrupted. "I think you're a drunk asshole who just attacked my girlfriend, your wife's sister, in her own home, with your kids sleeping upstairs."

He paled. "No, it wasn't like that. I only tried to kiss her."

"She felt compelled to defend herself physically from a kiss?"

He clamped his mouth shut, mutinous and petulant.

"Where were you Sunday night, between midnight and 4:00 a.m.?"

"Asleep in bed."

"At home, with your wife?"

He wet his lips. "No."

"We can discuss this at the station, if you'd rather."

"I have a girlfriend, okay? My wife and I haven't been getting along."

"What's her name?"

"Elisabeth. She's my secretary."

Marc glanced across the cab at him. "How trite," he murmured.

He turned on Carlsbad Village Drive, following the sports car's handy navigational system while Greg dozed. After they arrived at Greg's posh estate, he roused and invited Marc in for a drink. Either Greg had completely forgotten what he'd done to Sidney just an hour before, or he was trying to smooth things over with liquid bribery.

Marc had a few minutes before patrol picked him up, so he accepted Greg's offer. Getting a look inside his house and extending the interview couldn't hurt.

"Cheers," Greg said, handing Marc a glass of Tennessee's finest.

He took a sip, not surprised to find the liquor smooth and of excellent quality. Greg couldn't buy class, or taste, but he'd apparently spent a lot of money trying. The interior of the house was spacious, modern and stark, with gray marble flooring, cubist art pieces and chic, sharp-edged furniture. From his position at the granite-topped wet bar, Marc couldn't see a hint of warmth. Or a single family photo.

"How long have you and Sidney been going out?" Greg asked.

"A few weeks."

"Has she given up the goods?"

Marc felt a flash of renewed anger. "No."

"Don't hold your breath for it," Greg predicted slyly, sounding pleased. "Her legs are tied together at the knees."

"Because she won't have you?"

"She won't have anyone. Doesn't date. Doesn't like to be touched."

"Why is that, do you think?"

Greg shrugged. "I always figured she was a dyke, and too uptight to admit it."

Marc smiled at his arrogance. "How long have you been in love with her?"

Greg downed his drink in one quick, angry gulp. "Get out," he spat. The violent overreaction was almost as good as an admission.

Marc drained his glass also. Standing, he met Greg's dark, glittering eyes, only inches from his own. "I'm going to let you off real easy this time," he said, "but if you ever touch Sidney again, you won't be holding on to your balls, whimpering like a baby." He shoved the empty tumbler at his chest. "You'll be choking on them."

He left Greg's house still wanting to put his fist through something. His concern for Sidney's safety hadn't been unfounded, but rushing to her defense could have tipped her off about the surveillance. He was treating her more like a witness than a suspect.

Maybe he was losing his objectivity, but he just couldn't see any artifice in her. Reluctantly he entertained the idea that her visions had some credence, and that she might be able to help him with the case.

When he got back to the hotel, Lacy was asleep. So was Sidney, judging from the sound of her soft, rhythmic breathing as he slipped on the headphones. He was supposed to let Lacy take second shift, but he didn't. Staring at Sidney's dark, curtain-shrouded windows, he stayed awake, listening to her breathe, finding that sound somehow more comforting than sleep.

Like a nightmare, the knocking wouldn't stop. Groaning, she rolled to a sitting position on the living room floor, every muscle in her body screaming in violent protest.

Samantha was sleeping peacefully on the couch, curled up in a bundle of rumpled sheets with Marley snuggled alongside her, purring.

"Traitor," she muttered, crawling to her feet.

Marc Cruz was at her doorstep. Again.

"What?"

"It's 5:45," he said. "I gave you an extra few minutes."

"How generous. Go away."

On the couch, Samantha moaned and stretched. Sidney closed her eyes, willing her sister silent, willing Marc gone, willing herself back asleep.

No such luck. Samantha came up beside her and draped her slender arm over Sidney's shoulder, striking a sultry pose. "Good morning," she said, her electric-blue eyes raking over Marc's muscular physique. Her mascara was smudged and her hair a riot of blond tangles, but Samantha made a hangover look like a million bucks. The hot-pink panties and matching lace camisole she was wearing didn't hurt.

Marc looked, proving himself a red-blooded man, and let his gaze linger, proving himself a shallow, horny bastard.

"This must be the handsome investigator you told me about," Samantha said.

Sidney felt her face grow warm. Why did her sister always insist on embarrassing her? "Do you want to come in and wait?" she asked Marc. "I'm not ready."

He ogled Samantha one more time. "Sure."

Sidney stormed away, wishing a lifetime of miseries on them both. She was staring at her pathetic, puffy-eyed reflection over the bathroom sink when Samantha hurried in, flapping her hands with excitement. "Oh, honey, you've got to get with him."

Sidney splashed cold water on her face. "Why?"

"So you can tell me if he's any good."

She began brushing her teeth vigorously. "Why don't you give him a test run yourself and leave me out of it?"

"Don't be so negative, darling. Men hate it."

Affecting total disinterest, Sidney shouldered past her. In the dryer, the only clothes she could find were a pair of blue terry-cloth shorts she sometimes used as pajamas. She pulled them on with a baggy T-shirt and stepped into her river-stained tennis shoes.

"Is that what you're wearing?" Samantha was horrified.

"Why don't I just parade around in see-through lingerie, like you?"

"Oh my God," she said, clapping a hand over her mouth. "You're jealous."

Sidney glared her sister into silence, motioning toward the living room.

"He went outside to make a phone call," Samantha explained. "He couldn't have been less interested in me."

"Sure."

"I mean it, Sid. I think he really likes you."

Sidney snorted her disbelief. Maybe Marc was pretending to be her boyfriend again, like last night. She was too tired to figure out what game he was playing. "I'll be back in a few hours," she said to Samantha. "Get some more sleep."

In his car, moments later, she was uncomfortably aware of his presence, her appearance, the amount of thigh exposed by her brief shorts and the feel of her bare skin against his all-leather interior. For some reason, whenever she was with him her physical reactions went haywire, while her other senses dulled. Last night, he'd put his hands all over her face. He'd brushed his lips over hers. And yet, the only feelings she'd experienced were her own.

Was animal attraction the cure for her condition?

Closing her eyes, she replayed his kiss in her mind, unable to stop torturing herself with the memory.

"About last night," he began, pulling at his collar. "I was thinking I could have handled things differently."

She hazarded a glance at him. "What do you mean?"

"I wanted to talk with Greg privately, so I misrepresented our…relationship, and put my investigation above your feelings. You can still press charges, of course."

"No," she said quickly, flushing at the thought of complaining to his superiors about a harmless little kiss.

"I should have offered you that option last night. It was selfish."

She shrugged. "It's no big deal. I hardly felt it."

"Hardly felt what?"

"Your…" She trailed off, seeing his confusion. "What are you talking about?"

"You, pressing charges against Greg."

"Oh. Right."

"What were you talking about?" His lips curved into a slight smile. "Me kissing you?"

She felt her cheeks heat even more.

He arched a brow. "Hardly felt it, did you? Hmm."

"Where are we going?" she asked, changing the subject.

"Guajome Lake."

Those two words dispelled any romantic notions she'd been entertaining.

Guajome Lake was a small body of water along the eastern edge of Oceanside, close to Bonsall, where Sidney grew up. The lake was surrounded by a quiet camping area and RV park. A month ago, Anika Groene's nude body had been found there, half-submerged, tangled in reeds.

As Marc pulled his car into the shaded parking area, Sidney felt mildly nauseous. She wished she'd eaten something this morning to settle her stomach, and was glad, at the same time, that she hadn't.

"What do you want me to do?"

He shrugged, getting out of the car. They walked the perimeter of the lake with a flock of ducks waddling around their feet, changing the mood from macabre to bizarre. Sidney didn't feel anything supernatural, but she hadn't expected to. She didn't get readings from the air, or the sky, or the soles of her shoes.

At a clearing along the shore, she stopped. It was a dry dirt bank, close to the road, and the kind of place where a person wouldn't leave muddy footprints. "Was she found here?"

Instead of answering, he shoved his hands in his pockets, looking across the silent expanse of water.

"Hold my hand," she requested.

His dark gaze searched her face, but he did as she asked. Closing her eyes in concentration, she grasped for an impression and got nothing more from him than she ever had. He put up a resistance around himself like a brick wall.

Sighing, she gave up on trying to read his thoughts. Instead she felt the warmth of his skin, the slightly rough texture of his palm, the banked strength in his hand.

"You weren't here," she said. "When they pulled her up."

It wasn't a question, so he didn't bother to reply. He did meet her eyes, and for a second, the wall between them fell away.

Through him, she saw herself, not standing on the shore of Guajome Lake, but in the outdoor shower at her own home. With her head tilted back and her hands in her wet hair, every detail of her naked body was on provocative display.

She dropped his hand from hers like it had been burned. "You saw me in the shower," she whispered. Not only had he been spying on her, but he'd been listening in. "You heard..." Shame and betrayal stabbed through her, as sharp as a knife. She pressed the back of her hand to her trembling mouth. "How could you do that?"

Guilt flashed in his eyes. "Sidney—"

With a muted cry, she turned and ran, almost losing her footing on the slippery, freshly watered grass on the hillside leading up to the women's rest room. Inside, she locked herself in the last stall, pulse beating wildly in her throat, a cold sweat breaking out on her skin.

Night before last, he'd seen her naked. He'd heard her *masturbating.*

She put her forehead against the stall door, unable to stifle a humiliated moan. The hand she'd felt on her pillow had been his. He'd been in her house. He'd violated her sanctuary.

Last night, he hadn't knocked on her door because he'd been "in the neighborhood." He'd been listening to her and Greg grapple on the living room couch.

She stood there for a few moments, writhing with mortification, blinking back angry tears. Although she wanted to hide forever, Sidney wasn't a coward, so she squared her shoulders, lifted her wobbly chin and walked out of the stall to face him.

She paused at the sink with the intention of washing her hands, and maybe splashing a bit of water on her flushed cheeks.

When she reached out to turn on the faucet, her reflection in the stainless steel mirror faded. In its place, there was a strange man, his features gaunt and steeped in shadow…

Just thinking about her made him hard.

He watched her sink down into the water, unable to breathe, unable to move. She was helpless. Hopeless. Mindless with terror.

She kicked. They both had, thrashing wildly under the surface, releasing a flurry of bubbles. He witnessed her last breath.

God.

He was in control of her. Complete control.

His own breathing roughened, and he unbuttoned his black jeans, freeing himself. He was pulsing, hard and hot in his slender hand.

Hot. He was so hot.

Moving feverishly toward release, he pictured them tied, gagged, frozen in fear. He imagined their mouths flooded with the tinny taste of it, with brackish water, with him.

Gasping, he jerked toward the sink, squeezing his eyes closed in ecstasy, knowing the next woman who came in would get a wet, hot handful of him.

Chapter 7

"Sidney?" Marc listened at the open doorway of the public rest room, waiting patiently.

He couldn't hear anything. If she was crying, or peeing, or throwing up, she was doing it silently. "I'm coming in," he warned. The last thing he wanted was to embarrass her further, but he was worried she'd had another…panic attack.

He found her slumped in the corner by the door, unconscious, but breathing. Cursing himself for causing her distress, he picked her up and carried her out of the stuffy rest room, barely noticing the strain in his shoulders as he bore her weight. He laid her down on the soft grass in the shade of a gnarled oak and shook her gently.

"Wake up, Sidney," he said, trying to force himself to stay calm. Murmuring something unintelligible, she turned her head. "Please wake up," he urged again, surprised to hear fear quavering in his voice.

"Marc," she whispered, licking her dry lips.

"You need water. Let me get you some—"

"No!" Her eyes flew open. "He was in there."

A chill trickled down his spine. "Who?"

"The killer."

Sitting up, he scanned the immediate area, drawing his Glock 9mm from his shoulder holster in one fluid motion.

"He was…" She looked down at her hands. "He…"

As a homicide investigator, and a man, Marc recognized semen when he saw it. "Son of a bitch," he muttered in a low voice as he rose to his feet.

With swift, efficient motions he checked every stall in both rest rooms. At the women's sink there was more than enough seminal fluid for a DNA sample, although it appeared to be several hours old, at least.

When he came out she was shivering, staring at her hands. Without a word he holstered his Glock and helped her into the men's room, where she washed them repeatedly, chafing her skin with harsh powdered soap.

"That's enough," he said, pulling her away gently. The trembling began again, racking her entire body, and he knew she was in shock. Under the shade of the oak, he drew her into his arms and held her there while she cried.

"I hate you," she said, sniffling.

"I know." He took a handkerchief out of his pocket and handed it to her. She used it noisily, and he knew he was in trouble, to find the way she blew her nose endearing. "Tell me what you saw."

"He was watching himself in the mirror. Fantasizing about…them dying."

"What did he look like?"

"I don't know. It was dark. His features weren't clear."

"He had dark hair?"

"I'm not sure."

"Short hair?"

"I don't know."

He summoned patience. "Picture what you saw, Sidney. Study his reflection. Was he taller than you?"

"Maybe. Or he could have been standing closer to the mirror. He wasn't short," she said decisively. "And he was wearing dark clothes."

"Okay. Good. Was he thin, fat? Round-faced? Clean-shaven?"

"Thinner than you," she said, studying the breadth of his shoulders. "Scary-looking. I couldn't see much of his face. He was standing in shadow."

"Was he black, white, Hispanic?"

"White. Maybe."

"What else?"

"I don't know," she wailed, covering her face with her hands.

"You were in his mind, right?" he persisted. "What was he like? What did he remind you of?"

"A bully," she said with a shudder. "Maybe it's the wrong word, but that's what he reminded me of."

"Why?"

"Something about him made me think of a boy I used to know in grade school. He would pull my hair, call me a witch, stuff like that." She ran a hand over her cap of short black hair, as if remembering. "He liked to inflict pain. Isn't that what bullies do?"

He took out his cell phone and called CSI, requesting they rope off the area to collect evidence. It was a logical move, even without Sidney's vision. Violent, sexually motivated criminals often returned to the scene for physical gratification.

Upon ending the call, he studied her carefully. It was getting more and more difficult to discredit her impressions. And impossible to control his attraction to her.

She was facing away from him, arms crossed over her chest, head down, exposing the pale skin at her nape. Drawn to that tender, vulnerable place, he put his hand there, tracing the top of her spine with his thumb.

She flinched at his touch, but didn't pull away.

"I'm sorry," he said.

She was silent for a moment. "I guess we're two of a kind." She jerked her chin toward the rest room. "Me and him."

"What makes you say that?"

She stared at him over her shoulder, anguish in her eyes, until he caught her meaning.

"That's ridiculous," he said. "Do you get off on raping women? Torturing them? Watching them die?"

"Of course not."

He wanted to shake some sense into her. "What you did, in the privacy of your own bedroom, is nothing like what he did here. It's nothing to be ashamed of."

"How would you feel if someone watched you? Listened to you?"

He dropped his hand from her neck, feeling the muscles in his own shoulders tighten in frustration. He searched for the right words to justify his actions, when there were none. "There's no excuse for my behavior," he said. Not only was it contrary to protocol, it was completely at odds with his moral code. "You're beautiful—"

She turned to face him, disbelief apparent on her slack features.

"That's not the only reason I did it," he admitted, shoving his fingers through his hair. He'd invaded her privacy, and yet he was the one who felt totally exposed. Never had he been less able to govern his emotions. Had she put some kind of spell on him? "I knew it was wrong, but I couldn't look away." He forced himself to meet her gaze. "If the room had been on fire, in that moment, I couldn't have looked away."

She stared back at him, thunderstruck.

"You are so clueless," he said softly. "How can you see everything else, and not know how much I want you?"

Her smoky, wet-lashed eyes wandered over his face like a silken caress. "You what?"

"I want you," he ground out, meaning the words as a warning this time.

When she moistened her lips, as if in anticipation, he took control of the only thing he could: her mouth. He pulled her body against his, wanting to punish her for making him want her so much he'd become reckless and impulsive, the kind of man he despised.

To his amazement, her lips parted and she kissed him back, tentatively at first, shyly touching her tongue to his. Then she moaned, flattening her breasts against his chest and lacing her fingers through his hair, driving him right over the edge from inappropriate to insane.

Groaning, he deepened the kiss, tasting her thoroughly, plumbing the sweet recesses of her mouth. His hands, no less eager to explore, moved down to cup her bottom. With a slight shudder, he pressed close, unable to contain his excitement, or his arousal.

There were advantages to her height, he discovered. He didn't have to lift her to get her in the position he wanted. They fit together perfectly.

He felt the soft apex of her thighs cradling his erection, and was overwhelmed by the need to have her hot, wet, naked, now. Changing the angle of his kiss, he backed her toward a concrete picnic table, seeking a flat surface on which to lay her down. When her bottom hit the table, she sat on its edge and wrapped her long, silky legs around him.

At that moment, he abandoned common sense in favor of raw sensation.

Desperate for the feel of her bare skin, he rode one hand up her sleek thigh and slid the other underneath her T-shirt, filling his palm with her breast. Through the thin fabric of her bra, he felt her nipple, tight with need. He circled his thumb over the pebbled tip as she cried out, twisting her fingers in his hair.

Her small sound of pleasure rang out in the open space, reminding him of where they were. Lifting his head, he searched the deserted park for somewhere more private than a picnic table and more romantic than a public rest room.

Across the street, Crystal Dunn's news van was parked. One of her cronies was pointing a telephoto lens out the passenger side window, straight at him.

Marc saw his entire career flash before his eyes.

"I shouldn't have done that."

Her eyelids fluttered open. "Wh-what?"

One moment, he was kissing her ravenously, moving his strong, eager hands all over her body, taking everything, holding nothing back. The next, he had completely withdrawn.

"I didn't mean to do that." He jerked his hand out from beneath her shirt like a kid caught in a cookie jar. His eyes swept down her body, coming to rest at the top of her thighs, making her all too aware of the sensual image she presented, legs splayed before him, her soft terry-cloth shorts barely covering what was necessary.

"CSI will be here any minute," he said, pushing himself away from her.

Did he still think she had something to do with that…monster who defiled women? Indignation burned through her like wildfire, and she hated him, hated herself, hated her body's traitorous reaction to his touch. Even now, she wanted him to continue, to put his hand back under her shirt, or better yet, between her legs, to soothe the torment he'd created.

They waited for his team in bitter silence. When crime scene investigators arrived on the scene, he gave them a few terse instructions and pulled Detective Lacy aside. "I need you to check with residents about a suspicious character hanging around last night."

She darted a glance at Sidney. "Do you have a description?"

"Not really. Possible Caucasian. Thin build. Average to above-average height."

Nodding, she hurried away to complete the task. Marc turned back to Sidney. "Come on. I'll drive you home."

Unless she wanted to be stranded, Sidney didn't have much choice, so she quickened her stride to keep up with him. He was rushing toward his car, which wasn't unusual, as he was a man who lived at a fast pace. Before they got there, she realized he had another reason to hurry: Crystal Dunn and her omnipresent news crew.

"Get that goddamned camera out of my face," he ordered, opening the door for Sidney. When she got in, he slammed it, effectively cutting her out of the conversation.

Crystal asked the cameraman to give her five.

"Slumming, Marc?" she asked, standing between him and the driver side, a not-so-sweet smile on her pretty face.

Sidney's jaw dropped. Although she was inside the car, she could hear every word, and had no trouble catching the slight.

"I went slumming once," he replied, giving her a pointed look. "It wasn't that good."

Crystal laughed with the confidence of a woman who knew she was being lied to. Sidney wanted to rip her perfectly coiffed platinum hair out by its dark blond roots.

"Look, I don't have anything for you. Go chase another bone."

"I guess I'll go over your head, then," she said, smoothing her hand over the front of his shirt. "Talk to Stokes."

His features hardened. "What do you want?"

"An exclusive. With her."

Sidney's stomach clenched in apprehension. If Crystal Dunn wanted a story on her, it meant the end of her privacy, her peace, her only protection.

"No," he said flatly. "This is a murder investigation, not an entertainment opportunity."

"I'm running it, Marc. With or without her."

"We'll see about that. Stokes holds some sway with Carlisle, too, you know. And she didn't have to go down on her knees to get it."

Unlike their earlier exchange about slumming, this barb hit its mark. Her expression as brittle as ice, Crystal turned on her pencil-slim heels and walked away.

When he got in the car, she let him stew for a few moments.

"Who's Stokes?" she asked.

"My boss."

"And Carlisle?"

"Hers."

Sidney nodded, needing no further elaboration. If Marc had caught Crystal sleeping her way to the top while they were involved, it was no wonder he didn't trust women. "Does she know about me?" she asked.

"She wouldn't want an exclusive if she didn't."

"Can I sue the station?"

"You can threaten to. But that only works if they're planning to say something about you that isn't true."

"Even if it compromises your investigation?"

"Even then. Professional ethics aside, what the press finds out about, they can use. It's my job to protect information we don't want out."

He didn't say it, but she knew he thought he'd failed. Because he was the kind of man who judged his self-worth in terms of self-control, he was probably angrier with himself than with Crystal Dunn. He couldn't stop the leak of information and he couldn't prevent the killer from taking more women off the streets.

The fact that he was having a hard time, in more ways than one, did little to assuage Sidney's anger. By invading her home and violating her privacy, he'd made her his enemy.

If her lawyer was anyone but Greg, she'd be looking forward to making Marc pay.

At OPD, Deputy Chief Stokes was on a rampage.

After Marc dropped Sidney off at her house, he went down to headquarters, dreading the inevitable confrontation. It came sooner than expected.

As he sat down at his desk, Lacy made a gesture from across the room, slicing her forefinger across her throat, indicating his current status as dead meat. Instead of running scared, he got up and walked into Stokes's office.

Like a good boy, he'd take his medicine and get back to work.

"What the hell is this?" she asked the instant he showed his pseudohumble face.

He looked down at the photos littering her desk. Digital technology, he decided, was a real bitch. The pictures were very thorough, and at an excellent angle, showing all of his sensual trespasses to maximum effect. "Amateur porn?" he quipped.

"Sit down and shut up," she ordered.

He did.

"You let Crystal Dunn catch you with your pants down."

His pants had been up, but he thought it best not to quibble over semantics.

"Sexually harassing a suspect, in itself, is bad enough—"

He picked up one of the photos of Sidney's body plastered against his, her hands in his hair. "Does she look like she's being sexually harassed?"

Stokes didn't even glance at it. "As a high-ranking police official, you were in the position of power."

He had no comeback for that.

"You used incredibly poor judgment and allowed yourself to be photographed in the process. It's inexcusable."

"They won't run it," he said with certainty. "This is—" he gestured at the photos "—a mistake. A very stupid, very careless mistake. But it's not a story."

"They won't print the explicit ones, no. As long as she makes no complaints."

"She won't."

She quelled him with a look. "Are you psychic now, too?"

He rubbed a hand over his face, wishing he'd had more than three hours' sleep the past two nights combined. "Chief, I apologize for my unacceptable behavior. To tell you the truth, I really don't know what came over me." He felt his jaw tighten, and had to force himself to relax. "But I assure you, this stays here. I will not end up in court, or the papers, just because I kissed a woman in public."

"You kissed a suspect while on duty. At a crime scene."

He conceded that these were very sound points.

"What they will run is this—Oceanside Police Department Consults Psychic."

"They've done that before. So what?"

"I won't let you make this department a joke. And having her name in the paper, when we're in the middle of undercover surveillance, will hardly work in our favor."

He cleared his throat. Now was not the time to tell her they'd already been made. "She's not a suspect," he asserted.

"Oh, really? I don't need you making decisions for me, Cruz. Especially when you're letting your dick think for you."

He winced at the well-deserved insult. "My instincts say Sidney Morrow is not involved. Most homicidal criminals are loners. They don't recruit women."

"It's not unprecedented," she said. "Women can be used as a lure, to draw in victims, to gain confidences. She's good with dogs, and we don't know how the killer managed to get past them. She's the perfect accomplice. Perhaps she's pulled the wool over your eyes, too."

"Bring Lacy in here," he requested.

Sighing, Stokes buzzed her in. They both listened to his account of Sidney's "vision" in the bathroom, Stokes with her arms crossed over her chest, expression closed.

"Do you believe this?" she asked Lacy.

Lacy darted a glance at Marc. "No, Chief," she lied, throwing him right under the bus.

Stokes studied him for a moment, her eyes narrowing into dangerous slits. "You've always been a loose cannon, Cruz. Yesterday you went Rambo in a homeless camp. Today you're Romeo on a picnic table. Your personal issues are interfering with your police work. Not all women are damsels in distress or targets for seduction."

That hit him where it hurt. He struggled not to let it show.

"I can't have a wild card on my team right now," she decided. "You know that vacation you've been putting off? As of right now, you're on it. Two weeks. Now get out of my sight."

Refusing to meet Lacy's apologetic gaze, or Stokes's assessing one, he pushed himself away from the seat and strode out of her office.

Marc was more pissed off at himself than at Stokes or Lacy, but having his boss tell him he had "issues" was humiliating. If his problems with the opposite sex were so pronounced, why was he the only officer on homicide with a female partner?

"I'm sorry," Lacy said, hurrying to catch up with him. "I was afraid she was going to take me off the case, too."

He grabbed his keys off the top of his desk. "Any luck with the door-to-doors?"

"No. The park is popular with joggers and strollers, that's about it. No one noticed a shady character. There are vehicle records I could pull. It's a two-dollar charge to park inside, at a pay box, but it's infrequently monitored. Some people don't fill out the ticket, or bother to pay. Of course, there are places to park along the street, too."

"He also could've walked from home, if he lives nearby."

"It's a residential area," she said, nodding.

And a needle in the haystack.

She followed him out to his car. "I feel really bad, Marc. Stokes doesn't have to know everything. I'll keep you informed."

"You're goddamned right you will," he muttered, getting in and slamming the door. If Stokes thought he wouldn't continue investigating on his own, she'd completely underestimated his psychological flaws.

She thought he had problems with women? They were nothing compared to his control issues.

Chapter 8

Pacific Pet Hotel had been open for business less than five minutes when Crystal Dunn burst through the front doors, microphone in hand, a pair of bulky cameramen behind her.

The pint-size reporter's heels clicked self-importantly on the tile flooring as she approached. Her tailored black suit hugged her trim figure, and the ruffled blouse beneath showed only a tasteful hint of cleavage, but she still managed to look more like Barbie than Barbara Walters. Her makeup was flawless: pale skin translucent, hair a golden halo.

"Miss Morrow, is it true that you've been employed as a psychic by the Oceanside Police Department?"

Sidney's throat went dry. She couldn't help but feel awkward standing next to Crystal Dunn, staring at the flashing red light on the video camera. Even with Crystal's big hair and high heels, Sidney towered over her. "No, it's not," she said, forcing herself not to slouch. "And I don't want to be interviewed. Please leave."

Undaunted, Crystal continued her questioning, her baby-blue eyes wide with excitement. "Have you revealed the identity of the serial killer?"

"I'm calling my lawyer," Sidney decided. Maybe she wasn't the type of woman who commanded instant respect, but Greg, in a professional capacity, was a bone-crusher.

Making a cutting motion, Crystal handed the microphone off to one of her beefcake assistants and sent them both outside with a brusque dismissal. As Sidney picked up the phone to dial, Crystal shoved a full-color photo under her nose.

Sidney's jaw dropped.

The photograph was a stunner. Marc was carrying her away from the public rest rooms. Her eyes were closed, head cradled against his chest. He looked every inch the hero, concern clear on his chiseled features, the muscles in his arms delineated under the strain of her weight.

"Nice shot," she said quietly.

"You like it? I've got some even better ones."

She blanched, knowing Crystal had her. The photo had been taken several moments *before* their very public make-out session. It was the reason he'd stopped, she realized. He'd spotted Crystal's camera crew and wanted to spare her the humiliation of knowing they'd been caught on tape. Why?

"This could ruin his career, you know."

Sidney worried her lower lip with her teeth.

"You give me a sit-down interview, and I promise to keep the most incriminating pictures out of the news."

She crossed her arms over her chest. "No way."

"You don't seem to understand the gravity of the situation, Miss Morrow. I have proof of sexual misconduct."

"Why do you think I care about his career?" she bluffed.

"Oh, please. You're so soft you probably cry watching *Bambi*."

Her temper flared. "Living in the slums has toughened me up."

Crystal looked her up and down, reassessing her as a competitor. "I apologize for the lowbrow remark. You're—" she swept her eyes over Sidney, arching a brow at her attire "—not his type. Perhaps I was jealous." She leaned in conspiratorially. "He broke my heart."

Sidney believed her, and resented her for being honest. Marc might think Crystal had wronged him, but she apparently felt it was the other way around. "Even if I wanted to help you, I couldn't,"

Sidney said, feeling depressed and confused. "I don't know anything."

Crystal made her last play. "Sign the release for this photo," she said, handing her a pen and paper, "and I won't destroy him in the papers."

After a moment of indecision, Sidney signed the form, knowing from the smug look on Crystal's pretty face that she'd just been manipulated.

The interior of his house was stifling.

Marc turned on the A/C as soon as he came through the door. He tore off his shirt, shoulder holster and sweat-dampened undershirt, wondering when the weather would break. The shady motel room he'd been living out of for the past two days was more comfortable than this. Along the coast, the air was cooled by refreshing ocean breezes. Ten miles inland, where he lived, it was muggy as hell.

Tossing his discarded items on the living room couch, he strode into the kitchen, grabbed a beer out of the fridge, popped off the top and took a long pull. He desperately needed something to take the edge off.

He'd never felt so keyed-up.

Staring out the window above the kitchen sink, he noted that his backyard needed attention. The grass was dry and sunburned, the plants slowly dying. Groaning, he rubbed a hand over his weary face. His fatigue went bone deep.

"Hell with it," he said aloud, abandoning the kitchen in favor of sprawling out in front of the TV on his leather couch. 10:00, the blinking red numbers on the DVD player read.

"Christ," he muttered, taking another fortifying swig. Only losers drank beer by themselves on a weekday morning.

Instead of finding something more productive to do with his time, Marc indulged himself further by replaying every moment of his kiss with Sidney in slow motion. It was the reason for his "vacation," after all. Why not reflect upon it?

Hell, why not embellish, while he was at it?

This time, as he explored her wet, hot mouth with his tongue, he gave his hands, and his imagination, free rein. He didn't just reach underneath her T-shirt, he made it disappear, along with her bra, and feasted his eyes on her luscious breasts. He didn't just brush his thumb across her tight little nipples, he flicked his tongue over them, enjoying the soft gasp of pleasure she made while he tasted her.

His cock stretched and swelled, pushing against the fly of his pants the same way it had pushed against the cleft of her thighs.

Groaning, he lifted the bottle to his lips, letting the cool liquid slide down his throat as he considered his options. There were women he knew—skillful, enthusiastic women—who would come over and take care of him if he asked. It wouldn't be the first time he'd called a woman just for sex.

More often than not, when he was between girlfriends, like now, he went without. Sometimes, even when he had one, he took matters into his own hands, so to speak. Calling another woman to slake his lust for Sidney didn't appeal to him in the least.

He didn't want to touch another woman. He didn't want to look at another woman. He didn't want to think about another woman.

He wanted to think about Sidney touching herself.

With his free hand, he released the buttons on his pants, picturing her lying naked on her wrought-iron bed. He saw her as he thought she'd been, eyes closed, head thrown back, breasts jiggling slightly as her hand worked feverishly between her sleek, open thighs.

While he watched, and enjoyed, her brow puckered in concentration and her slick fingers moved faster. Moaning, she arched her back, thrusting her dusky-tipped breasts forward as she shuddered her exquisite release.

God, what he would have given to really have been there. To watch her come.

He stroked himself slowly, extending the fantasy until he was in the room with her. Leaning over her, he brushed the damp hair off her forehead, touched his lips to the fluttering pulse point at the base of her throat, lapped a drop of perspiration from between her breasts. When she smoothed her fingers over his hair, he caught her hand and brought it to his mouth, tasting her, inhaling her scent.

Needing more, he lowered his head to the silky black curls

between her legs and tasted her there, too, savoring the sweet aftermath of her orgasm.

In her, he found his own release, and it was so intensely satisfying he closed his eyes and gritted his teeth against the pleasure of it. With his head pounding, and dark flashes pulsing across his eyelids, he wondered if the reality of touching her could ever live up to the fantasy.

Too bad he'd never find out.

Greg called during her lunch break. "Where are Samantha and the girls?"

Sidney pressed her fingertips to her aching temple. "Still at my house, I suppose." If he was really worried, why hadn't he called earlier? "She came in late."

He cleared his throat. "Did you two, uh, get a chance to talk?"

"No."

His relief was almost palpable. "Listen, Sid, I'm sorry about last night. I don't really remember what happened, but I do have the vague notion that I made a total ass of myself. Forgive me?"

She didn't, and his insincere apology, in which he couldn't even own up to what he'd done, let alone take responsibility for his actions, only salted the wound. "Since you called, I need help," she said, refusing to pardon his behavior. "You know my…boyfriend—" she felt her cheeks heat, even though no one could see her "—the investigator?"

"Yeah. I don't like him."

"Oh? Why not?"

"He threatened to beat me up. I think. Details are a little fuzzy."

Sidney was absurdly pleased Marc had bothered to defend her. "Well, he's been, um, videotaping me. And recording me. Is that legal?"

"Not if you don't agree to it, baby."

She frowned into the phone before she caught up with his dirty mind. "Oh! No, not like that. I mean I'm under police surveillance."

"What the hell for?"

Sidney told him about finding Candace Hegel's dog and falling under suspicion. Like most of her family members, Greg knew about Sidney's "special abilities" and dismissed them as hysterical female silliness, so she didn't go into too much detail.

She never should have given Blue that first, comforting pat, she thought with a sigh. Her need to touch and be touched, despite its inherent dangers, was so often her undoing.

Greg's mind was elsewhere. "Last night, when your boyfriend came over, it was because he heard me?"

"Yes," she said, wondering how many other private moments and personal conversations Marc had been privy to.

"That son of a bitch," Greg said, terribly concerned for his own welfare.

Every cloud had its silver lining, she supposed. Apparently Greg remembered more than he let on. Making him feel accountable, after he knew he'd been taped, was better than nothing.

"So is it legal?"

"Yeah, it is. A judge has to sign an order first, but it's just a formality."

She let out a frustrated breath. "What can I do?"

"Let me get this straight—a homicide cop is dating his suspect? You can sue his pants off, and the department, for gross misconduct."

"No," she said quickly. "I don't want to get him in trouble."

He was silent for a moment. "Okay. Leave it to me. I'll take care of it."

That sounded even worse. Her brother-in-law had always been protective of her, in a way that was disturbingly unfamilial. "No, Greg. Just drop it. You have enough to worry about with Samantha." She paused for a moment, dreading what she was about to do. "She says you want full custody."

"Stay out of this, Sidney," he warned. "It's none of your business."

"You made it my business last night. On tape," she reminded.

Greg was wise enough to bite back his anger, and his response.

"Don't drag her through the mud, Greg. If you can't come to an agreement with her, fine, use your lawyers. But don't try to get the girls on grounds of infidelity. Don't make Dakota and Taylor pay for Samantha's mistakes."

"She's a drug addict, Sid," he said softly.

Tears flooded her eyes, spilling over onto her cheeks. This was an incredibly ugly thing to face, and she didn't want to. God, she hated getting involved in Samantha and Greg's problems, being pushed and pulled between them, stuck in the same role she'd been forced to play with her own parents. "Let's do something about it," she urged. "Put off the divorce, and convince her to go to rehab."

"My girlfriend wants to get married," he said. "I've been trying to convince Samantha to kick the habit for years. I can't do it anymore, Sid. I need to get on with my life."

After Sidney hung up the phone, she stared at it for a long time, wondering why she was so worried about everyone else's life when she couldn't begin to manage her own.

Marc drank himself into a mild stupor, slept it off all afternoon, and woke up feeling refreshed instead of hung over. He showered, raided the refrigerator and went for an early evening jog even though it was still hot.

On impulse, he stopped by his next door neighbor's house on the way home. Tony Barreras was the kind of friend he never knew he wanted and wasn't sure why he had. Whatever the reason, they'd been close for years, and he was always there when Marc needed him.

Tony answered the door shirtless, barefoot, clad in ragged fatigue shorts. A colorful hand-woven bandana held his dark, shoulder-length hair out of his eyes, giving him the look of a bohemian vigilante. At his feet, an ancient white pit bull thumped his tail against the ground.

"Hey," Tony said in greeting. "Where've you been?"

Marc shrugged. "Around. Working. You know."

He walked away from the door, leaving it open in welcome. The dog, having known Marc too long to expect any kind of attention, returned to his lounging area beneath the front window. "You want a beer?" Tony asked, looking over his shoulder. "Water?"

"Yeah. Water."

He grabbed a plastic bottle out of the refrigerator and chucked it at Marc, then plunked himself back down on the couch in front of the tube. "So what's up?" Tony asked, his eyes on his favorite video game, Doom or Duel or Death—whatever the name of it was. His focus was on the screen, but Marc knew the way his friend's mind worked. He could hold a conversation, wield the video controls and listen with another ear for the phone or the doorbell, one of which was always ringing.

Tony had some warped kind of ADD. He multitasked like a whiz, but couldn't concentrate on one thing at a time. Trying to talk to him when he wasn't also listening to music or playing video games was actually more difficult.

"Hard day?" he continued when Marc didn't respond. Tony didn't need to look at his face to know his mood.

"You know homicide," he said vaguely, watching a soldier bloody everything in his wake on screen. Having first met Tony in Saudi Arabia during the Gulf War, Marc had always found his taste in entertainment strange. "It's always hard."

"Another body? A woman?"

"Yeah."

"Damn."

That pretty much summed it up, so he drank his water in silence. He didn't know how he'd forged this strange friendship, but it had become a comfortable one, in which he didn't have to explain himself or even talk, if he didn't want to. Sometimes he sat on Tony's couch and watched him play video games while his mind drifted, neither of them saying a word.

"You know what you need?" Tony asked.

"To get laid?" he replied, feeling moody.

"Well, yeah. Always." Then he frowned. "What happened to that hot little blonde? She dump you?"

Marc didn't know which one he was talking about, but it didn't really matter, because his relationships always ended the same way. "A while ago."

"What's wrong with you, dude? Don't you know how to tell a woman what she likes to hear?"

Marc pondered that. "What if you didn't have to? Wouldn't you rather find one you could be totally honest with?"

"Being honest is one thing. Doing it with finesse, rather than brutality, is another."

"Thanks for the advice, Mr. Finesse," he muttered. "Where's your woman?"

Tony didn't have an answer for that, because his notoriously short attention span extended to his dealings with the opposite sex. He stood up and switched off the video game monitor abruptly. Reaching into the cigar box that was always on top of the television, he pulled out a Baggie and some rolling papers. "This is what you need. Maximum Relaxem."

"No," Marc said shortly. "I don't."

"Sure you do. You're wound up so tight you're about to snap." Tony sat down and started rolling a joint. "This stuff here is purely medicinal. Like taking a pill for anxiety."

Marc didn't like being thought of as anxious, or uptight, but compared to Tony everyone was. "You know I can't. Besides, pot makes me paranoid."

"Not this kind. It's one hundred percent guaranteed to cure whatever ails you. Either that, or knock your ass out." Tapping a silent tune with his bare foot, he licked the paper, securing it in place.

"You do realize you're soliciting an illegal substance to a cop."

Tony just laughed. Marc had been looking the other way while Tony sold pot for years. He'd known what Tony did long before he moved in next door to him, so Marc didn't think it would be fair to bust him now. "This isn't solicitation. It's a gift." He put the joint into a plastic bag to keep it fresh. "Give it to your mom if you don't want it. Maybe it'll help her more than that *curandero* you're always complaining about."

Marc shoved the bag in his pocket, having no intention of turning his mother on to marijuana. The so-called faith healer she visited once a week had been fleecing her (and Marc, for it was he who supported her) for the better part of a decade. Once, she'd even stopped taking her insulin for a short period of time because that damned witch doctor said he could cure her diabetes with "spiritual cleansing."

His mother's mental and physical health was fragile enough; she didn't need to start doing recreational drugs. "Can dogs get stoned?" he asked suddenly.

"Sure. Whispers ate my stash once," Tony said. "He got really faded."

Marc glanced at the dog lying beneath the window, whose tail had started thumping at the sound of his name.

"Want to go to the gym?"

He shrugged his assent, and when Tony left the room to get ready, Marc took out his cell phone to call Gina at the lab. "Did you run Blue for marijuana on the toxicology screen?"

"No. We don't usually add it on, unless specifically requested."

"Can you?"

"Sure, if I had another sample. THC stays in the system for quite some time, so urine would work."

He thanked her and hung up, his heart rate quickening, not because he may have discovered a break in the case, but because he had an excuse to see Sidney again.

Chapter 9

Thursday morning dawned in dismal gray layers, peeling away inch by inch until the sun was revealed like a hazy, shimmering orange fireball. Thunderclouds rumbled in the distance, more bluster than threat, for there was only a twenty percent chance of precipitation.

As he jogged in a steady loop around the beautifully manicured grounds of the San Luis Rey Mission, Marc prayed for rain, and release. The oppressive air surrounded him like a steamy blanket, and his mood was as heavy as the weather.

He hated having time off.

If he had any control over the situation, he might have breathed a little easier. Instead Sidney Morrow had turned his life, and his investigation, upside down.

By the time he got home, the morning newspaper was resting innocuously at the base of his front steps. Sweating up a storm, he sat on the stoop and opened it, cursing when he saw the headline: "Police Department Works With Psychic."

He should have known Crystal would approach Sidney for the

story on her own. She was infamous for her back door dealings; he'd discovered that the day he showed up unannounced at the station and caught her blowing her boss in her dressing room.

It was three years ago, but he remembered the scene, and how he'd felt coming upon it, like it was yesterday.

He could still see himself, standing like a fool in the open doorway, the flowers he'd brought to surprise her slipping from his hand, forgotten. If he'd arrived a moment later, he might never have known. If he'd arrived a moment earlier, Crystal might have been able to jerk away from Carlisle and leap to her feet before Marc walked in on them.

In a cruel twist of fate, he entered the room at the exact moment another man was coming in his girlfriend's mouth.

Marc didn't say a word, he just turned and left her doing what she did best.

Shaking away the remnants of that unpleasant recollection, he turned his attention to the newspaper in front of him. The caption below the photograph read: "Lieutenant Marc Cruz carries a fainting Sidney Morrow away from the public rest rooms at Guajome Lake Park, near the scene where the body of Anika Groene was found."

It could have been worse. He read on, considering himself lucky the article wasn't entitled "Police Officer Suspended for Hitting on Suspect."

"Local psychic Sidney Morrow may be aiding the homicide division with their latest investigation. Victims Candace Hegel and Anika Groene were taken within weeks of each other, under similar circumstances, and perhaps by the same assailant. Lieutenant Cruz had no comment on Morrow's involvement with the case, and Deputy Chief Amanda Stokes has stated that the Oceanside Police Department does not consult psychics.

"Sidney Morrow has offered her assistance to the police department before. More than fifteen years ago she helped solve a missing persons case in neighboring Bonsall. A local girl, Lisa Pettigrew, was found trapped in a well on a rural piece of property. Miss Morrow disclosed the girl's location to police officers, stating she'd seen the place in a 'psychic vision.'

"An unidentified source at the Bonsall Fire Department indicated Pettigrew couldn't possibly have fallen into the well without sustaining considerable bodily damage. Due to the minor nature of her injuries, it was suspected that Pettigrew and Morrow, who were in the same grade at Bonsall Middle School, had perpetrated a preteen prank.

"Deputy Chief Stokes has named no lead suspects in either of the latest killings, nor has she confirmed the brutal slayings are related..."

As he sat there, glaring at the page and condemning Sidney Morrow to an eternal damnation he no longer believed in, the clouds overhead broke open and it began to rain.

When Sidney arrived at Pacific Pet Hotel, Marc was already there. He'd called last night to ask if he could pick up a urine sample from Blue.

Ignoring her jittery pulse, she opened the gate and drove through it, parking in her usual spot beside the building. When she got out of the truck he was striding toward her.

From across the expanse between them, she could feel his anger, shimmering like a mirage on hot asphalt. It had rained for a few moments, just a teasing sprinkle, before the relentless sun returned and evaporated every drop of moisture from the baking earth.

Now the air was as muggy as shower steam.

Judging by the hard set of his jaw, another kind of storm was brewing. It was too bad he looked mouthwateringly good in a plain white T-shirt and navy-blue trousers, because she had a feeling he was going to ruin the effect when he opened his mouth.

"Here," he grated, shoving a sterile cup at her chest.

Refusing to rise to the bait, she took the small container placidly and retrieved Blue from his kennel. True to form, the dog growled at Marc, teeth bared, hackles up.

Again, Marc didn't seem surprised by the dog's reaction, and Sidney wondered at the animosity between him and man's best friend. Once bitten, twice shy?

"Will he piss on cue?" he asked.

"He's a male, isn't he?"

"What's that supposed to mean?"

"Intact dogs like to mark their territory," she explained.

"Intact?"

"Not neutered."

She led Blue through the front gate to a tree-lined median, letting him sniff the area's most popular target. Sure enough, he lifted his leg. She stuck the cup under him, capped it when he was finished, and thrust it at Marc, a self-satisfied smile on her face.

"Thanks," he said tersely, his expression far from grateful.

"So what are you testing for?" she asked as he walked away. Her eyes lingered on the way his T-shirt fit across his broad shoulders, the fading scratches on the back of his neck, the still-raw patch on his elbow.

He arched a backward glance at her. "Marijuana. Do you think that's what he was on?"

She shrugged. "Could have been, I guess."

"Aren't you familiar with the effects?"

"I've never tried it."

"Right," he scoffed, setting the sample on the top of his car.

"I suppose you have?"

"Many times."

Sidney wasn't sure she believed him. He didn't strike her as a free-loving, experimental type, but perhaps he hadn't always been so iron-willed. "Were you one of those wayward boys who turned his life around by joining the other side of the law?"

"No."

She urged Blue to sit by tugging on his leash. "What were you like, as a child?"

He shoved his hands into his pockets. "I was very responsible."

"So you went away to college and cut loose?"

"No. I went away to Saudi Arabia. And I wouldn't call killing people cutting loose, although some of my comrades seemed to find it entertaining."

She searched his face. "I would never have guessed that. Are you saying you were introduced to drugs in the military?"

"Yes."

"Did it help?"

His whiskey-brown eyes met hers. "No."

The intensity with which he spoke, and the underlying rage she sensed in him, made her uneasy. "You have to know I didn't have a choice about the photo in the newspaper," she said to fill the silence. "Is that why you're angry?"

"I don't know anything about you," he replied, quite honestly.

Turning his back on her, he got in his car and drove away, leaving her standing there, speechless, confused and very much alone.

At LabTech, Marc found Gina hunched over her laptop. "Anything interesting?"

"Yes," she said, taking off her reading glasses as she straightened. "Preliminary reports show consistencies between the semen samples obtained from both victims and the one from the Guajome Lake rest room, but it could take weeks for DNA confirmation. And still no hit in CODIS." She closed the screen. "What have you got?"

He placed the container of urine on the desk. "If he tests positive, can you match the results to a specific crop or plant?"

She looked skeptical. "Maybe, if the grower used a certain kind of fertilizer, pesticide, or another traceable chemical. Your homegrown variety can also have unique qualities, such as astronomically high THC levels, but it's a long shot, either way."

Most investigative techniques were, he thought, taking Tony's joint out of his pocket. "Can you run this?"

"Sure. Is it from the scene?"

"No."

"From a suspect?"

"Not really. Not firsthand, anyway."

She arched a dark, curvy brow. "So the paper isn't evidence?"

"No."

She tore open the joint to see its contents. "It's definitely fresh, probably local. Good quality. You want me to have narcotics take a look?"

It was a good idea, but Marc didn't want to bring the heat down on Tony, or his customers, who were mostly harmless, fresh-faced college kids. Like Anika Groene, he thought suddenly. "Not yet. See if you can match it first. I'll take it from there."

She smiled at his secrecy. "By the way, I'd make myself scarce, if I were you."

He grew instantly wary. "Is Stokes around?"

"Not that I know of, but I heard she's breathing fire."

"She saw the paper this morning?"

"Yes, and your little psychic friend got herself a lawyer. Slapped homicide with a cease and desist order first thing this morning."

When Marc caught up with her again, it was really raining. Huge, fat drops saturated Sidney's clothing as she walked from the parking garage to her front doorstep.

He was waiting for her there, getting soaked, although he appeared oblivious to the downpour. His hair was thick and damp in the moisture-laden air, and his T-shirt clung intriguingly to the muscles of his chest. From his half-lidded eyes to his pseudo-casual stance, every aspect of his demeanor suggested barely restrained fury.

The amount of tension between them spiked higher than the humidity.

"What do you mean you didn't have a choice about the photo?" he asked. "Did your lawyer advise you to go public?"

She took her keys out of her front pocket with a trembling hand, feeling the rain permeate her tank top. "What lawyer? Greg?"

"Your brother-in-law is your lawyer?" he asked, eyeing her with derision. "That is dysfunctional on so many levels."

"Would you move? I'd like to get out of the rain."

He didn't budge.

"Did you read the article?" she asked, exasperated.

"Of course."

She stared at him, for that explained it all. He didn't appear convinced. Wiping the rain from her face, she said, "The picture they printed was taken before…"

"We almost had sex on a picnic table?" he finished for her.

Hot color suffused her face. "I wouldn't have…"

"Oh, yes, you would have," he countered smugly. "And so would I, if we'd been alone."

She opened her mouth to deny it, and found the lie impossible to utter. "Crystal said she would destroy your career," she murmured, returning to the subject of most importance.

His expression changed. "That's why you consented? Because of me?"

"Yes. Now can I please get by?"

He moved aside a half step, giving her access to the front door, but only if she wanted to plaster her body against his. Refusing to let him intimidate her, she put her shoulder in the middle of his chest and grinded her elbow into his hard, flat abdomen as she turned the key.

He seemed to take a perverse pleasure in her attempt to harm him. To her chagrin, she couldn't deny her own enjoyment in his proximity.

Why did he have to smell so good? Like freshly laundered cotton and rain, testosterone and Old Spice. At the base of his throat, his skin was dark and damp against the collar of his T-shirt. She closed her eyes, overwhelmed by the urge to put her mouth there and taste him, too.

"You should have asked me," he said. "The *Explorer* isn't a tabloid press. They would never have printed anything explicit."

She moistened her lips, still staring at his neck. "She lied?"

"Yes."

The door opened in, but she didn't push it. Her eyes drifted up to his face. "Greg contacted your office?"

He was fixated on her mouth. "Yes."

"What did he say?"

"That you would sue for harassment if we continued surveillance."

She put her head against the door, more weary than astonished by her brother-in-law's underhanded machinations.

"He lied?"

"Yes," she said, casting him a sideways glance. Her eyelids felt very heavy, and she wanted nothing more than to lean in to him, to taste his mouth again, to flatten her breasts against his chest and feel how his body responded to hers.

Then the hurtful words he'd said to her this morning came rushing back, and she squeezed the doorknob tightly, willing her hand to make it turn.

He didn't know her. He didn't want to know her.

Marc wanted her the same way Greg wanted her—in a base, purely sexual way. The only difference was that she wanted him back.

If he really knew her, he'd run the other way, she reminded herself. No one wanted a freak for a girlfriend. What man would feel comfortable around a woman capable of invading his mind, guessing his secrets, stealing his thoughts?

"Come on in," she said, pushing open the door. "I'll get you a towel." Going in ahead of him, she grabbed a towel off the rack in the bathroom. She avoided glancing into the mirror, afraid of the raw need she would see reflected there.

Marc stood in the doorway, his broad shoulders filling the frame. He seemed unsure if he wanted to commit himself further by stepping into the room, and his reluctance to impose upon her was twice as appealing as his tough guy façade.

"Here," she said, shoving the towel at him.

He hesitated, his eyes on the way her wet tank top molded to her chest. "I think you need it more than I do," he said gruffly.

She didn't have to glance down to know the circles of her nipples were revealed by the damp fabric. She could read it in his hot gaze. Clenching her hands into fists, she whirled away from him, storming up the staircase to change her shirt.

Outside the door to her bedroom, she stopped dead in her tracks.

Someone had been in her house. Someone had… "Oh God," she said, clapping a hand over her mouth. "Marley."

In the middle of the bed, the cat was stretched on its back, spread-eagled, tied to the wrought-iron posts with black thread. Its coat was dark with congealed blood, and it appeared to have been disemboweled.

"Oh my God," she repeated, nausea rising to her throat.

Taking the stairs two at a time, Marc pushed her back against the open door, putting his body in front of hers protectively. "Go outside," he said after looking into the bedroom. "I'll check the rest of the house."

She nodded, tearing her eyes away from the mutilated cat. Above the bed, a newspaper clipping was pinned to the wall with a large kitchen knife. She didn't need a closer look to know what it depicted. Shuddering, she navigated the stairs on weak, rubbery legs.

Marc waited until she was safely outside before moving. Feeling numb, she closed the front door behind her and hugged her arms around herself until he came out again.

"It wasn't your cat," he said.

She squeezed her eyes shut, trying not to see the horrifying image.

"Your cat is under the bed."

"Are you sure?"

"Yeah. Grumpy-faced little calico, right?"

"Tortoiseshell," she corrected, intensely relieved.

"I have to go."

"You—what?"

"Lacy and some others are on the way."

She blinked at him in confusion. "Aren't they close by? Watching? How could they have let this happen?"

"Your lawyer's cease and desist order put a halt to surveillance this morning."

"I didn't know."

His expression indicated he thought otherwise. "Don't go back inside until they get here," he suggested, then got in his car and drove away, his tires making slick tracks in the dark, still-wet street.

Detective Lacy and two uniformed officers gave her house a perfunctory search, using the bare minimum of effort, resources and congeniality.

Sidney gathered that Greg's oh-so-helpful interference had not endeared her to the Oceanside Police Department.

The newspaper, knife and thread the perpetrator used were hers. Other than the dead cat, there was no evidence of a break-in. One of the officers took a few photographs, another dusted for prints, and after Sidney offered to take care of the carcass, they left.

As soon as they were gone, Sidney locked and relocked all the windows and the doors, checked and rechecked them, ran her hands over every edge and corner, searching for the point of entry. Finding nothing, she also felt around, groping furniture and rummaging through shelves, looking for an impression of the cat-killing vandal.

If he'd worn gloves, that explained the lack of fingerprints, but had he also done it to thwart her? Then again, how could he know she used her sense of touch for psychic readings?

The newspaper article had maligned her character and attacked her integrity, but it hadn't revealed that particular secret.

Sidney secured Marley in a pet carrier, afraid she would try to hide again or run away, and went about the unpleasant task of dealing with the remains. She cut the makeshift bonds and folded the limp, lifeless body into a heavy-duty garbage bag, then stripped the bed. Into another bag went the sheets, pillow covers, mattress pad and even her beloved chenille blanket. Thankfully the mattress itself wasn't damaged.

The bag of linens went in the trash, the cat in her freezer. It would have to keep until tomorrow when she would drop it off at Vincent Veterinary Clinic.

That done, she decided to clean and sanitize every square inch of her house. She felt dirty, just standing inside it, almost as if the villain had soiled her belongings the same way he'd soiled the ladies' room at Guajome Lake Park.

She scrubbed down the floors, walls, bathrooms, windows and countertops. She sprayed the mattress, pillows and couch cushions with disinfectant. When the doorbell rang she was dusting the top of the bookshelf. Sidney was so startled by the sound she almost fell off the chair she was standing on.

It was Marc. Folding her arms over her chest and tapping her foot, she made it clear his presence was unwelcome.

He took in her frazzled appearance, from the dusting rag in her gloved hands to her hair, covered by a hillbilly handkerchief, and had the nerve to smile. "How's your cat?"

"Which one?"

"The live one."

"She's edgy. Like me. What do you want?"

"I've been assigned to protect you."

"Spy on me, you mean?"

"No. That would be grounds for a lawsuit."

She rolled her eyes.

"Look, Sidney, I can make sure anyone who comes in here has to get by me first, but I can't do it from outside."

"And if I refuse?"

He sighed. "Then I guess I'll wait for you to go to sleep, jimmy that loose latch again and come in anyway."

"What loose latch?"

He winked at her. "Let me in, and I'll fix it."

God, he was infuriating. And so charming, when he wanted to be, that she felt some of her anger seep away. "Where will you sleep?"

He breezed by her. "I'll take the couch."

She shut the door behind him. "I was going to sleep there. My bed is…" Her throat closed up around the words.

His eyes wandered over her face. "Have you eaten?"

She shook her head, swallowing back tears.

"You need to," he decided, striding into her kitchen and browsing the fridge. "What have you got?"

"There's some fresh meat in the freezer," she said, unable to stop the hysterical laughter bubbling up inside her.

He looked. "Very funny. Why is it in there?"

"I'm taking the body to Bill tomorrow."

"For an autopsy?"

"Just a disposal," she said, coming up behind him. "Why? Do you think he could find out something?"

"It's worth a try." He transferred the plastic-wrapped body from the freezer to the refrigerator. "Freezing can alter the evidence, disrupt the consistency of the organs, change the weight of body fluids."

She suppressed a fresh wave of nausea.

He slammed the fridge shut. "Let's go out to eat."

Chapter 10

Marc awoke with a start, momentarily disoriented. His hand was reaching out to pick up his Glock before he knew what he'd heard to alert him.

The sound of an intruder outside reminded him where he was. At Sidney's house, playing bodyguard. Stokes would have a conniption if she found out.

Rolling off the couch, he made his way to the kitchen window and crouched under it, staying low. Sure enough, someone had removed the screen and was trying to wiggle the window until the faulty latch disengaged.

They didn't know he'd already fixed it.

From his vantage point, he could see the glint of blond hair and hear muffled curses. Lowering his weapon, he stood and flipped on the backyard lights.

Samantha Parker jumped sky-high.

"You scared the hell out of me!" she shrieked when he opened the door.

"Sorry," he lied. "Someone broke in today. I thought you were a burglar."

Her glassy eyes slid down the length of his body, pausing on the gun he held at his side. "Sid was robbed?"

"Nothing was taken, that I know of."

"Thank God," she said with a wicked smile. "I was going to ask her for a loan."

Sidney's sister was spoiled, self-absorbed and drop-dead gorgeous. She was also clever enough to know her own faults, and unpretentious enough to laugh at herself. Against his will, he liked her.

"Ah, Detective, you're a heartbreaker when you loosen up," she said as she passed by.

"Lieutenant," he corrected.

She arched a sultry glance over her shoulder. "Look good in your boxer shorts, too," she said. "Are you screwing my sister?"

"Not yet."

She laughed. "Still working on it, huh? She's a tough nut to crack."

He gave the patio a once-over before he turned off the light and locked the door. "That's what your husband said."

Her spine stiffened at his words. "Oh really?" she asked. "And when did the two of you have the pleasure of meeting?"

"The other day, when you dumped off your kids with Sidney and disappeared. He came by looking for you."

She whirled to face him, her blue eyes icy. "I've been going through some emotional turmoil lately," she defended. "Why should Sidney be the only one who gets to act loony?"

"Does it run in the family?" he asked, intrigued by her admission.

"Mental illness? Sure it does. Mama's *Southern.*" Rearranging her features from snow queen to sex kitten, she settled herself in the spot where he'd just been sleeping. "Daddy met her in Lafayette, Alabama, on leave. Whatever she had must have been contagious because he's been crazy in love with her ever since. Or—" lowering her voice, she slid her hands over the rumpled sheet in the guise of smoothing it "—just plain crazy."

"He was in the service?"

"Bomber jet pilot," she said, her tone softening with pride. "Won a medal in Korea, another in Vietnam."

Marc was surprised. "You two were Air Force brats?" he asked, setting his Glock down on the empty chair.

"Oh, no. Mama made him quit. She blamed him for the way Sidney turned out, too. Said Agent Orange mutated her genes."

Marc couldn't tell if she was serious, or if Samantha was one of those women who told wildly exaggerated stories just to get attention. "Where are they now?"

"They have a condo in Miramar, close to the base. He watches the jets fly by every day. It's the saddest thing you've ever seen." She tilted her head to one side, assessing him. "If you're looking for a way to get to Sidney, asking about Daddy is a good start. She was the apple of his eye." Her lashes fluttered. "It's *so* Elektra."

"Were you jealous?"

"No, but Mama was." Her gaze traveled over him again, lingering on his bare chest. "I'd love to talk all night, sugar, but I'm wore out. You wanna share this couch with me, or go upstairs to work on Sidney?"

He tried not to react to the provocation. "I'm not here to work on her. There's a killer out there somewhere, in case you haven't been keeping up with the news."

With a wide yawn, she unsnapped her designer jeans and pushed them off her hips, revealing a tiny pair of black lace panties.

Marc wondered why Sidney's plain cotton briefs turned him on more.

"No man would rape me."

His eyes rose to her face. "Why not?"

"'Cuz I'm easy." Stretching out on her belly, she smiled. "Tempted?"

"I'd have to be dead not to be," he said, although he wasn't having any trouble resisting her. Samantha was just his type: sexy, blond and available, in a no-strings-attached kind of way. But when he looked at her, he saw her only as Sidney's troubled sister.

Gathering up his clothes, he went to the woman he really wanted, instead of staying with the one he could actually have.

Sidney stretched like a cat, reveling in the sound of raindrops hitting the windowpane and the smell of freshly washed sheets.

She loved sleeping in on a rainy day.

The weather had broken. A cool, misty breeze drifted through the open window, and it was a welcome respite from the stifling heat of the past week. Snuggling deeper into the covers, she let herself doze off again, knowing the alarm would wake her in time for work.

In her dreams, Marc was there with her, a tantalizing warmth against her back. She arched against him, wanting to feel more.

He slipped his arm around her waist, smoothing his palm over her belly and brushing his lips across her nape. Her nipples tightened with arousal and heat pooled in her lower body. Encouraging him, she covered his hand with hers, pushing her bottom against his erection. With a low groan, he drew her even closer, sliding his naked thigh between her bare legs. The skin-on-skin contact was shocking; the hard pressure of his muscular thigh nudging the sweet ache between her legs, exquisite.

The hand on her belly moved up under the hem of her T-shirt. He cupped one breast, then the other, teasing her taut nipples with his fingertips until she moaned her pleasure. When that hand wandered down beneath the waistband of her panties, her eyes flew open.

This was *way* too real to be a dream.

Sidney scrambled off the bed, taking the sheet with her, clutching it to her tingling breasts. Too late, she realized the error of her ways.

She should have left the sheet with him.

Marc was stretched out on her bed, mostly naked, a devastating image of masculine perfection. He was all sinewy muscles and dark skin, the thin cotton boxer shorts he was wearing showcasing rather than concealing his heavy arousal.

"What are you doing?"

"Uh..." He followed her gaze to his erection. "Getting you off?"

She threw the sheet at his chest. "Getting yourself off, more like."

"That, too," he admitted with a wince. "Your sister came in last night and stole my spot on the couch."

"And that gives you the right to touch me?"

"No," he said, pushing the sheet away and rising to his feet. "When you started rubbing your sweet little ass all over my hard-on, I considered it an invitation."

"I was asleep!"

He located his pants on the floor and jerked them up his hips. "Some parts of you were awake," he said, glancing at the points of her nipples, poking at the front of her T-shirt.

She flushed darkly.

"I don't know what you're so upset about," he continued. "The other day you were panting for it."

"That was before…" She gestured to the middle of the bed, where the cat had been. "And then you just took off afterward, with no explanation." Her eyes narrowed. "If anyone's been running hot and cold, it's you."

"I couldn't stay," he said, pulling his T-shirt over his head. "Don't you get it? I can't be seen with you."

"But you said—" She broke off. "Who assigned you to protect me, then?"

"I assigned myself. No one else believes you."

"You believe me?"

His gaze moved from her bare thighs, and the pale blue panties peeking out under the hem of her T-shirt, to her face. Instead of answering, he collected the rest of his belongings, slipping on his shoulder holster and pocketing his keys.

"I can't stay here with you again tonight," he said.

"Fine," she said, crossing her arms over her chest. She didn't need a bodyguard. Or a babysitter.

"I'll pick you up after work," he added.

"Why?"

"You'll have to spend the night at my house."

Marc left Sidney's, bagged cat in hand, and drove to Vincent Veterinary Clinic. After the late dinner last night, he'd slept very little, and knew from the restless sounds Sidney made upstairs that she'd had similar trouble.

Her futon couch wasn't comfortable, but he'd slept in worse conditions, on cots and in chairs and atop the desert sand with only his fatigues between him and the sun-baked ground.

The problem wasn't physical comfort, but his own hyperawareness of her. Every time he heard the bedsprings shift, he imagined her long, silky legs, kicking off blankets. He wondered what she was wearing and ached to know how she smelled.

He hadn't meant to touch her this morning. Hell, he'd been half-asleep himself, and fully aroused by the time he knew what he was doing. The hand he'd reached into her panties still itched to test her heat, but he hadn't felt anything more than her silky pubic hair under his fingertips before she pulled away. A mere wisp of a touch, the memory of which was powerful enough to make him hard all over again.

He pulled into the parking lot at Vincent Veterinary Clinic, shelving his bedroom fantasies. A glance in the mirror before he left Sidney's showed a shadowed jaw, wrinkled clothes and bloodshot eyes. He already looked like he'd been on a bender; he didn't need to walk in with a stiff cock, too.

Inside the clinic, Bill was as sunny and insincere as ever, chatting with a pair of pretty receptionists who gazed up at him through worshipful eyes. When he saw Marc, his expression cooled. "Lieutenant Cruz," he said. "To what do I owe this pleasure?"

"Dead cat," Marc replied, setting it down on an aluminum examination table with a thud.

"How delightful. Did you run it over with your car, or did your personality kill it?"

One of Bill's girls giggled uneasily, not sure of the joke.

"I found it on Sidney's bed, actually," Marc said, watching the other man's face for a reaction. "Tied up on its back. Guts all over the place."

"Go on up front, ladies," Bill murmured, dismissing his receptionists. With businesslike concentration, he let the cat out of the bag. "Refrigerated?"

"Overnight."

His eyes raked over Marc's unshaven face and disheveled clothing. The implication that he'd been with Sidney all night did not appear to sit well with Bill. "She's not one of your two-bit bimbos, you know," he remarked as he examined the remains.

"I defer to your greater experience with bimbos," Marc replied, his voice laced with sarcasm.

"I mean it," Bill said, looking up. "If you hurt her—"

"You'll what?"

Bill's face flushed an angry red. He was much too reserved to engage in a fistfight.

Marc wasn't. At that moment, he would have gone a round in the parking lot with the smarmy vet, for no greater reason than he didn't like picturing Bill with Sidney.

"I care about her," Bill said defiantly, gaining more respect from Marc than if he'd rolled up his cuffs.

"Speaking of bimbos, Sidney's not really your type, either, is she?" He lowered his voice. "And let's not pretend we don't both know exactly what your type is."

Bill took out a scalpel, cutting into what was left of the cat's stomach cavity.

"Did she discover you had a secret life, Vincent? Follow you to one of those late-night, underground clubs, catch you out on the prowl?"

His mouth thinned with displeasure.

"She didn't have to, did she? All she had to do was touch you to know where you'd been."

Bill's patience broke. "And what will she find out about you, Cruz? How will you feel when she touches you and recoils, when her face goes pale as she unearths your dirtiest secret? Mommy never loved you? Daddy was never around? The neighborhood priest took you into his rectory for a private confession?"

"Don't get my lurid past confused with yours, Doc. I'm sure you were every padre's favorite altar boy."

Bill lifted his chin a notch, maintaining a thread of dignity. "We all have skeletons, Lieutenant. That's why Sidney's not for you. You can't compartmentalize her, keep her out of your personal life, hold her at a safe distance. It's all or nothing with her."

Marc resented being told how to treat Sidney by a man who couldn't possibly have handled her well. "Tell me what you know about this cat," he said, changing the subject.

Bill sighed, giving him a brief overview. "It's emaciated. Not spayed. Nothing in the digestive tract but plant material and mouse bones. Just your basic barn cat, I'd say."

"Why not a city stray?"

"Teeth are worn and stained. With the coyote population around here, most strays don't live long enough to get this old."

"A pet, then?"

"Not one that was well cared for."

Marc nodded. "What else?"

"Died from blood loss, as far as I can tell."

From the amount of it on Sidney's bed, that much had been obvious. The man had killed the cat inside, but had he drugged it first? "Do you know anything about the effects of marijuana on animals?" he asked, thinking aloud.

Bill raised his brows. "Sure. I get a client in every few months with a dog that 'ate the neighbor's plant,' or a cat who 'got into something.'"

"Doesn't anyone ever tell the truth?"

"No. It's silly, because I have no legal obligation to report them to the ASPCA or the police. Nor would I, if asked to," he added, letting Marc know his patients were granted confidentiality. "The effects are varied, from excitability to extreme lethargy."

"Loss of consciousness?"

"In extreme cases."

"As a sedative, how effective would marijuana be?"

Bill shrugged. "Unreliable, in my opinion, but I'm no expert. There aren't a lot of clinical studies on accidental ingestion of illegal drugs."

Marc decided it was time for another trip to the crime lab. "Can you bag the stomach contents?"

Sidney brought her cat to the kennel for boarding because she was afraid to leave her at home by herself. Those brief moments she'd thought Marley had been tortured and killed had been excruciating.

She went through her workday in a daze, disturbed by images both sensual and sadistic, seeing dead cats and live men around every corner. By closing time she was completely strung out, awash with sexual frustration and reluctant to engage in another test of wills with Marc.

Sidney wasn't used to interacting with men, period. Using her sense of touch as an investigative tool and facing the atrocities of a serial killer were scary; spending another night with Marc, terrifying.

As promised, he picked her up from work and took her home with him. He was even hospitable enough to feed her before he disappeared upstairs. While she waited for him to come back down, she munched on an apple and a peanut butter sandwich, studying her surroundings. His house was bigger than hers, his appliances newer and his furniture more expensive, but the place had no soul. It was…boring.

She sat down on his leather couch, discovering it was more comfortable than it looked, and flipped on the TV to see what channel he'd been watching. Sports. Sighing, she turned it off again, disappointed that his personal belongings were as rigid as his personality.

"Getting any 'impressions'?"

Sidney turned at the sound of his voice, low and intimate in the darkening room. They'd arrived at just before sunset; now night was fast approaching. "I don't try to get impressions," she replied, offended by the sarcastic question. "They just come."

He took a seat at the opposite end of the couch, close enough for her to smell his Old Spice. In worn jeans and an old T-shirt, he should have appeared relaxed. He didn't. He looked ready to pounce.

Tucking her legs in, she curled one arm behind her head, getting cozy. When his eyes darkened, she suppressed a smile. Taunting him wasn't nice, but he deserved it. "Why are you so distrustful?"

"I'm a cop."

Pursing her mouth in concentration, she surveyed the living room once again, looking for clues with her eyes, not her hands. "You have a cross."

He followed her gaze to a carved wooden cross hanging near the front entrance. It was the only wall decoration he owned from what she could see. "So?"

"Faith implies trust."

"My mother put it there," he explained with a scowl.

Laughing, she stretched her arms over her head, feeling lazy. She hadn't slept very well last night, but she didn't need to be alert to pick up on his concern for his mother. She could hear it in his voice. "You worry about her," she murmured. "She trusts too much."

"She spends too much," he corrected, eyeing her derisively. "On second-rate con artists and religious scams."

Sidney's jaw dropped at the implication. "You think I'm a second-rate—"

"No," he interrupted in a soft voice, his gaze lingering on her breasts. "You're first-rate all the way."

A war of emotions waged inside her. She was angry with him for insulting her, and with herself for wanting him anyway. The only consolation was that she knew he fought the same battle. He thought if he kept pushing her away, he wouldn't succumb to temptation.

She also felt closer to understanding his motivations than ever before. "You believe me," she said, stunned by the realization. "You're mad at yourself, because you believe me, and you're afraid I'll scam you."

Something dangerous flashed in his eyes, and she felt an answering jolt in her stomach. Marc was not a man who liked to be told how he felt. He was also quite adept at reasserting himself into the position of power with women.

Bracing her hands on the couch cushions underneath her, she scooted back a few inches, trying to put some space between them. Not about to let her off so easy, he grasped her bare ankle and tugged her back toward him.

Just like that, she was struck by another insight: The last time he'd been on this couch, he'd been fantasizing about her. "You..."

He leaned into her, focusing his attention on her mouth. "I what?"

She moistened her lips. "You were thinking about me. That day we went to Guajome Lake."

"I was doing a lot more than thinking," he said, bending his head to kiss her. He probably just wanted to shut her up, but Sidney offered no resistance. At the first touch of his mouth, every reason she had for not getting involved with a man like him just sort of...burned up. She melted against him, her mental protestations evaporating like mist. Flattening her palms on his chest, she kissed him back shyly, nibbling at his lower lip.

Her pulse throbbed with sensual awareness. Her body ached for his touch.

He pulled her over his lap, fitting his erection into the notch of her thighs, and she gasped at the intimate contact. Then she moaned, pressing herself harder against him, digging her fingernails into his shoulders and twining her tongue with his.

His hands snuck up under her shirt, splaying over her bare back.

Breaking the kiss, she drew her shirt over her head, offering him even more. Her nipples pebbled under his gaze, jutting against the soft cotton bra, and she reached back to unfasten the clasp. Letting it fall from her shoulders, she watched his face, holding her breath in anticipation.

He slid his hands up her rib cage to the undersides of her breasts. "You're very beautiful," he said, cradling her in his palms.

"So are you," she sighed, brushing her lips over his once again.

At the sound of someone approaching the front door, he froze. Looking over her shoulder, Sidney watched in horror as a small, dark-haired woman walked into the room, chattering in a foreign language.

With a tiny yelp, she clutched her shirt to her chest, preparing to flee.

"Don't you dare," he said in her ear, holding her in place. "It's just my mother."

"Marcos?" she said, squinting in the dim light. *"¿Que haces?"*

"What *am* I doing?" he translated in a mutter, as if he wondered that himself.

"You live with your mother?" she whispered.

"No, she's just visiting. How was bingo?" he inquired politely, as if he didn't have a half-naked woman in his lap, hiding his erection.

"It was fine," she said in heavily accented English, regarding Sidney with undisguised curiosity. "Who do you have there?"

Sidney blushed to the roots of her hair, visualizing the debauched picture she made. "Oh my God," she moaned, burying her face in Marc's shoulder.

Chapter 11

When Sidney awoke to the smell of good things cooking, she was so surprised she almost fell off the couch in a tangle of blankets.

Remembering where she was, and what she'd been doing the night before, she groaned, pulling the covers over her head in shame. She couldn't believe Marc's mother had walked in on them last night. Hasty introductions had been made, after which Mrs. Cruz had gone to bed early, Marc had retreated to the safety of his study to work and Sidney had spent a lonely evening trying to figure out the secrets of digital television.

Although she'd been exhausted, sleep had eluded her. Maybe it was the way Marc's borrowed sleeveless undershirt and cotton boxer shorts felt against her bare skin, or the faint smell of his laundry soap on them. Maybe it was the cool, smooth leather of his living room couch, the comfy blanket from his closet, or the pillow off his own bed.

She lay awake for what seemed like hours, all of her senses on overdrive, her body humming with frustration. Now, the clock on the DVD player said seven-thirty. She was going to be late! The kennel didn't open until nine, but she needed to go home and get ready first, and she still had to feed and clean. Saturday was her busiest day.

Hurrying away, she ran into Marc at the foot of the stairs. Literally.

"What's the rush?" he asked, steadying her.

"I have to shower and change clothes," she said, her voice throaty from lack of sleep. "I can't go to work like this."

"Shower here," he offered. "And borrow my clothes."

Her gaze dropped to the fly of his jeans, which was well-worn and well filled out. "Your clothes won't fit me," she said, feeling her cheeks tinge pink.

"They can't fit any worse than yours," he countered. "Breakfast is almost ready." He gave her a mildly insulting swat on the behind. "Hurry up."

In the master bath, she took a quick shower, using his masculine-smelling soap and shampoo sparingly. She wrapped a towel around herself and opened the door to let out steam as she rifled through the contents of the cabinet for toothpaste. When she found his deodorant, she pulled off the cap and inhaled, delighted to have found his scent.

"You can use that if you want," he said, standing in the open doorway.

She applied the deodorant to her underarms nonchalantly, as if that had been her intention all along.

With a slight smile, he pulled one of his T-shirts out of a drawer and handed it to her. "All I have is large," he said, getting an eyeful of her bare legs beneath the hem of the short towel.

"It's okay," she said, hugging the shirt to her chest. "I can wear it with my jeans from yesterday."

She got ready quickly before joining him downstairs.

At the kitchen counter, there was an abundance of scrambled eggs, coffee, orange juice, whole wheat toast and fresh fruit. "Did your mother make this?" she asked.

"No, I did. She's at church."

"Hmm." Taking the plate he offered, she piled it high and sat next to him at a small table overlooking the backyard. "Who takes care of the lawn?" The grass looked freshly clipped, if a bit dry in places, despite the recent rain.

"Me. Why? Can't you picture me engaging in domestic duties?"

"Cooking, maybe. Cleaning, definitely. Mowing a lawn? No."

"I think you just offended my masculinity," he said dryly.

"You know what I mean. You aren't the power tools and monkey grease type."

He smiled. "And yet, you are. I'm having a wild fantasy about you tinkering around under the hood of my car."

"Is that some kind of innuendo?" she asked.

"No," he said with a low laugh.

"You know what you need?" She gestured with a forkful of eggs. "A dog."

"I suppose you have a candidate in mind?"

"Yes," she said in triumph. "Blue."

His smile disappeared. "Even if I wanted a dog, which I don't, I wouldn't take that one. He's a maniac."

"I think he could get over his aversion to men, if he found a trustworthy one."

His expression was bland. "If you think I'm trustworthy, you don't know me very well."

"Maybe not with women, or relationships," she conceded. "But you take care of what's yours." When he didn't argue, she knew he wasn't interested in pursuing the conversation. "Tell me why you hate dogs," she continued anyway.

"I don't hate dogs," he said after a pause. "I just never really understood their…appeal."

"You never wanted one, as a boy?"

"I suppose I did." He paused, as if remembering something. "I fed a stray once. Several times, actually, behind my mother's back. I thought if I kept feeding him, he'd stay. He didn't."

What he'd said was so incredibly revealing that for a moment she couldn't breathe. It embodied every childhood wish, every lost hope, every unfulfilled dream he'd had growing up. The stray dog was a metaphor for his absent father, whether Marc realized it or not.

Then he continued, having never known how much he'd given away. "In Saudi, there were strays everywhere. I hated the sight of them. They were mangy, ill-bred and ill-kept, like the dogs that roam the streets in Mexico. I couldn't understand why people with so little to spare would feed an ugly mongrel instead of their own children."

"I thought Saudi Arabia was a wealthy country. Oil-rich."

"It is, for the minority elite, but most people just scrape by. In the refugee camp next to the base where I was stationed, the residents were dirt poor."

"Go on," she urged.

"There was one dog the other soldiers took a liking to. He was always getting into the chicken coop, making a nuisance of himself, stealing hens. But he was so sneaky and clever he gained their respect. They called him Houdini because they couldn't figure out how he was getting in and out. I caught him once while I was on night watch, skulking away with a dead bird. I could have shot him then, but I followed him instead, just to see where he was going."

Sidney nodded, finding the sound and cadence of his voice wonderfully pleasant.

"He was taking the chicken to a little girl. A family, I suppose, although I only saw her. She plucked the bird right out of his mouth, and he gave it up so easily. I couldn't believe it.

"After that, I looked at the camp dogs differently. Not all of them were loyal and selfless, like the chicken thief, but the people who tossed them scraps were genuinely fond of them, and I finally realized why they did it. It was just basic human nature, to give. To share. To see something hungry and feed it."

"This is a nicer story than I thought it would be."

He laughed harshly. "No. It isn't. We'd all grown fond of the dog, had taken to giving him our leftovers in hopes that he wouldn't raid the coop. I didn't see him around for a while, but one afternoon I spotted him walking down the deserted dirt road next to camp.

"It was clear something was wrong with him by the way he was moving. Unsteady, and sort of convulsing every few steps. When he got closer I saw the foam around his mouth."

"Oh, no," she whispered.

"I didn't have any choice but to shoot him. But just as I raised my rifle, the little girl came running out to him."

"My God."

"I walked toward them, shouting at her to get away, to get out of the line of fire. She only understood that I was going to kill her dog. Even half-crazed with rabies, he was protective of her. When he lunged at me—" he stared down at his open palms "—I broke his neck."

She raised her hand to her mouth, speechless with shock.

He was silent for a moment, then he arched a brow at her. "What do you think? Was it as good as the ones Daddy told?"

"No. Although I don't doubt he had some similar tales, being a veteran himself."

"That's what your sister told me. Right before she took off her clothes."

She bristled at the provocation, which was too strong to ignore. "I know you didn't sleep with her."

He smiled smugly, telling her he could have if he'd wanted to. "And who would you be mad at if I did?"

"You. She probably considers it her sisterly duty to test you."

"To see if I'll cheat?"

"No," she said. "To see if you're any good."

He studied her face. "Did you two compare notes about Greg, as well?"

"You're not fooling me," she said, tamping down her anger. "You didn't want to expose yourself emotionally by telling that story, so now you're pushing me away."

"Honey," he said, his expression one of great pity, "I don't have any emotions to expose."

"You saved a girl's life," she argued. "Why did the dog's death affect you more?"

A light flickered in his wary brown eyes, but his voice remained flat. "The dog meant more because he represented compassion, a phenomenon I've rarely encountered in life and scarcely understood. And when I found it, I killed it with my bare hands."

As warnings went, his couldn't have been clearer. He substituted sex for intimacy because he had nothing more to offer, although he was so skilled at what he did, women probably didn't complain.

And if they did, he moved on.

Her heart began to beat a rapid tattoo in her chest, and she turned her back on him, afraid her face would reveal her feelings.

This was not a man to fall in love with, logic warned.

Too late, fate replied.

Marc left a note for his mother before he took Sidney to work. She'd be disappointed if he couldn't accompany her to the San Luis Rey Mission that afternoon, as planned, but she wouldn't be surprised. His work often superseded all other aspects of his life, and attending religious gatherings had never been high on his priority list.

It wouldn't be the first time Alma Cruz had only her faith to keep her company.

"You don't have to stay," Sidney insisted.

"Yes, I do."

Alone at the kennel, she was just as vulnerable as she was at home, but instead of dogging her footsteps, he retreated to her office to make phone calls.

"Gina's got a match on your reefer," Lacy reported. "Stomach contents from the stray cat and the joint you gave her are consistent. Homegrown, high THC level, same basic color and maturity. Tests on the dog were also positive, but inconclusive for a specific strain."

He sat back in his chair, letting the ramifications of her words sink in. If the man who broke into Sidney's house was the killer, Marc had discovered an indirect link to his identity: his friend and neighbor, Tony Barreras.

Finding everyone who had access to a certain marijuana crop was like playing six degrees of separation. A local grower often sold bulk amounts to a few big-time dealers, who in turn hooked up with small-time guys like Tony, who then distributed the product to a dizzying range of nickel and dime customers.

Still, it was worth a shot. "Let's assume the perp is drugging dogs with marijuana. He may be hiding it in food, giving it an hour or so to kick in before he strikes. If he waits too long, the dog won't be in the mood to go for a walk, right?" He drummed his fingertips on Sidney's desk, considering. "Leak it to Crystal Dunn. Giving female dog owners a head's-up can't hurt."

"You really think he'll stick to that MO?"

"Not after it's been all over the news. But what choice do we have? If he tried it a few times before he actually abducted a victim, maybe we could jog someone's memory."

Lacy groaned, probably thinking of the task force hours that would be sacrificed to old ladies calling to say Muffy had been sluggish after her morning walk six months ago. "I'm already burning the midnight oil here, Marcos."

"Public service is a thankless job, Meredith," he returned, completely unsympathetic.

Marc hung up, no more satisfied with the direction of the case than she was. The "grasping at straws" investigative technique was rarely fruitful. Neither was sitting on their hands, however.

He toyed with the idea of calling Tony then discarded it. His friend adhered to the drug dealers' code of ethics, an unspoken set of rules that included being deliberately vague over the telephone and never naming names. Tony might give up his source in person, but he wouldn't do it on a live wire.

After spending another hour trying to piece together a puzzle that didn't fit, Marc gave up and left Sidney's office. He'd kept a surreptitious eye on every customer she interacted with throughout the day, studying vehicles, facial expressions and demeanors.

If the killer had been among them, he didn't know it, and neither did she. Sidney treated all of her clients with the same deference. Her manner was reserved and her professionalism exemplary. Owners spoke of their pets as though they were members of the family, and Sidney cared for them as such.

It was all very bizarre.

Confounded by interspecies dynamics, Marc wandered to the kennel and roamed the fence line, hands shoved deep in his pockets. What had drawn Blue here? The sound and scent of other dogs? Sidney's psychic connection?

Shaking his head, he studied the surroundings. The industrial park looked nothing like Candace Hegel's neighborhood, or any other residential area. Pacific Pet Hotel was part of a business zone, a concrete jungle with scant vegetation and few trees.

He flipped open his cell again.

"What?" Lacy answered, exasperated.

"Where did Anika Groene get her dog?"

"At the pound, same as Candace Hegel."

"Follow up on the prior owners."

"I already have. Both dogs were picked up by animal control on opposite sides of the city during routine patrols. No tags, no microchip identification and no prior owners."

Marc mulled it over. Like Blue, Anika Groene's dog was an odd-looking specimen. What else did they have in common? "Are Dobermans a German breed?"

"As far as I know."

"Check out local breeders, especially the disreputable kind, those who might sell dogs of questionable pedigrees. And trainers. Maybe Hegel and Groene used the same trainer."

"They didn't. Neither dog had ever been to a trainer."

Marc frowned, thinking of the commands Sidney had given Blue. It wasn't just a habit; she didn't use them with other dogs, and half the time, she didn't seem to have any idea what she was saying. "Did Candace Hegel speak German?"

"I don't know."

"Find out."

Lacy was silent for a moment. "You're enjoying this, aren't you? You do all the thinking, I do all the legwork?"

"Yes," he said with a grin, and hung up.

Whistling, he wandered over to Blue's kennel. For once, the dog didn't lunge or bark at him. Instead he regarded him warily through strange, colorless eyes.

"Hey there, sport," he said, keeping his voice amiable.

Blue lowered his head and issued a low, rumbling growl.

"Oh, yeah," Marc muttered. "You're a keeper."

"Bonding?" Sidney asked, coming up behind him.

"Best friends," he agreed, jerking his chin toward the dog.

Blue bared his teeth.

She threw back her head and laughed, the same guileless,

throaty laugh he'd been intrigued by from the start. He hadn't heard it very often, because things between them had hardly been jovial, but he liked the sound. Even more, he liked the way she looked, unselfconscious and unadorned, her simple beauty complimented by his plain white T-shirt and her cap of short, black hair.

He smiled back at her, wishing for a moment he had a fraction of her innocence. When she noticed his appraisal, the happiness drained from her face. "I'm done," she said, stepping away from him. "I always close at noon on Saturdays."

"Do you think he misses her? Candace?"

She raised her eyebrows, perhaps surprised by the sentimental question. "Yes. He mopes and sighs and takes very little joy in life."

"Maybe he was like that before."

"No."

"And his aggressiveness? Is that also a symptom of grief?"

She hesitated. "With most dogs, aggression is a learned behavior, although some animals seem to be naturally more inclined to it."

"What is your professional opinion, in his case?" he asked, adopting her clinical tone.

"I think he was abused or mistreated before the abduction."

"By Candace Hegel?"

"Of course not," she protested, as if defending a close friend.

"Could he have been trained that way?"

"I don't know. Most formally trained dogs are very controlled, very well-behaved. Their owners spend a lot of time caring for them. Are police dogs aggressive, off-duty?"

"No," he admitted. Even the most vicious attack dogs were the best of canine companions, according to their human cohorts. Examining Sidney's face, Marc shelved thoughts of the investigation temporarily. It was Saturday afternoon, she rarely had time off and she looked tired. "Would you like to go with my mother and me to the mission?"

She rubbed at her eyes with her fists, an endearing, childlike gesture. "Actually, I'd like to go home and go to bed."

"That can be arranged."

"Alone," she clarified.

He bit back another smile. "I knew what you meant." Not that he wouldn't enjoy joining her there—when she was no longer a part of this investigation. Last night, once again, he'd gone too far with her. He'd known his mother had been due back any minute, but he'd gotten lost in the taste of her mouth, the feel of her body, the scent of her skin.

He would have her, Marc told himself. Just not yet.

"If I go home, will you follow me?" she asked.

"Yes."

She sighed. "Then I'll feel guilty for keeping you."

"Don't. I'd rather work than go to church."

"And here I thought you were a good Catholic boy," she teased. "Responsible, God-fearing, dutiful."

"I said I was responsible, not obedient." With his mother, he'd always felt more like a parent than a child. She was emotional and reactive, all sense, little sensibility. He'd taken advantage of her fragile nature and ignored her admonishments more often than a good son should. People with weaknesses were easy to exploit, he'd discovered at a young age, and had hardened himself accordingly. "I'd rather commit sins than atone for them," he added, his eyes on the curves of her body.

"I don't have anything to wear," she said, crossing her arms over her chest.

"I'll take you home first. You can pack an overnight bag."

She scowled at him. "Presumptuous, aren't you? You think I'm spending the night with you again?"

"I'd prefer it, but don't get any hopes up that I'll ravish you. My mother isn't leaving until tomorrow morning."

While Marc waited downstairs, Sidney packed her bag, casting a longing glance out her bedroom window. It was a beautiful day, crystal clear and not too hot, the recent rain having scrubbed away both the smog and the humidity.

She would have loved to spend the afternoon at the beach.

Sighing, she shoved some clothes and toiletries into a green canvas tote, then searched her closet for a dress to wear. She only had one appropriate for the weather, so there wasn't much to deliberate over.

Her shoe collection was also woefully inadequate. She'd never thought she needed flirty summer sandals until this very moment. Shrugging, she grabbed a pair of simple white Keds. They weren't new, but they were cleaner than her work sneakers, so she called it good.

"I have to talk to my neighbor about something," Marc said after they'd arrived at his house. "I'll be over in a few minutes."

Sidney glanced at the front door anxiously. "What about your mother?"

"She doesn't bite."

Clutching her bag to her chest, she knocked on the front door.

"Just go in," he said over his shoulder.

She made a shooing motion with her hands, waving him away. He may not care what his mother thought of her, or of him, for that matter, but she did.

Alma Cruz answered the door with a warm smile on her face. "*Mija!* You don't have to knock," she said, ushering her in. "Where is Marcos?"

"Next door."

"Oh, good. I wanted to apologize for last night. I'm so sorry for embarrassing you."

"Um," she murmured, feeling her cheeks heat.

"Are you going to *La Misión* with us?"

She smiled hesitantly. "If that's okay."

"Of course," she said, her eyes alight with pleasure. "Have you eaten *lonche?*"

"No."

"Come, come. I made enchiladas. You like?"

Sidney shrugged, puzzled by her excitement. As the older woman's hand clasped around her upper arm, the reason for her hospitality became clear: Alma thought she was speaking to her future daughter-in-law.

Apparently Marc didn't make a habit of introducing his lady friends to his mother. Nor did he have them spend the night on the couch while she was visiting, or invite them to church the next day.

"I think you've got the wrong idea," she began.

"Oh, no," Alma countered, fixing them both a serving of spicy, aromatic food. "I see how young people are nowadays, hopping from one bed to another. I can tell you're not that type." She sat down at Marc's kitchen table, patting Sidney's hand. "How long have you and Marcos been dating?"

Sidney stared down at the plate in front of her, wondering if her cheeks were as red as the enchilada sauce. "Not long enough," she muttered.

Alma put a hand over her heart, sighing as if Sidney had said something romantic. "It doesn't take long, with that special someone. I fell in love with his father at first sight."

Her eyes got a misty, far-away look Sidney associated with mourning. "Are you a widow?"

"No, *mija,*" she said with a trilling laugh. "He was a handsome devil, and I was young and foolish. We never married."

Of course. Marc had admitted to the circumstances of his birth, had he not? And hinted at more, even less pleasant details, albeit unwittingly. Not sure if condolences were in order, Sidney tasted a bite of the chicken enchilada. "This is delicious," she said, and meant it. It was hot and flavorful, but not so spicy it burned her tongue. "Do you live nearby?"

"In San Ysidro. I take the bus from there one weekend a month."

"Don't you drive?"

"Oh, no," she said quickly. "Too dangerous."

"Won't Marc pick you up?"

"Yes, but I don't ride in cars, either. So many accidents." She clucked her tongue in sympathy. "Just last week, in *El Chisme,* there was an article about abduction. An entire family in a minivan was taken by *extra-terrenos.*"

"Extra-terrenos?"

"Sí," she nodded. "Space aliens."

Sidney hid a smile, finding Mrs. Cruz's eccentricities endearing. It was refreshing to meet another person at least as crazy as she was. Thanking Alma for lunch, Sidney excused herself to Marc's room to change.

Primping more than usual, she applied a touch of lip gloss and a hint of eye shadow before she donned the navy cotton halter dress. Her lashes were thick and black without mascara, and her cheeks didn't need any more color.

Stepping back from the mirror, she surveyed her reflection with a frown. The dress was nice enough, showing off her tanned shoulders and cinching in at the waist. It was calf-length and demure, sort of a fifties style, so it didn't look ridiculous with tennis shoes.

She tapped her lower lip with her forefinger thoughtfully. "My hair," she breathed, running her fingers through it. She never bothered with bows or frou-frou, and it hadn't occurred to her to bring any.

"Mrs. Cruz?" she called into the hallway, her voice rising, exposing her nervousness.

"Call me Alma," she insisted, poking her head out of the guest bedroom.

"Do you have a hair clip? Or a barrette?"

Her eyes lit up. "Yes! I have the perfect thing." She came out a moment later with a white silk rosette attached to a bobby pin.

Sidney smiled at the whimsical decoration, pushing a lock of hair away from her forehead and pinning the flower in place.

"You look lovely," she said, squeezing her bare shoulders.

Alma was right. For once, she looked pretty, feminine and composed. "Thanks," she answered, smoothing a hand over her fluttering stomach and wondering if Marc would be as pleased as his mother by her transformation.

Chapter 12

Marc found Tony at his usual station, parked in front of the TV, playing video games. Taking a seat next to him on the couch, Marc tapped his fingers against his jeans-clad thigh, wondering how to broach the subject.

"You know that joint you gave me?" he asked finally.

Tony's dark brows drew together. "You actually smoked that?"

"No. I sent it to the lab."

He shut off the video game, for once giving Marc his undivided attention. "Why?"

"Just a hunch. You said it was knockout stuff. I think the guy I've been looking for has been using it to drug dogs before he attacks their owners."

"You don't know for sure?"

Marc told him about the dead cat at Sidney's house and explained her involvement with the case.

"I can't give you any names," he said, coming to his feet. "This is my life, man. This is my livelihood."

"I know your customers, Tony. I see them come and go, and I don't need you to tell me their names. I want your connect."

Cursing, he paced the living room. Marc was silent for a moment, giving him time to think it through. "The guy I deal with is not a psycho," Tony said. "He's just a man trying to make an honest living, like me."

Marc didn't bother to point out that selling controlled substances did not fall under the scope of honest living. "Does he get it from someone else? Sell it to anyone else?"

"I don't know," he muttered, not meeting his eyes.

"Don't lie to me. Please."

Tony paused, considering how much to reveal. "I think he grows it himself, and I have no idea who else he sells to. He's not big-time, but he doesn't mess around with amateurs."

"I would never tell him you gave me his name."

"You wouldn't have to," he said with a frantic gesture. "Don't you see? I'm one of his only guys. The only one, maybe. The process of elimination would be swift and deadly."

"Deadly?"

Tony scowled. "Not that kind of deadly. The 'I'll never work in this town again' kind of deadly."

Marc wouldn't mind if Tony sought more reputable employment, but he refused to turn the argument into a moral discussion. In his current state of disgrace, he was in no position to judge. "Women are being murdered, Tony. I can't pass up a good lead."

"I'll tell you his name," he finally agreed. "But if you talk to him, I'm toast."

"Maybe I won't have to," he murmured, formulating a plan that, once again, involved Sidney.

To her great disappointment, Marc barely noticed Sidney's appearance. His mind must have been distracted by other things, because he hadn't said two words to her since returning from his neighbor's house.

The mission was less than a mile away, so they set off walking, his mother several strides ahead of them. Sidney assumed she was giving them privacy, not that they needed it. Sighing, she stared at Alma's sturdy calves between the hem of her skirt and the tops of her sensible black shoes. The colorful umbrella she was carrying shielded her head and shoulders from their view.

"Is your neighbor a woman?" Sidney asked.

He snapped out of his reverie. "What? No." Then a smile curved his lips. "Why?"

"Just wondering," she said, feeling ridiculous and pathetic.

To her surprise, he took her hand in his. "I'm not seeing anyone else."

The gesture was just a simple touch, an easy show of affection, and yet it meant more to her than any of his sexual advances. He knew it, too, judging by his guarded expression.

She looked down at his hand, strong and dark in her own. "Good," she said, not interested in playing coy with him.

He laughed at her possessiveness. "I like your dress."

"Thanks." Feeling her cheeks turn pink, she resisted the urge to fidget with the silly flower in her hair.

"I was just thinking about the case," he added, offering an excuse for his inattention.

She nodded in understanding. Any woman he became involved with would take a back seat to his job. Then she scolded herself for assuming she held any place in his life, let alone distant second.

Sidney had lived in Oceanside for five years, and was born and raised in neighboring Bonsall, but she'd never visited the San Luis Rey Mission. It was a tourist attraction, a historical site and a piece of local tradition. More quaint than grand, it boasted lush gardens and bubbling fountains, Spanish-style architecture, and an old graveyard.

Afternoon mass was held in a small rectangular chapel with polished pews and a high, domed ceiling. In an alcove at the entrance, there was a small porcelain bowl. Alma wet her fingertips with the holy water and made the sign of the cross.

Sidney paused, not sure if she should follow suit. Taking the matter into his own hands, Marc dipped two fingers into the bowl.

"*En el nombre del padre, el hijo, y el espíritu santo.*"

As he touched her forehead, the valley between her breasts, and each bare shoulder, Sidney was intensely aware of the damp traces his fingertips made on her skin, like the remnants of a butterfly kiss. In a response that was far from spiritual, her nipples contracted, pushing against the bodice of her dress.

Watching her intently, he repeated the gesture on himself then urged her toward the back of the church, away from his mother. She slipped into the last row, expecting him to follow.

At the base of the pew, he knelt, making the sign of the cross again before entering.

Sidney blushed, embarrassed by her ignorance about his faith and her own inappropriate reaction to his touch. Only a depraved person would get turned on in church.

Oblivious to her inner struggle, he picked up a prayer book and began thumbing through it. Perhaps because she was striving to think of anything but sex, it was foremost on her mind. His dark hands looked positively sinful against the white pages. They were long-fingered and beautiful, much larger and more forceful than her own.

She looked away, but she could feel his hand in hers, strong and warm. Worse, she could feel the blunt tips of his fingers, brushing the naked spot between her breasts, and remembered just how intimately he'd touched her the night before.

Sneaking another peak at his hands, she wondered how she could find the least private part of his body so arousing, and when she'd become such a wanton.

"Get on your knees," he said.

Her eyes flew to his face. "What?"

"You have to kneel for this part." He pointed to a cushioned bar at their feet.

"Oh." Her entire body tingling with awareness, she knelt beside him, trying to deny the obvious sexual parallels.

For an indeterminable length of time, the ups and downs of the ceremony kept her physically occupied, if not mentally. Catholics apparently spent a lot of time on their knees. The sermon was in Spanish, and although Marc knew all of the proper responses, his voice sounded wickedly seductive, as if he were whispering dirty things in her ear during sex.

They were sitting again when he did whisper something suggestive. "Are you hot?" he asked softly, his lips brushing her neck.

"What?"

"You look flushed."

She followed his gaze to the neckline of her dress. Not only was she hot, she was sweating. While he watched, a tiny bead of perspiration rolled from the base of her throat down into the hollow between her breasts.

She swallowed dryly. He moistened his lips.

"Come on," he said, urging her to her feet, impervious to God's watchful eye. Just outside the side door, a set of narrow concrete steps let to an underground tomb where esteemed religious figures had been reverentially interred. The instant they were alone, shrouded in cool, blessed darkness, he pulled her close.

"You did that on purpose," she accused, refusing to let him kiss her.

"Did what?"

"You know what. Taking me to the back row. Acting all…sexy."

He laughed, curving his arms around her waist. "I took you to the back row so we could sneak out early. But if austere surroundings put you in the mood…"

"It wasn't the setting," she defended, her cheeks burning in shame. "It was you. Your voice. Your hands."

In the dim light, his eyes went opaque with desire. "My hands?" he repeated, bringing one hand up to her collarbone, rubbing his thumb across the base of her throat. "What about them?" He pushed aside her bodice, exposing the pale upper curve of her breast, which he knew made an erotic contrast with his own dark skin.

She closed her eyes, covering his hand with hers. "What am I going to do with you?" she whispered.

He touched his lips to her bare shoulder. "The possibilities are endless."

Before he could rouse her to mindlessness, she arched away from his eager mouth and extricated herself from his embrace. "Let's see if you can channel that energy for another intimate activity."

"What?"

"Conversation."

He leaned against the wall inside the tomb, wearing a pained, frustrated expression. "You are such a pain in the ass."

Smiling, she offered him her hand. He took it, but fell into silence as they rounded the deserted graveyard. "Tell me about your father," she ventured.

"What about him?"

"Were you close?"

"No."

She squeezed his hand. "Did he hurt your mother?"

He jerked away from her, misreading the gesture. "Yes, he hurt her," he muttered. "Thankfully he wasn't around that often. What other misery do you want to pull out of me? Did he hit me, too? No. He was good to me, the son of a bitch. Taught me everything he knew."

"About what?"

"Conning people. Picking pockets. Sleight of hand. He was the lowest kind of criminal, a petty thief, but he was handsome, and he was charming. My mother couldn't resist him. No woman could."

Sidney swallowed her emotion, feeling as though he was hurling the words at her, pelting her with them. But she'd asked for it, hadn't she? "What happened to him?"

He shoved his hands in his pockets. "He came by the house just before I got deployed. I threatened to beat the hell out of him if he didn't stay away from her." He looked out across the well-manicured grounds, then back at her. "She never forgave me for it."

"He didn't come home again?"

"No. A few years later, he got stabbed by a vagrant in the cab of a train. She took the bus all the way to El Paso to see him before he died."

"Did she make it?"

He shook his head.

"I'm sorry," she said.

"I'm not."

Sidney wasn't sure she believed him, and wanted nothing more than to take his hand again, not to read the truth, but to comfort him. She kept her arms at her sides, knowing he would reject the gesture.

Those she cared about the most always avoided her touch.

By the time they returned to his house, it was early evening and Sidney was exhausted. She wanted nothing more than to curl up in a little ball and retreat from the world.

Marc had other plans for her. "I need you to meet someone," he began. "Get a read off him, if you can."

She groaned, rolling over onto her stomach. They were in his bedroom, having just eaten dinner, and the combination of cozy bed and full stomach was lulling her to sleep. "Who?"

"My next door neighbor's drug supplier."

"Why?" she whined, burying her face in his pillows.

"Because he's a suspect," he said, taking the pillow out from under her. "You know that dead cat in your house? It had a bellyful of pot, the kind this guy grows."

She glared up at him. "You are so annoying."

He grunted a response, digging through her overnight bag. "Wear this," he said, throwing a pair of shorts and a purple tank top at her. "No bra."

"Oh, great," she muttered, clenching a fistful of fabric. "Are you going to have me jiggle my way to an introduction?"

"Whatever works."

He drove her truck past the outskirts of Oceanside all the way out to Bonsall. As they wound through the rolling hills of a middle-class neighborhood, she rolled down her window to study the scenery, struck by a wave of nostalgia.

"I grew up near here," she said.

"I know."

"How?"

"I do my homework." As they went miles beyond city limits, the houses became few and far between, and Sidney saw more horses than cars. Finally he pulled off the side of the road. "See that house? The one with the brick retaining wall?"

She squinted down at it. "Yes." Sidney knew the house well, actually. A friend of hers used to live there.

"Drive down there and slow to a halt, like you ran out of gas. Then bend over and look under the hood."

Giving him a disgusted look, she said, "Why don't I just knock on the front door?"

He deliberated for a moment. "Do that if he doesn't come out."

"Who am I looking for?"

"A young guy. Your age."

"What if he's the one?"

"Then get the hell out of there. And no matter what, don't go inside the house."

She sighed. "I don't enjoy these adventures, you know."

"You think I do?" Unfastening his safety belt, he got out of the truck seat. "I'll be right here," he said, watching her slide over into the driver's seat. "With my gun."

To her surprise, his ruse worked like a charm. She rolled the pickup to a stop, popped the hood and looked under it like a clueless bimbo. In less than a minute, she heard a screen door slam shut and approaching footsteps.

Who knew it was so easy to pick up men? She straightened uneasily, wiping her sweat-slick palms against the sides of her shorts.

The man walking toward her stopped in his tracks. "Sidney?"

For a second, she couldn't place him. He was tall and lanky, his dark blond hair on the long side, face partially hidden by about a week's worth of stubble. "Derek?" His blue eyes lit up with delight, and she launched herself into his open arms, forgetting her fear.

Derek DeWinter had been her best friend in junior high, the closest thing she'd had to a boyfriend in high school and quite possibly the only person in her life who knew her secret and had never treated her like a freak.

When she was fifteen, his family had moved from Bonsall to Scripps Ranch to be closer to Children's Hospital. His little sister Trina had a rare kidney disorder, and the disease had brought the family both heartache and financial ruin.

Sidney and Derek wrote to each other sporadically, but lost touch, as teenagers were wont to do. In all this time, she'd never forgotten him, or thrown away his letters.

He hugged her so tight she laughed at his enthusiasm. Then he pulled back to look at her, as if he weren't quite sure she was real. "My God. You're beautiful."

She couldn't help but flush from pleasure at his words, although he'd always been effusive, and a little nearsighted. "You're not so bad yourself. What are you doing here?"

"I live here," he said, jerking his shoulder toward the house. "We moved back."

"Your mom and dad?"

A shadow darkened his eyes. "No. Just me and Trina."

The smile fell off her face. It was terrible of her, but she never thought the sick girl would survive this long. "How is she?"

"She has her good days and bad," he hedged. "Want to see her?"

"Of course," she said immediately.

"What's wrong with your truck?"

"I think I ran out of gas." She toed at the dirt in front of her, trying to look sheepish.

"Come on in. I've got a gas can in the garage."

She glanced at the tree-shrouded hill in the distance, remembering her promise to Marc. Following Derek, she made an okay sign behind her back, hoping he wouldn't freak out.

Trina DeWinter remembered her, although they hadn't seen each other in more than ten years, and she was just a little girl when Sidney and Derek had been friends. At twenty-two she should have been a vibrant, full-grown woman. Instead she was painfully thin, the illness keeping her as small and undeveloped as a child.

For one so sick, she was in great spirits. She had a colorful silk scarf over her head, covering her baby-fine hair, and her soft speech was punctuated by light laughter. The conversation invariably turned to the foibles of youth, and some of the scrapes Sidney and Derek had gotten themselves into as wild hooligans.

"Remember the well?" Trina asked suddenly. "Who fell in there?"

"Lisa Pettigrew," Sidney said with a smile. "Derek had a major crush on her."

"No, I didn't," he protested. "I had a major crush on you."

"Well, Lisa chased after you, I remember that. And you didn't run very fast to get away. Neither did Kurtis," she added wryly, thinking of the boy who'd taunted her throughout grade school. "Whatever happened to him?"

"He's still around," Derek said, his eyes hard. "We're neighbors, in fact. He bought old man Frasier's property.

Sidney hugged her arms around herself, feeling a sudden chill. Kurtis Stalb had lured Lisa down into the well and then abandoned her there. Afraid of the repercussions, he didn't tell anyone where she was. If Sidney hadn't bumped into him inadvertently and discovered his shocking secret, Lisa might never have been found.

"Hopefully he grew up to be a decent person," she said. She cut him some slack because twelve-year-old boys couldn't be held accountable for, or even expected to understand, the consequences of their actions.

"Are you kidding?" Derek snorted. "People like that don't change. He was born bad."

Sidney felt a rush of sympathy for Derek, recalling how often he and his sister had been the subjects of Kurtis's ridicule. With her long, black hair and freaky ways, Sidney had also been one of the bully's favorite targets.

After a few more minutes, Trina's eyelids began to droop. Hefting her easily, Derek carried her off to bed, calling her a sleepyhead with warm affection.

"Where are your parents?" Sidney asked when he returned.

"Dead," he answered shortly. "There was a pile-up on the 15. Mom was killed instantly. Dad hung on just until he heard."

She placed a hand over her heart. "Oh God, Derek. I'm so sorry."

"Yeah."

"You must be…" She was about to say buried in debt then rethought her words. "How are you managing? Trina's medical care alone—"

"We're getting by," he interrupted.

"How?"

"You don't want to know."

She bit down on her lower lip, trying not to show her pity. It was the last thing he needed. He found his gas can and dumped it into the tank, smiling with pleasure when her truck started without a hitch. She promised to keep in touch, and he claimed the same, neither of them believing it, or each other.

Whatever they'd had, once upon a time, was a childhood dream, a sweet, purely innocent fantasy, lost in the harsh miasma of reality.

Chapter 13

Marc had been going out of his mind since Sidney disappeared. One moment he was admiring her gorgeous legs as she bent over the engine, the next he was watching some hippie drug dealer put his dirty hands all over her.

He'd been crouched in an orange grove, seething, for almost an hour.

Finally she came out and said goodbye, driving away as the last vestiges of daylight slipped into darkness. Marc could see the younger man's forlorn, almost hangdog expression in the fading taillights.

It was only then that Marc lowered his weapon.

Straightening, he holstered his gun and waited for Sidney to round the corner, every nerve in his body as taut as a wire. She was safe. Why wasn't he relieved?

She pulled up alongside him, killing the engine and stepping out when he made no move to get in. "I gave you one simple instruction," he said, enunciating each word carefully.

"He's harmless. I've known him since we were kids."

A hot, prickly sensation crept up the back of his neck. "I asked you not to go in the house," he reiterated.

"His sister is extremely sick," she said, crossing her arms over her chest. "He invited me in to see her."

The reasonable excuse did nothing to assuage his anger. It still boiled inside, straining for release. "Did you give him your phone number?"

Her demeanor changed from defensive to coy. "If I did, would you be jealous?"

"No," he lied, "I'd be furious. He's a key component in a murder case. Someone he's connected to is mutilating women. Do you want to become one of them?"

"I didn't give him my number, he gave me his, and I accepted it for old times' sake. We were friends once. Nothing more."

He laughed harshly. "You are so naïve. He hugged you close to feel your tits against his chest, and his eyes were glued to your ass every time you turned around."

"You're the one who wanted me to dress sexy," she pointed out. "To bend over under the hood. To go without a bra." Each detail brought a sensual image to mind, and he had to force himself to keep his focus on her face. "If having other men look at me disturbs you, maybe you shouldn't use me as bait."

"That's not it," he said, shoving his fingers through his hair. "I had no idea what you were doing in there. I was worried about you."

She examined his face then stroked her eyes down his body. "Careful, Marc," she said in a low voice, leaning forward and putting her hand in the middle of his chest. "You're getting dangerously close to revealing your—" she touched her lips to his ear "—feelings."

He gaped at her in shock. She'd disregarded his only request, put herself in a great amount of danger and now she had the nerve to jerk his chain?

Splaying her fingers over his rib cage, she stepped closer, insinuating every inch of her body along the length of his. He was breathing heavily, instantly aroused, and he knew she could feel it, but she didn't back away. As her fingertips trailed over his leather shoulder holster, he realized she was toying with him, the same way he'd toyed with her at the mission. The difference was he hadn't been bluffing. If she thought he wouldn't give her exactly what she was asking for, right here, right now, she was in for a hell of a surprise.

"Don't play with that, sweetheart," he warned, moving her hand away from his gun. "It might go off."

"I was kind of hoping it would," she replied breathlessly.

He pushed her back onto the hood of the truck, hooking his hands under her knees and placing himself between them. Wrapping her legs around his waist, she threaded her fingers through the hair at the nape of his neck and brought his mouth down to hers.

Groaning, he crushed himself against her, thrusting his tongue into the heat of her mouth and shaping her body with his hands. He was desperate to touch every part of her, taste every inch of her. She kissed him back hungrily, accepting everything he had to offer, letting him know he could have her any way he wished.

Too keyed-up to wait, he wrenched his mouth from hers. "Take off your shorts," he said hoarsely, stepping back to release the buttons at his fly.

She stood, fumbling with the clasp and zipper, then pushed her shorts down her hips. After a brief hesitation, she hooked her thumbs in the waistband of her panties and stripped them off, as well. Then she boosted herself back on top of the hood of her pickup truck and spread her long, lovely legs for him.

He thought he might go off then and there.

"Lift up your top," he added, as an afterthought. Her eyes burned into his, smoke-dark, as she raised the hem, exposing her breasts. While he watched her nipples tighten in the cool night air, he felt more blood pulsing to his groin, making him painfully, impossibly hard.

Sinking to his knees before her, he laved each one thoroughly, flicking his tongue over the wet, puckered tips. Gasping, she braced her hands on the hood of the truck and arched her back. With a low groan, he dragged his mouth from her breasts to her belly, sliding his hands along her inner thighs. The scent of her arousal beckoned, and his mouth watered for her taste, but he didn't go lower until she writhed and whimpered, pushing down on the top of his head.

Her loss of inhibitions was his undoing. Abandoning any attempt at delicacy, he thumbed aside a damp, silky curl and licked at her slick flesh until she stiffened and cried out. Clutching her fingers in his hair and holding him to her, she climaxed against his mouth.

The last of his control shattered with her.

Half carrying, half dragging her inside the truck, he laid her down on the bench seat. The space was tight, barely enough room for him to get on top of her, but it offered a semblance of privacy. If someone drove by, at least they wouldn't see her spread-eagled on the hood.

Pushing her thighs apart with his hands, he freed his erection and thrust himself inside her, showing even less finesse with intercourse than he had with oral sex.

Her body tensed at the intrusion, and he knew she'd paid the price for his impatience. With a phenomenal effort, he held himself motionless. She was sleek and tight, pulsing around his cock like a silken fist. He was afraid he might come even if he didn't move.

"Are you all right?" he asked, scarcely able to form coherent words.

"Yes," she said, raising her knees slightly, as if seeking a more comfortable position.

The subtle movement sent him right over the edge. Gritting his teeth, he pulled back and drove deep, again and again, feeling how wet she was, tasting her on his lips, wishing he could make the incredible sensation last forever.

Instead it lasted about ten more seconds.

He withdrew as far as he dared and buried himself in her snug heat one last time, his entire body quaking with the power of his release.

Afterward, he lay stretched out on top of her, panting, too sated to consider the full ramifications of his actions. It had been the fastest, most ill-planned, and least well-executed sexual experience of his life. But by far the best.

As she shifted beneath him, he became aware of how uncomfortable she must be, pinned to a vinyl seat under about one hundred eighty pounds of dead weight. He was in a damned awkward position himself, his legs sticking out the open passenger door, the gearshift prodding his ribs, the steering wheel pressing into his right shoulder.

He lifted himself up and pulled out of her, a warning bell clanging through his head. "I didn't use anything."

"I noticed."

"You did? When?" Jerking his pants up, he buttoned them haphazardly.

"When you, um, started."

He found her shorts and panties on the damp grass at his feet and handed them to her. "Why didn't you stop me?"

"I should have," she agreed.

Stunned by his lapse in judgment, he slammed the passenger door and went around to the driver's side. He waited for her to dress, growing more appalled by his own behavior with each passing second. The least he could have done was to pull out before he came. In the heat of the moment, the thought had never even occurred to him.

Beside him, Sidney zipped up her shorts with a slight wince and fastened her seat belt.

He groaned, covering his eyes with his hand and putting his head against the steering wheel. Not only had he failed to protect her, but he hadn't been any good. He'd fallen on her like an animal, pounded into her like a madman, and gone off quicker than a teenager.

So much for waiting until she was no longer a part of his investigation.

He snuck another glance at her, noting the displeasure on her face. She'd probably felt nothing more than annoyance. Hell, she'd been so tight, and he'd used her so carelessly, he might even have hurt her.

He'd never lost control like that. Ever.

"I'm sorry," he said. Apologizing for an abysmal sexual performance was another first for him.

She stared out the window, tears filling her eyes.

Muttering a curse, he started the engine and drove home, all of the satisfaction he'd taken from her body dissolving into cold, hard remorse.

Sidney sat beside him in miserable silence, feeling like a total failure. Experiences like this were the reason she'd given up on sex.

A flood of past disappointments washed over her, leaving her feeling awkward, empty and bereft.

At twenty, tired of Samantha's taunts and Greg's unwanted advances, she'd given her virginity to a sweet but clueless college boy who'd pretended she was his ex-girlfriend the entire time.

Her second attempt at intimacy had been even worse. Samantha had set her up with one of Greg's law school buddies, and Sidney found that she actually enjoyed his company. Adam was charming, handsome and experienced. She'd been genuinely infatuated with him until, after a dozen chaste dates, they'd finally gone to bed together.

Sidney had tried to relax and go with the moment, but it was difficult not to read a man during prolonged physical contact. Adam had been thinking he might have to embellish upon his performance when he gave Greg a detailed account of their sexual encounter, because it wasn't going very well.

It was kind of hard to derive any pleasure from his touch after that.

Her last and most recent effort before Marc had been with Bill Vincent. She was reluctant to enter another relationship that would fizzle as soon as it got to the bedroom, but they'd been friends long before they became lovers, so he knew about her psychic abilities. Having been forewarned, Bill was quite skilled at blocking his thoughts from her. He was also warm and generous, but she never lost herself in his embrace like she did with Marc.

After a lackluster courtship, they parted as friends, and Bill told her a secret of his own: he preferred men.

It topped off her trio of shame.

Samantha's promiscuity had also soured her on sex, and Sidney began to think of most men as cowards, liars and cheats. She was just too tenderhearted to suffer a man's embraces—reading his dirty mind, knowing he wished she was more experienced, more beautiful, someone better, someone else.

Marc had never given her the impression he'd rather be with another woman, but he was hard to read, like Bill. Younger men wore their hearts, and their fantasies, on their sleeves. If she didn't know better, she'd believe Marc when he said he didn't have any softer emotions. Instead she suspected they were buried so deep even he no longer recognized them.

The disappointment, this time, fell on her shoulders. Lost in sensation, she wasn't sure where she'd gone wrong. Her cheeks burned as images of her wanton behavior assaulted her like hot flashes. She'd practically begged him to make love to her. After he'd succumbed to her advances, she'd been too wrapped up in her own responses to pay any attention to his. One moment she was lying underneath him, drowning in pleasure, the next he was heaving himself off her and saying he was sorry.

It had been the most profound experience of her life, and he was sorry.

She took at least half the responsibility for their unprotected sex, having instigated it. He'd felt so good she hadn't wanted him to stop. Ever. She'd actually wanted him to come inside her. For a brief, monumentally naïve instant, she'd entertained a foolish dream about them starting a life together.

Judging by the horrified expression on his face as he realized what they'd done, he would rather adopt a family of rabid dogs than tie himself down to her.

When they arrived at his house, she got out of the truck quickly, depressed about having to spend more time in his stilted company. As she stood, gravity worked its magic, and she felt an embarrassing wetness soak through her panties.

"Oh," she breathed, touching her fingertips to the crotch of her shorts.

He glanced at her sharply, his features taut with tension. "What?"

"Nothing," she said, taking her hand away. Face flaming, she walked gingerly, hoping the moisture wouldn't spread until she was safely upstairs.

Alma Cruz would think she was such a slut.

Thankfully his mother had already gone to bed. Planning on doing the same, Sidney trudged up to his room and grabbed her tote bag.

"Where are you going?" he asked.

"Downstairs. To the couch."

"You can sleep here."

"Marc—"

"Goddamn it, Sidney, you can have the bed. Don't make me feel more like a bastard than I already do."

She stared at the ground, wishing he would leave her alone so she could wash and change clothes.

"Do you want to take a bath or something?"

"It's too late, you know. The damage is done."

He had the grace to look chagrined. More than that, he seemed stricken. "I just wanted to make sure you were—forget it," he broke off in frustration. "Do you need anything?"

"Yes. Some privacy."

"Fine," he grated, leaving the room without another word.

When she got out of the shower, she found a fluffy white bathrobe on the bed, a cup of chamomile tea on the dresser, a cold pack and some over-the-counter pain relievers. What the hell? Her mother had coddled her less after she'd had her first period.

She put on the robe and drank the tea, ignoring the pills. Placing the cold pack against her hot forehead, she stretched out on top of the comforter, and just like that, she fell asleep.

When Sidney awoke it was late morning, judging by the sunshine streaming into the room and warming the bed. Sometime during the night, she'd gotten overheated and shed the robe.

Now she was covered by a thin white sheet.

Partially covered, anyway. She had it cuddled up to her front, leaving her naked back completely exposed. The bedroom door was wide-open, so anyone walking by could see her.

At the breakfast table on the opposite side of the room, Marc had a particularly unrestricted view.

With a tiny gasp, she sat up, clutching the sheet to her chest and pushing her short, tousled hair off her forehead. "How long have you been there?"

He transferred a mug and a glass of orange juice from a tray to the table. "A minute."

"Did you cover me up?"

"Yes."

She closed her eyes with a moan. "Your mother probably thinks I'm an exhibitionist."

At that, he smiled. "She left before I checked in on you."

Warm, wonderful smells were wafting across the room. Securing the sheet above her breasts, she climbed off the bed, lured by hunger. "What's that?"

"French toast."

"Mmm. You made it?"

"Yes."

Touched by his thoughtfulness, she settled herself into a chair and started to dig in. "Aren't you having any?"

"I already ate."

As a mouthful of crisp, sugary French toast literally melted on her tongue, she closed her eyes in pleasure. When she opened them again, he was staring at her. "What?" she asked.

"I like watching you eat," he murmured, his eyes on her mouth.

"And sleep?"

"Hmm?"

"You were watching me sleep?"

His dark gaze traveled over her. "Yes," he said in a gruff voice, perhaps ashamed that he'd ogled her nude body during a moment of vulnerability. Again.

Her breasts tingled at the thought of his eyes there, and her nipples tightened, thrusting against the thin cotton sheet. She crossed her arms over her chest, plumping out her breasts, a movement that had the dual effect of easing her discomfort and increasing his.

"I have to take a shower," he rasped, his eyes glazed. His arousal was apparent when he stood, but he made no move to touch her.

Obviously he'd rather go without than have her again.

Tears stung at her eyes, and she lost her appetite, but she forced herself to eat every bite, not wanting to give him the satisfaction of knowing he'd hurt her feelings. After a few minutes, he came out of the bathroom, a dark god with a white towel wrapped around his waist.

Did he have to rub it in?

"I'm going to change," he warned.

"Go ahead," she challenged, sipping from her mug like she couldn't care less. Then he dropped his towel, and she almost sputtered coffee all over the table.

Sidney thought she'd seen it all, but he hadn't really undressed last night. She knew he had an awesome upper body. She knew the way he filled out his jeans could make a grown woman weep. What she hadn't directly laid eyes on, she'd felt against her and inside her.

Even so, the entirety of his naked form was even more impressive than those extraordinary individual parts. He was muscular, but lean, and…very well proportioned. Judging by the lack of steam in the small bathroom, he'd taken a cold shower.

It hadn't worked.

As he pulled a pair of snug boxer briefs up his hips, along with his jeans, she felt heat pool to her lower body.

Annoyed with her reaction to him, she walked across the room, stripping off the sheet she was wearing and throwing it on the bed. Intent on giving him a glimpse of what he was missing, she bent over to take a fresh pair of panties out of her tote.

He inhaled sharply.

Her satisfied smile turned into a slight grimace as she put on her underwear, feeling a tug in muscles she hadn't used in a while. She dressed in clean shorts and a tank top while he examined her with a keen interest that suddenly didn't seem at all sexual.

"Last night," he began slowly, "did I hurt you?"

She studied the tense lines of his face. "I'll get over it," she replied, mad at him for asking. He knew she was smarting from his rejection, and acting like he pitied her just added salt to the wound. "Can I drive myself to work today?"

"I'll take you."

"I'm going home after."

"I'll take you there, too."

She searched for another way to ditch him. "I was going to spend the day at the beach."

"Fine," he said with a tight little shrug.

Clenching her hands into fists, she picked up her tote and stormed out of the room, thinking he was really the most infuriating man.

Chapter 14

Marc let Sidney drive herself to work, although he followed her. On Sunday she only had about an hour's worth of duties and she dragged her feet the whole time. He noticed, but didn't act impatient, and his casual acceptance grated on her frayed nerves.

When there was nothing more to do, or even pretend to do, they traveled to her house in separate cars. After parking, they walked in silence to her front door, with Sidney entertaining the hope that he would leave after making sure her house was secure.

As she touched the doorknob, an image burst into her mind, so disturbing that the keys slipped through her frozen fingers. "Samantha," she gasped, feeling a searing pain ripple through her midsection.

Marc swept up the keys and unlocked the door himself. "Get out of sight," he said, taking his gun out of his shoulder holster and pointing it toward the ground. He slipped inside, moving like a swift shadow.

She followed, too worried about Samantha to heed his warning. Her sister was on the floor in the living room, a fragile heap of tangled blond hair and limp, bloodied limbs. Marc crouched beside her and put his fingertips to her throat. "She's unconscious," he said, glancing up at Sidney. "Don't touch her."

He took out his cell phone to call an ambulance as he checked the rest of the house.

Again, she disregarded his instructions and sank to her knees at Samantha's side, smoothing her wild hair away from her forehead. If not for the bloody scratches on her arms and legs, she might have appeared peaceful. Her chest expanded with even breathing, and her beautiful, makeup-smeared face looked vulnerable and surprisingly sweet.

Sidney could smell alcohol and the stale hint of sweat, a strange odor for her meticulous sister. An uncouth man must have perspired on her. She was dressed in a skimpy black sheath, torn in a slit up to her hip, exposing most of her naked lower body. There was more blood on her thighs, and a thin line of red trickled from her nose to her upper lip.

"Bring a rape kit," Marc murmured into the phone before he closed it.

Sidney arranged Samantha's skirt more modestly over her legs. "He attacked her here," she said, her voice shaking. "I should have been home. I should have protected her."

He knelt down beside her. "Your kitchen window is broken. I think she cut herself on the way in."

She stared at him without comprehension. "She wasn't attacked?"

He studied her face, not answering.

Sidney grabbed her sister's hands, wishing desperately, for the first time in her life, that she could get a read. There was nothing. No image, no impression and no response.

"If she was assaulted, she may have evidence under her fingernails."

Sidney dropped her hands, sobbing with frustration.

"Who has she been with?" he asked.

"I don't know."

"Does Greg get rough with her?"

"No. Never."

"Have they been sleeping together?"

"Not that I know of."

"Who has she been with?" he repeated.

"Greg's business partner," Sidney whispered, blinking back her tears. "His appeal is more about sticking it to Greg than anything else. I can't imagine him hitting her."

Another idea occurred to her. "Did you tell her about the cat?"

He shook his head in one short, choppy motion. "I mentioned the break-in. She was more interested in coming on to me than your well-being. And in the morning, she was gone."

A flash of anger surged through her. How could he speak badly of Samantha while she was tangled in a broken little heap upon the floor? "Maybe you were distracted, too, *Lieutenant.* She showed you her panties, and you forgot to mention that an animal had been murdered in my bed just hours before!"

He dragged a hand over his jaw.

"You won't let me go to the bathroom by myself, but Samantha was on her own." She glared up at him. "Wasn't she worth protecting?"

His tone became dangerously low. "Don't ever—ever—question my commitment to a victim. I don't care if she's a crack whore or the mayor's wife, I always give one hundred percent. Always."

"Is that what you were doing with me last night?" she asked softly. "Giving one hundred percent?"

His eyes darkened, but he didn't reply. Instead he turned from her, holstering his weapon, and they both waited in silence for the ambulance to arrive.

Paramedics couldn't rouse Samantha on the floor of Sidney's house or in the ambulance on the way to the hospital.

Whatever she'd taken, it had been some strong stuff.

Marc stayed behind to brief Lacy on scene while Sidney accompanied her sister to Tri-City Medical. There was actually very little to investigate. Until Samantha woke up, he couldn't be sure a crime had been committed.

She'd thrown a potted plant through the kitchen window, the same window Marc had just repaired. Dirt, glass and pieces of orange clay littered the floor. On her way in, she must have cut herself on the glass shards adhering to the window frame, because there were smears of dried blood on the sink and countertops.

Once inside, it appeared she'd stumbled into the living room, fallen down and passed out where she landed. Whether she was attacked before, after, during, or not at all remained to be seen. The blood on her face and thighs could have been sustained during her clumsy break-in. Or, as Marc strongly suspected, it may have been the result of a consensual act.

For the first time, Marc wondered if Samantha could have been responsible for the dead cat on Sidney's bed. She was volatile, emotionally unstable and she had a great motive, if she knew Greg was sniffing around her little sis.

Marc made arrangements for the window to be repaired before driving to Tri-City Hospital, where Samantha was being treated. He learned she'd been admitted to a private room and was expected to make a full recovery. The doctor's exam indicated she'd engaged in intercourse sometime over the past twenty-four hours, and they were running a blood toxicology. Marc requested a sample be sent to the crime lab as well. He'd be interested to find out if Samantha had some Maximum Relaxem in her system, on top of everything else.

Sidney didn't look up from her sister's bedside when he walked in.

He took a seat in the corner of the room, knowing he wasn't welcome. He was still smarting from her earlier criticism and pissed off that he hadn't crawled into bed with her this morning to redeem himself.

He'd wanted to. God, how he'd wanted to. Her gloriously nude body, bathed in pale morning light, stretched out on his rumpled comforter, was the most arousing, tempting, heart-wrenching sight he'd ever laid eyes on.

Her back was so elegantly curved he could have spent an hour nibbling his way down her spine. Her breasts were lush and inviting, her nipples blush pink and soft in repose, her face achingly beautiful under the blanket of sleep.

As he imagined sliding his palm over her smooth belly, watching it grow round with his child, he felt his already throbbing erection become even harder.

That was when he panicked.

He was getting off on an idea that terrified him. Something was wrong with him, he'd decided. Drastically, fundamentally wrong.

He had thrown a sheet over her and fled to the kitchen, hoping whatever illness he'd come down with was temporary, and resolving not to touch her until he'd recovered. Of course, she'd teased him without mercy over breakfast. Even a cold shower couldn't calm his raging hard-on.

What had brought him under control, finally, was her wince of discomfort as she put on her panties, reminding him how rough he'd been the night before.

He stifled an agonized groan, hating himself for hurting her.

"I called Greg," she said. "He's not coming."

Shaking away his regrets, he looked over at Sidney.

"He told the girls Samantha was in the Bahamas. He doesn't want them to worry."

Marc tried to put his thoughts in order. "Is he aware that she's fooling around with his business partner?"

"Maybe. She certainly knows about Elisabeth, his secretary."

"Does she know about you?"

Sidney glanced back at Samantha, guilt and sorrow apparent on her features. "No. I never told her he—"

"He what?"

Her eyes flew to the doorway, and a strange expression crossed over her face. It was a mixture of hope and uncertainty, as if she wasn't quite sure the recipient of her gaze returned her affection. "Mama," she said softly, rising to her feet.

Sidney's mother was fine-boned and delicate, dressed in a wispy silk blouse and pencil slim trousers. So insubstantial was her appearance that her heavily coiffed hair and chunky jewelry seemed to weigh her down. Her eyes were blue and feral, like Samantha's, but also cold. When she embraced Sidney with open arms, Marc found himself letting out a breath he didn't know he'd been holding.

"I asked you to talk to Samantha," she said when she released Sidney, her voice dripping Southern scorn. "To look out for her. Instead you left her alone and helpless all night."

Sidney's mouth trembled at the reprimand, but she didn't open it to defend herself.

"Aurelia," a man scolded, putting his hands on her thin shoulders. At six-four or taller, he was a veritable giant, yet Marc hadn't noticed him until he'd spoken. His salt and pepper hair was cut military short, and though he had the rigid stance of a drill sergeant, his authoritative presence was muted by the tiny blond fury standing in front of him.

Her eyes narrowed on Marc, who felt her disapproval like a blast of frigid air. "Where were you?" she asked Sidney, crossing her arms over her flat chest. "What were you doing?"

"Oh, lay off, Mama," Samantha mumbled from the hospital bed. Her lashes fluttered open then closed again. "Maybe if you'd actually had sex in the past twenty-five years, you wouldn't begrudge the rest of us for getting it when and where we can."

Mrs. Morrow's lips pursed with displeasure, but she swept across the room to kiss her daughter's ashen cheek. "Tell us what's happened. The police thought you'd been ravaged."

"I'm fine," she said, accepting a sip of water. "I just, um, fell and hit my head climbing in through Sidney's window. I guess I was out for a while."

Everyone in the room knew she was lying. "There, there, dear," Mrs. Morrow said, smoothing her hair. "Sidney thought you might want some time away from it all. We know a nice place near Dana Point where you can get all the rest and rehabilitation you need—"

"Rehab?" Samantha said, straightening. "I'm not going to rehab." She turned to Sidney, changing from protective older sister to vindictive brat in a split second. "Why did you call them? I had a little accident and you've got to blow it all out of proportion, alerting the police like it's a national freaking emergency! Did you blab to Greg, too?"

Sidney's eyes filled with tears.

Samantha let her head fall back on the pillow. "Oh God, Sidney, why don't you just sign over custody of my kids, and have me committed, while you're at it?"

"Now, Samantha, you don't have to go anywhere you don't want to," Aurelia soothed. "Everything will be just fine."

"My head hurts," she whined. "Can't they give me something?"

"I'll see what I can do, dear."

"And get everyone out of here," she said, her eyes shooting daggers at Sidney. "Can't I recover in peace?"

While Mrs. Morrow hurried away to procure Samantha more drugs, the last thing she needed, everyone else shuffled out of the room. Sidney stood in the hallway, her slim shoulders shaking with emotion. Although Marc normally ran the other way when he saw a woman's tears, he couldn't stand the sight of her in pain.

But when he stepped forward to comfort her, Sidney walked past him, right into her father's arms. "Oh, Daddy," she said, pressing her face to the front of his shirt. Mr. Morrow patted her back gently, avoiding Marc's eyes and pretending he hadn't noticed Sidney had thrown him over.

Instead of relief, he felt an astonishingly sharp stab of pain at her rejection. Feeling like an unwanted intruder, and a fool, Marc turned and walked away.

After Samantha was released, against the doctor's recommendation, she talked Sidney into sharing a cab with her from the hospital to Las Olas, a down-and-dirty beach bar less than a mile from Sidney's house.

Samantha had parked her SUV there the previous evening.

"You walked to my house from here?" Sidney asked, relieved her sister hadn't been driving last night, on top of everything else.

She shrugged, disengaging the car alarm and climbing into the driver's seat.

"Who were you with?"

"Some guy. What's it to you?"

"I'm afraid for you, Sam. If you keep doing this, you won't have to worry about losing the girls. They'll be losing you."

Samantha groaned, looking both ways before she pulled out onto Pacific Coast Highway. "Give me a break, okay? I'm not exactly proud of myself."

"Maybe you should think about rehab, like the doctor said."

"Please, Sid. I have a splitting headache. I can't think about anything right now." She grabbed a pair of designer sunglasses from the visor to shade her bloodshot eyes.

"Let's go to that place in Dana Point. I'll drive. You won't have to think, or worry, or punish yourself anymore."

Samantha gritted her teeth and pressed her foot on the gas, a not-so-subtle hint for Sidney to shut up. Taking the threat seriously, Sidney waited until Samantha pulled over at a local convenience store to continue the conversation. "Did Marc tell you about the break-in?"

"I did *not* do that," she defended hotly.

"Whoever did left a dead cat on my bed. Tied it up and tortured it first."

"Are you serious?" she said, wrinkling her nose in distaste.

"I think it was the same guy who's out there killing women." She cast Samantha a worried glance. "When I saw you lying there, bleeding…I thought he'd gotten to you, too."

"Maybe he did," she whispered.

Sidney's stomach turned over. "What do you mean?"

"I don't remember who I was with. I don't remember anything." Beneath her sunglasses, tears rolled down her gaunt cheeks. She stuck out a wavering hand. "Here, see for yourself."

Sidney reached out to take it tentatively, afraid of what she might encounter, but just as when Samantha had been unconscious on her living room floor, she felt nothing. This time it wasn't due to a lack of extrasensory perception. The drugs and alcohol had completely obliterated her sister's psyche.

Her face must have revealed dismay, because Samantha jerked her hand back with a muted sob. Sidney hugged her fiercely. "You didn't do anything wrong."

"Besides get so wasted I don't remember who I screwed."

"Whoever it was, he took advantage of you," she said, smoothing her hand down her sister's back, feeling more bones than flesh. "Samantha, I love you. You need help, and you need protection. If you go out partying by yourself again, I'm afraid you'll never come back."

Samantha pulled away, her face showing an obstinate determination to do just as she pleased, the world, and herself, be damned. Then she rummaged through her leather purse, coming up with a few crumpled dollars instead of a vial of pills. "Will you go in and get me a Diet Coke, Siddie? I've got such a migraine."

Unable to resist the pet name, or Samantha's dulcet tones, Sidney unlatched her seat belt and went into the convenience store. She was standing in the parking lot, soda in hand, when she realized that Samantha had driven away without her.

"Damn it," she whispered, feeling the hot sting of frustration. Around its edges, panic was creeping in. Slam-dunking the soda in a nearby trash can, she dug some coins out of her pocket and picked up the grimy receiver at the pay phone.

She dialed Marc's cell phone number from memory, having stared at his business card for so long it was stamped on her brain.

"Cruz," he answered tersely.

"It's Sidney."

"Where are you?"

"At the 7-Eleven on Oceanside Boulevard."

"I'll be right there."

After he hung up, she stared at the receiver in annoyance. Couldn't men ever say goodbye? When he pulled in the parking lot less than five minutes later, she forgave the impertinence.

"What happened?" he asked.

"Samantha ditched me."

"Why didn't you call me before you left the hospital? And what the hell were you doing here with her anyway? Scoring some smack?"

Anger flared inside her, and she grabbed onto it, desperate to feel something other than deep, all-consuming fear. "You didn't check in with me before you left, either, *honey*. I thought maybe you'd given up surveillance."

Without another word, he turned onto Oceanside Boulevard and headed west, toward the beach. It was another glorious day, sunny and hot, absent of the stifling mugginess that had been pervasive during the week. Perfect weather for swimming or sunbathing, what she'd planned to do this afternoon rather than chase down runaway sisters.

The tears she'd been fighting since she found Samantha this morning, or to be more accurate, since Marc's scathing rejection of her, threatened to resurface, clogging the back of her throat. She forced herself to take a deep, steadying breath.

"What's wrong?" he asked.

"What could possibly be wrong?" she said, the hysterical quality of her voice betraying her emotions. "You're acting like a stranger. My sister's sleeping with strangers. My mother blames me for Samantha's drug problems and failed marriage..."

"Your sister is a grown woman," he said. "Older than you. Her problems are her own." He tightened his hands around the steering wheel. "I can't believe you took off with her."

She studied his tense mouth. "Were you worried?"

Across the console, his eyes met hers. "I would never forgive myself if something happened to you."

Sidney fell silent, reading the hidden message in his words. She was a burden, a responsibility, a weight on his shoulders, nothing more.

When the case was over, he'd be gone.

At home, Sidney changed into the bikini Samantha had given her and padded downstairs in her bare feet. Marc was treating her like an invalid again, placating her by offering to spend the last few hours of the afternoon on the beach.

She found him in the kitchen, putting some snacks into a basket.

"You're going to make some lucky woman an excellent wife," she said, more annoyed than charmed by his domesticity.

"I certainly wouldn't make a good husband," he admitted.

She couldn't argue with that. Instead she dug her beach bag out of the linen closet and found a clean white sheet to spread beneath them on the sand. When she turned around, she caught him staring at her backside.

He averted his eyes, taking bottled water out of the refrigerator and giving her the chance to ogle him. Husband material or not, his bare chest was a beautiful sight. The tan shorts he wore rode low on his hips, exposing his flat abdomen almost to the point of indecency.

Or maybe it was just her dirty mind, stripping him naked.

"What happened to your other swimsuit?" he asked.

Her eyes jerked up to his face. "Hmm? Oh, that," she said, remembering he'd seen her demure black Speedo, and everything underneath it, only a week before. "I thought you would make fun of it."

After he checked the lock on her new kitchen window, they left, walking across a wide expanse of sand before staking claim to a free spot close to the water. "Why do you dress the way you do?" he asked as she unfurled the bed sheet on the sand. "Are you trying to hide your—" his eyes dropped to her breasts, pushed together by the triangle top of the bikini "—body?"

"Not really," she said with a frown, looking down at herself. "I wash dogs and clean kennels for a living. There's no need to be sexy."

"Why didn't you go on to vet school?"

She stretched out on her tummy, hating the way his seemingly unrelated questions painted an accurate, and not very flattering, picture of her. "Too much touching," she replied honestly.

"Do you ever think about going back?"

"Yes," she said, although she didn't feel as though she was wasting her talents at the kennel. She took pride in caring for animals and running her own business. In her heart of hearts, what she truly longed for wasn't more money or a better education, but the intangible rewards of a happy home and a loving family. "Do you ever think about having a long-term relationship?"

"Yes," he said, surprising her. "But women tend to give up on me well before we get to that stage."

Her lips twisted wryly. "And whose fault is that?"

"Theirs," he said, meaning his. "Has Samantha met Greg's girlfriend?"

Sighing, she rested her head on her arms and closed her eyes, too weary to analyze his insinuation. "I imagine so. She's his secretary."

"Are you ever going to tell me what happened between you two?"

She squinted up at him. "Why?"

"Because like it or not, you're part of this investigation."

"What does that have to do with Greg? He's no prize as a husband, but he's not a murderer."

"Yes, well, as accurate as your perceptions are at times, they don't work as well with people close to you."

Incensed, she rolled over and sat up. "Just because I can't always read you—"

"Or Samantha."

"She was blacked out!"

"Greg has been in love with you for years. Did you know that?"

She drew her knees up, hugging them to her chest. "He only thinks he's in love with me because he's a perverse asshole. He loves Samantha, he's just too stupid to admit it."

Marc smiled at her assessment. "Did he ever touch you, before they were married?"

Taking a deep breath, she stared out at the crashing waves, trying to channel the strength of the Pacific. "He was like a brother to me, at first. I was a tomboy, more interested in sports than dating, and he's very athletic. We would pal around together. It was harmless."

"Until when?"

She felt her cheeks grow warm. "Until I got breasts, okay? The same ones you're always staring at. He would…tickle me and stuff. I finally figured out he was trying to cop a feel."

"Is that all he did?" he asked in a low voice, although it appeared to be enough information for him to want to smash Greg's face in.

"He grabbed me once, at the wedding reception. I struggled to get away from him, and he finally let go. After that, I made sure never to be alone with him again, or get close enough for him to touch."

"Did you tell Samantha?"

"No. She was pregnant. They were young. I hoped they could work things out."

Instead of criticizing her naiveté, as she expected, he remained silent. It didn't matter, because she already blamed herself. Maybe if she'd been honest with Samantha from the beginning, her marriage could have ended more peacefully.

And maybe if Sidney weren't so gullible, she wouldn't have let her sister slip away this afternoon at the convenience store.

Disheartened and depressed, she lay on her stomach again. Emotionally drained from the day's events, she let the rhythmic pounding of the waves breaking along the shore lull her into a troubled sleep.

Chapter 15

She awoke to the delicious sensation of Marc massaging sunscreen into her shoulders. All but purring her enjoyment, she arched her spine and stretched like a cat.

"I didn't want you to burn," he said, apologizing for waking her.

"Mmm," was the only response she could muster. The sun was hot on her back, the breeze cool against her skin, and his masterful hands on her tense muscles…they were magnificent.

When he smoothed lotion down her arms, his fingertips brushed the sides of her breasts, and her lassitude morphed into sexual awareness. Then his hands were on her legs, caressing the sensitive skin behind her knees, stroking his way up the backs of her thighs.

By the time he reached her bottom, her breasts felt full and heavy, her nipples were tight and a sweet, hot ache pulsed between her legs.

When his fingertips slid up and down the length of her spine, she closed her eyes, murmuring her pleasure. When they dipped below the waistband of her swimsuit to trace the crease of her buttocks, her eyes flew open.

"I don't think I'm going to get burned there," she said, her voice husky from sleep. Unless he didn't stop, and then she would surely burst into flames.

His eyes traveled up to her face, then looked out at their surroundings. Over the crash of the waves, she could hear children playing. He jerked his hand out of her bikini bottoms, seeming to realize what he was doing, and where. "Sorry," he muttered, rolling onto his stomach in an obvious attempt to hide his arousal.

The incongruity of his behavior baffled her. Last night, he'd brought her to orgasm with his mouth on the hood of her truck. Afterward, he'd pushed her legs apart and thrust inside her with so little forethought he hadn't remembered to use a condom. Now, less than twenty-four hours later, he'd rather go unsatisfied than slake his lust in her again.

She inhaled sharply, feeling her throat close up and her chest grow tight with pain. Before she could make a bigger fool of herself by crying in front of him, she leaped to her feet and ran into the surf, letting the cold shock of the Pacific wash away her shame.

She didn't know he'd followed her until she felt his hand clamp around her arm. With wild abandon, she wrenched away from him, falling headfirst into the waves and getting a mouthful of saltwater for her efforts. As he pulled her to her feet, she gasped and sputtered, pummeling his chest with her fists and making raw, animal sounds in the back of her throat.

"Stop," he said, holding her by the forearms, his body flush against hers. "Stop," he repeated, holding firm when she continued to struggle.

With no way to escape his embrace, or the deluge of emotions that assaulted her, she tucked her head into his chest and sobbed her frustration. In the periphery of her awareness, she felt his body tense. After a moment, he relaxed his grip on her, wrapping his arms around her waist and holding her gently while she cried.

In slow measures, she began to calm, aware of her hot, wet face against his chest, her labored breathing and the pounding of her own heartbeat. The waves crashed into them, breaking at hip level then receding, lapping around their knees.

Knowing she was unattractively teary-eyed and runny-nosed, she turned away from him, cupping handfuls of saltwater to wash her face. He watched with a mixture of humor and concern in his eyes, as if he found her lack of dignity amusing.

No wonder he didn't want to go to bed with her—she was an absolute mess.

"Lacy put a 'be on the lookout' for your sister's SUV. We'll find her."

Rather than admit she hadn't spared a single thought for Samantha since awakening, she sank deeper into the water with a low groan, ducking her head under the curl and swimming away from him.

He caught up with her easily. "That's not why you were crying?"

"Why don't you want me anymore?" she asked, deciding to make her humiliation complete.

His eyes widened. "Not want you? Are you crazy?"

"Probably," she murmured. "This morning, you didn't..."

It took him a moment to get her meaning. "You said I hurt you."

She frowned at him in confusion. "You thought I meant physically?"

"Yes."

"That's why you haven't touched me?"

"Of course. You were acting sore. Uncomfortable. I asked if I hurt you, and you said yes. What was I supposed to do, throw you down on your back like an animal again?"

When she thought about the pain relievers and the tea, the breakfast in bed and the cold pack she'd put on her forehead, she couldn't help but laugh.

"What's so funny?"

Once she got started, she couldn't stop. Holding her midsection, she doubled over with giggles, only to get knocked off balance by the incoming waves. She fell unceremoniously on her bottom in the shallow water, laughing harder.

He crossed his arms over his chest, finding no humor in the circumstances.

"You didn't hurt me, Marc," she said when she'd collected herself, wiping tears from her eyes. "It's not like I was a virgin."

"You felt like one."

Her amusement wilted. "Oh," she said in a small voice, letting him help her up. "What did I do wrong?"

"What did you do wrong?" he repeated, as if the question were beyond his realm of comprehension. With a harsh laugh, he pulled her close, turning his back to the shore. "You were too hot," he said, touching his lips to her collarbone. "Too tight," he added, sliding his hands down her lower back, "and too wet," he finished, cupping her buttocks.

"I'll have to work on that," she breathed, curling her fingers through the hair at his nape.

"I'll help you," he replied, covering her mouth with his. He kissed her slowly, tenderly, expertly, more to soothe than inflame her desire. Even so, she found herself moaning and rubbing her naked belly against his.

A wave hit her backside, cooling her off right where it counted. She laughed softly, putting her face against his warm, brown throat and stroking his shoulders until they were ready to return to shore.

Making a tacit agreement to call it a day, they gathered up their belongings and left the beach. Sidney didn't feel her feet hit the sand once.

In the outdoor shower, they explored each other languidly, his mouth on hers, her hands gripping his water-slick back. She stripped away her bikini and he dropped his shorts, but their intimacy didn't go beyond kissing and light touching for a long time.

"I want you in bed," he whispered, burying his head in the curve of her neck.

She wanted him against the shower wall, but she acquiesced readily enough, needing no special intuition to realize he wouldn't be fast or rough with her this time. Wrapping a towel around her body and handing him another, she slipped into the house ahead of him, pretty sure the terry cloth wasn't keeping her bottom decently covered. Maybe it was cruel to tease, but the way he was looking at her, all lean cheeks and hungry eyes, made baiting him irresistible.

As they mounted the stairs, his tension was palpable.

In her bedroom, the oscillating fan whirred lazily, circulating whatever breeze was coming off the Pacific through her open window.

"Lay down."

A hot thrill raced down her spine, turning her knees to jelly. Dropping her towel on a nearby chair, she crawled across the bed naked, watching him through half-lidded eyes. His body was truly gasp-worthy, every inch of it hard and strong. When he took away his towel, she stared at him unabashedly, wetting her lips in anticipation. It was all she could do to keep herself from spreading her legs and pulling him down on top of her.

Setting a different pace, he stretched out beside her and kissed her moist lips. He cupped her breasts, pushing them together and tracing her cleavage with his tongue. He licked and sucked at her nipples until they were wet and rock-hard.

"Marc," she moaned, reaching out to curl her hand around his throbbing erection.

He let her stroke him for a moment, closing his eyes, as if her touch pained him. Then he brought her hand up to his mouth and kissed the center of her palm.

Desire flowered between her thighs, hot and sultry.

Moving down her belly, he dipped his tongue into her navel, dropped a kiss on her hip, nuzzled the tops of her thighs. When he finally put his mouth where she really wanted it, his tongue was indolent, his touch designed to heighten, rather than assuage, her arousal.

"Oh, please," she breathed, lifting her hips.

To her intense frustration, he came up beside her and kissed her mouth again, stroking her parted lips with his tongue, sharing her taste. Easing a hand between her thighs, he explored the seam of her sex, separating her with his fingertip before he slipped it inside.

"You're so wet," he murmured against her mouth, sliding his middle finger in and out of her while she gasped and writhed. Then he withdrew, grazing his slick fingertip over her clitoris, barely touching her. With a feather-light motion, he rubbed her back and forth, using only enough pressure to drive her crazy.

Beyond self-control, she rocked her hips in a steady rhythm, straining toward ecstasy. When he replaced his hand with his mouth again, she begged for mercy, and he gave it to her. The instant his tongue came in contact with her sensitive flesh, she climaxed, lacing her fingers into his hair and screaming her pleasure.

Apparently drawing out the sensation also intensified it. Her scalp tingled, dark spots flashed behind her eyes and her pulse throbbed a wild beat in her throat.

Now *that* was an orgasm, she thought, resting her head on the pillows.

Before her vision cleared, he parted her legs and entered her slowly, bracing his weight on his outstretched arms. "Are you sure I didn't hurt you last time?"

Her eyes fluttered open. "Yes."

"When I first came inside you, you tensed."

She smoothed her hands over his sweat-slick shoulders, realizing what maximizing her enjoyment had cost him. "It had been a while," she said, touching her lips to his. "And you are rather…large."

Groaning, he began to move inside her, drawing himself in and out with deliberate precision, letting her feel every inch. She knew he was holding himself back, and that made tenderness well up inside her, along with a renewed excitement.

Last night, in the cab of the pickup, he'd been hard and rough and uncontrolled, and she'd loved every second of it.

Tonight, she had time to savor an experience that transcended physical sensation.

They melded, mouths and hearts and bodies. They rolled, him on top, then her, coming close to the brink, then edging back. He put her leg over his hip and took her on her side, facing him, always touching full-length, damp skin sliding against damp skin.

She stroked his back, his shoulders, his sinewy arms, his taut buttocks. He did the same, exploring every part of her, flicking his tongue over her tight nipples, brushing his thumb over her wet clitoris. She lost track of how many times he brought her to orgasm.

When she couldn't take it anymore, she straddled his waist and moved up and down on him with sinuous motions, milking him with her body, demanding his release.

"Sidney," he grated, gripping her undulating hips, trying to slow her.

"Let me," she murmured, moving faster, repositioning his hands on her bottom. Cradling his head to her chest, she let her breasts muffle his hoarse cry as he came.

Marc trailed his fingertips down Sidney's naked back, watching the room grow dim as evening fell. She wasn't asleep, but he wished she was, because every bachelor instinct he possessed was telling him to flee the scene.

He never slept with a woman after sex. Sometimes he stayed long enough for her to drift off, but he usually didn't bother. It was part of the convenience of using condoms. He had to get up to dispose of it, and then he was gone.

Why he was still lying beside her, not exactly cuddling, but caressing her, was a complete mystery to him. An anomaly. An aberration.

The sex had been...different, too. Better than last time, and last time had been amazingly good. For him, at least.

He'd remembered to use protection. He'd shown a little more finesse, and a lot more restraint. Somehow, the experience had gotten away from him all the same. God, he'd almost wanted to weep when he came, the pleasure was so intense.

He must have overdone it. Held himself back too long.

"I have to go to the kennel," she said finally, stretching her arms over her head.

"Fine," he said, rolling out of bed as if he'd been waiting for an excuse to get up. Which he had been. Hadn't he?

He watched her dress as he pulled on his own clothes, finding her yellow cotton panties and simple white bra impossibly alluring. Her baggy Bermuda shorts hung down to her tanned knees, and a blue dolphin arced across the front of her SeaWorld T-shirt.

His lips curved into a smile. At what point had her lame, sexless fashion sense become quirky and endearing? The answer hit him like a bolt of lightning: the same time he'd fallen in love with her.

For a moment, he was too stunned to move. He just stood there, his hands frozen at the fly of his jeans, as panic assailed him.

She sat on the bed to put on her shoes, oblivious to his plight.

He turned, buttoning up his pants and grabbing his T-shirt, every nerve in his body on red alert. He had to get out of here before she saw the dopey, lovesick expression on his face. He had to get away from her before she *touched* him.

Flipping open his cell phone, he strode out of Sidney's bedroom.

"Lacy," she answered, sounding breathless.

"I need you to do some surveillance."

He heard another woman's voice in the background, a muffled giggle. "On whom?"

"Sidney. Meet us at the kennel in fifteen."

"I just got off," she groaned.

"You can get off again later," he promised, hanging up.

He was shoving his cell phone in his pocket when Sidney came down the stairs, looking so positively dewy with female satisfaction that he gritted his teeth against the renewed urge to take her back to bed and screw her senseless.

After a few moments of silence inside his car, her pleasant afterglow faded. "What's wrong?" she asked.

"I have some work to do. Lacy's going to take over for me for a while."

"When will you be back?"

"I don't know. Do I have a curfew?"

Her face registered a mixture of hurt and surprise at his sudden personality change. Five minutes ago he'd been hanging all over her; now he couldn't meet her eyes. Adding insult to injury, when he dropped her off at Pacific Pet Hotel, he didn't say goodbye.

He headed home, needing some alone time to analyze the inconsistencies of the case. If he stayed overnight with Sidney, the only thing he'd be working on was going a few more rounds between her sleek, silky thighs.

As the headlights of his car hit his closed garage door, he noticed something taped to it. A manila envelope. Leaving the engine running, he got out, ripped the package off the door and sat behind the wheel to open it over his lap.

A dozen or so large, digitally printed photographs tumbled out.

At first, the images were so jumbled he couldn't make sense of them. As the lines and shapes began to take form, he saw that they were extreme close-ups. The first depicted a woman's round, supple breast, the upper curve framed by dark cloth, as if she'd lifted her top.

Sidney, he realized, his blood running cold.

Her legs, wrapped around his waist. The long, slender column of her throat. Her hands, clutching his hair as she climaxed.

There was only one full-length photo, and it was incredibly explicit. Their faces weren't in focus, but what they were doing was clear. He was on top of her, pinning her beneath him, his pants pushed down his hips. His buttocks were clenched. Her hands were curled into fists, resting against the driver side door.

In contrast to the other images, which were vague and erotic, this one was shockingly graphic. It looked like a rape.

"That bloodsucking bitch," he said, backing out of the driveway in a squeal of tires and heading south, toward Carlsbad, where Crystal Dunn lived.

Crystal was home, if the soft lighting visible through the small octagon-shaped glass window in her front door was any indication. She was also entertaining, judging by the dark green Jaguar in her driveway.

Straightening his shoulders, he knocked on the front door.

"Marc," she said when she answered it, her expression revealing genuine surprise. "What brings you here?"

"I need to talk to you. Alone," he added, knowing her latest plaything was lounging in the background.

Her eyebrows rose at his tone, but she stepped aside to allow him entrance.

It was a very cozy scene. Crystal was barefoot and casual in slacks and an ice-blue silk blouse, her pale hair cascading around her slender shoulders. Her coanchor was in his shirtsleeves, no tie or jacket, sipping red wine on her white leather couch.

"Brandon, why don't you run to the store for me?" Crystal asked as he stood self-consciously. "I need some Evian."

"Of course," he said, slanting a glance in Marc's direction. They'd only met once, but he knew the younger man recognized him. "Lieutenant Cruz," he said quietly as he passed by, acknowledging his predecessor.

Marc didn't grace him with a response. As soon as the door shut behind him, he strode forward, dumping the contents of the envelope out on her designer sofa.

Arching a brow, she perched her tiny little butt on the armrest and picked up the photos, studying them with mild interest. "This can't be you," she said unequivocally. Glancing up, she caught his sharp glare and looked again. "It is you! My God, were you drunk?"

"What's your angle?"

Taking a sip of wine, she flipped through the photos once more. "My guys didn't take these. Whoever did used a telephoto lens with a nighttime scope, an expensive camera, no doubt about it, but consider the shots. Not one of them is worth a damn. How would we use this? Obscure close-ups and indiscernible faces?"

"Don't mess with me," he warned.

"Like I would," she replied. Scorn blazing from her eyes, she shoved the pictures back into the envelope and returned them to him.

"You certainly have before."

"Not when I had nothing to gain. You were taken off the case—"

"Because of you," he interrupted.

"You have no leads, no suspects, no new information. I wouldn't waste a moment of my time following you."

He examined her cold, pretty face, knowing she was telling the truth. If he'd stopped to think, before flying off the handle, he would have reached the same conclusion. Crystal only made moves to feed her ego or her ambition; she was self-serving and unapologetic about it. Her ruthless personality had appealed to him at first, because he thought he'd finally found someone he didn't have to pander to.

As it turned out, having a woman treat him as casually as he'd treated all the others wasn't that much fun.

"Is she the one?" Crystal asked, her cool eyes assessing him.

"The one who what?"

Smiling slyly, she set her wineglass aside. "You never did me in the front seat of a car. Or on a picnic table."

"You were more comfortable on your knees, if I recall."

Her amused expression turned hard. "Do you even remember why you were there? In my dressing room that day?"

The question caught him off guard. They'd hurled insults back and forth, but never actually discussed the incident. Was she trying to claim he didn't know what he'd seen? "I remember everything," he asserted.

"Sure you do," she said with a laugh. "You brought me flowers. It was a grand romantic gesture, for someone like you. Why did you do it?"

Women obsessed over insignificant details, he decided. "What difference does it make?"

"We had a fight the night before," she continued, but it didn't jog his memory. "I said I wanted to see you exclusively. I told you I didn't want anyone but you."

"Then you're a liar and a cheat."

"Goddamn it, Marc, I said I loved you. At the very least you should remember that."

He shook his head wordlessly, surprised by her vehemence.

"Do you know what you said, in return? 'Love someone else.'"

The conversation floated back to him, like a dream. He *had* said those exact words. God, he was a bitter bastard. "And you took my advice to heart, didn't you?"

"You're goddamned right I did. I thought we were over. If I'd ever, for one moment, imagined you'd be knocking on my door to apologize the next day, flowers in hand, I would have told Carlisle to take a hike."

The self-righteous indignation he'd been carrying around for the past few years dissolved into faint regret. How ironic it was for him to be having this conversation with her, today of all days. Crystal was the only other woman besides Sidney he'd ever thought he'd loved, and the feeling was twice as unsettling the second time around.

"I'm sorry," he said finally.

"Why?"

"Because, once upon a time, you were the one."

"Oh, Marc," she wailed, her blue eyes filling with tears. Taking his hand, she allowed him to help her up, and put her head against his chest. "You are so insufferable."

Chapter 16

Marc left Crystal's residence with his mind reeling and his shoulders taut with tension.

The photos in his possession were career-destroying. Unlike the shots from Guajome Lake Park, which had caused a minor stir, these would be the end of him. If she saw them, Stokes would have his badge for sure.

It seemed unlikely that Derek DeWinter had been the photographer. His residence was below the hill Sidney's truck had been parked on, his line of vision obscured by orange trees. Even if he'd run to higher ground, he'd never have made it in time for the main event, which had lasted all of two minutes.

A friend or accomplice could have taken the shots from another vantage point, however, after a simple phone call. Marc would have to go out to Bonsall and scope the scene.

He decided to drop in on Tony first. It was late, and for once, his laid-back friend wasn't happy to see him.

That made two of them. Furious with himself for getting caught on film for the second time that week, and with Tony for having shady business connections, he jerked his best friend outside by the front of his shirt.

Whispers began barking hoarsely from behind the screen door.

"Tell me about everyone DeWinter deals with," he ordered.

"I already told you," Tony returned, shoving him backward. "I don't know."

He bit off a curse, feeling his anger fade away, replaced by desperation. "Have you seen anyone outside my house today?" he asked. "Taping an envelope to my garage door?"

"No. Why?"

He groaned, rubbing his hand over his eyes. A riot of sensations from the past few days assaulted him. Sidney, lifting her mouth to his. Her body tensing as he thrust inside her. Him, burying his face in her breasts as he came. What sorcery had she seduced him with? He'd completely lost control, not once, or twice, but every damned time he touched her.

"You have to go out to Bonsall with me," he said, shaking away the disturbing images. "Case the area."

"Are you out of your mind? I'm not suicidal."

"You said he wasn't dangerous."

"Men guard marijuana fields with shotguns, Marc."

He remembered what Sidney had said about Blue being spooked by a gunshot. "I'll bring my Glock. You still have that 9?"

"Christ," he muttered. "Yeah."

"I've got to change first," he said, looking down at the way his pale gray T-shirt caught the moonlight. After he went inside to put on a black one, he left a text message for Lacy.

Just in case.

Tony joined him on the driveway, dressed in dark clothing as well, his long hair pulled back, a brown canvas knapsack slung over one shoulder. He looked like Che Guevara.

"Why are you bringing me along, anyway?" he said after he got in the passenger side. "Short on deputies?"

"You should be glad I'm taking you instead of DEA."

He found the envelope on the floor mat beneath his feet. "What's this?" he asked, thumbing through the photos. "Whoa."

Marc felt heat rise to his face. With Crystal, he'd been too angry to be embarrassed. Now shame was setting in. Having a number of people bear witness to his most ham-handed sexual performance was excruciating.

"Where were these taken?" Tony asked.

"In Bonsall. A couple hundred feet from DeWinter's."

"Jesus, man. Couldn't you have found a more private place?"

"Obviously I didn't know we were being watched," he said through clenched teeth.

"Who took them?"

"I don't know that, either. Crystal said she didn't."

"Derek wouldn't do this," he asserted, replacing the photos.

"How do you know?"

"I stopped by his house earlier. He talked about her. Sidney."

His eyes narrowed. "Talked about her how?"

"Like a guy who wishes he could have her," Tony said. "Not like one who just watched her get it from somebody else."

Marc struggled to control his jealousy, and lost. "He was planning on calling her?" he asked, his voice hard.

"Nah. He has a girlfriend. He was just...speculating. You know."

"Bastard," he muttered. "Did he read about her in the newspaper? Know she was involved with the investigation?"

"No. He didn't mention it, anyway."

"What else did he talk about?"

"His sister's dialysis."

Marc turned on the radio, noticing his friend's nervous fidgeting. Tony's ADD was acting up again. "Did you take your Ritalin?"

He scowled. "Hell, no. It makes me feel like a zombie."

It made him act like one, too, so Marc was glad Tony wasn't on medication. They both needed their wits about them this evening.

He drove past the orange grove where he'd parked Sidney's truck the night before. Down the road a ways he found another secluded spot to park. From there he could see Derek DeWinter's house and the rolling green hills behind it.

"The photographer would have been up there somewhere," he said, pointing at a wide expanse of undeveloped land where sagebrush, beavertail cactus and manzanita grew wild. The native vegetation was interspersed with dry earth and flanked by rows of avocado trees.

It wasn't easy terrain to cover, but they managed, cutting through groves and trampling over the thick brush.

"Madre de Dios," Tony whispered when they found it.

The field was so well camouflaged they were practically standing in the middle of it before they realized where they were. Waist-high stalks, bushy with immature buds, quivered in the gentle night breeze. Marc guessed there were about a hundred individual plants. A hundred thousand dollars worth of high-grade stuff.

Tony's eyes went wide with greed and black with lust.

Marc motioned for him to circle the right side of the field while he started off toward the left. The terrain was loose and rocky, with no discernible path. Nor did there appear to be one particular vantage point from which the grower could keep an eye on the entire crop. It covered too much ground.

There was a flat stretch of land at the base of the hill where a number of large oaks stood alongside a tributary of the San Luis Rey River. A crop this size would require a lot of water, Marc reasoned. If DeWinter was hauling buckets by hand, he probably had to work all night, every night, toward the end of the growing season.

Even so, it wasn't a bad gig for the amount of cash he could rake in.

Under the cover of oaks, Marc waited, hoping he would hear the sound of splashing water or tromping footsteps. After listening to his own harsh breathing, the buzz of insects and the muted gurgle of the San Luis Rey for what seemed like an hour, he gave up and stepped out of his hiding place.

Looking for Tony, he ran into Derek DeWinter.

DeWinter raised his rifle before Marc could reach into his shoulder holster. "Keep your hands where I can see them," he ordered in a shaky voice, sounding more bewildered than authoritative. If Marc could take a guess, he'd say DeWinter had never pointed a gun at a man before, and wasn't enjoying the experience too much.

"I'm a cop," Marc said, lifting his hands slowly. "I've got a badge in my front pocket."

DeWinter took in a sharp breath, but he didn't respond.

"Drop the gun, Derek," a voice said from behind him, and Marc wanted to groan at the poor timing of Tony's interruption.

DeWinter whirled around immediately, pointing his rifle at Tony, and Marc had his Glock pressed against the back of his neck before he could blink. "Set it down, nice and easy," he murmured. "I don't want anyone to get hurt."

For a moment, Marc feared DeWinter wouldn't cooperate. If he shot Tony, Marc would have to shoot him, and that would be a hell of a mess. Infinitely worse than losing his job over sexual misconduct.

When Derek engaged the safety and laid his weapon down, Marc felt almost dizzy with relief. Tony secured the rifle, and Marc put his gun away.

"Are you stealing my plants, Tony?" Derek asked in a hoarse whisper.

"No," he replied, shooting a glance at Marc that promised vengeful retribution. "I would never do that."

Derek looked back and forth between them. "What are you doing here, then?"

Marc brought his badge out of his front pocket. "Why don't you invite us back to your place," he suggested. "I'll explain everything."

It was well after midnight when he arrived at Sidney's house. Lacy opened the door to him without a word, her eyes heavy from sleep, strawberry-blond hair tousled.

"What happened?" she asked.

"DeWinter's got a couple of different buyers, one who comes down from L.A., another who meets him in Yuma. Last year, someone ripped him off an entire plant. About a pound. He has no idea who, or even when, exactly." He shrugged. "It could have been anyone."

She studied him carefully. "Are you taking over for me?"

"Yeah. Go on home."

At the door, Lacy paused. Marc knew she was aware of his relationship with Sidney. She was a woman, and a cop, and therefore twice as intuitive. "Do you have any idea what you're getting involved with, Marcos?"

She used the name on purpose, to get his attention. Marc's greatest ambition in life was to be nothing like his father, who he'd been named after. In that, he'd failed. He couldn't make a commitment to save his life. The idea of staying with one woman and giving his heart to her, knowing she might take it with her when she left, as his father had done over and over again, paralyzed him.

Every time he looked in the mirror he saw the old man's face.

"No," he said, blinking away that image. "I don't."

"Be careful," she whispered, kissing the corner of his mouth. For the second time of the evening, he was caught in a tender, nonsexual moment with an attractive woman he cared about, but didn't want to sleep with.

He was definitely losing his mind.

Before going upstairs to Sidney, he showered in her outdoor stall on the patio and put his dirty clothes in the machine to wash. Raiding marijuana fields was sweaty work, and he didn't want her to know where he'd been.

It hadn't escaped his attention that the man who'd spied on them could have wielded something a lot more deadly than a camera. Such as a sniper rifle.

While under his "protection," Sidney had been in constant danger. He'd taken her to crime scenes, used her to lure out Derek DeWinter and allowed her to be photographed in a compromising position. Twice.

Yeah, he was doing a real bang-up job as her bodyguard.

In her room, she was lying on her side, fast asleep, both hands tucked under one cheek. Her chest rose and fell with even breathing, drawing his eye to the front of her dolphin T-shirt, which had ridden up above her cotton bikini panties to expose a silky strip of her stomach.

He lay down beside her carefully so he wouldn't disturb her, getting as close as he could without touching her. For a long time, he watched her sleep, memorizing the lines of her face and the curves of her body, as if her image could sustain him.

Maybe if he concentrated hard enough, he could keep this part of her, a picture locked away inside him, to take out and cherish after he'd gone.

Chapter 17

Sidney awoke before the alarm was set to go off, as usual, and she knew Marc was with her before she opened her eyes.

When she turned to look at him, all of the anger and confusion and disappointment she'd felt with him last night got mixed up in a rush of love so intense tears flooded her eyes.

He was lying on his back, his forearm draped across his lap, one knee bent, touching hers. Sometime during the night, he'd pushed the sheet down past his waist, revealing his naked upper body. His exceedingly masculine presence seemed to take up an inordinate amount of space.

She'd need to get a larger bed.

His face was troubled, even in sleep. There were faint circles beneath his eyes and a worried crease between his brows.

Her need to ease him was overwhelming.

Pressing her lips to the tips of her fingers, she touched the stubble shadowing his jaw, traced the hard line of his mouth. Trailing her fingertips over the long, brown column of his throat, she skimmed the sexy ridge of his Adam's apple. As she moved her hand down farther, exploring hard pectoral muscles and warm skin, he shifted, causing the sheet to inch farther off his hips, exposing a dark line of silky pubic hair.

Apparently his lower body was naked, too.

Heart thumping with excitement, she sat up and drew her T-shirt over her head, wanting to feel his bare skin against hers. She brushed her fingertips over her jutting nipples, stifling a moan. Feeling a dull ache throb between her legs, she rubbed herself there, too, watching his penis thicken and elongate under the thin sheet.

Her eyes flew up to his face.

"Take off your panties," he said in a rough voice, his heavy-lidded gaze fixed on the apex of her thighs.

She should have been embarrassed to be caught touching herself while she stared at him, but she was too enthralled by his arousal to be ashamed of her own. She also knew if she took off her panties, he'd bury his head between her legs and pleasure her with his mouth until she couldn't remember her name.

Which was all very nice, since he seemed to enjoy it as much as she did, except that making her lose her mind was his subtle, insidious way of maintaining control.

This time, she wanted him to forget *his* name.

Instead of removing her panties, she slipped her hand inside them and began to caress herself lightly, studying his face. He couldn't see what she was doing, but he didn't have to.

"Don't tease me."

"Tease you? Never," she promised, then bent her head to his lap and proceeded to do just that. Pulling down the sheet, she placed her open mouth on the inside of his thigh. His penis jerked, stiff and upright, saluting her efforts like a proper soldier.

"Sidney," he protested, his voice husky.

"Mmm," she replied, rubbing her cheek across his engorged flesh with a slight smile, basking in the glory of her feminine power.

He watched while she circled her fingers around his thick shaft and stroked him up and down. When a pearly bead appeared at the tip, she moistened her lips with it then licked his taste off them with delicate slowness.

Groaning, he let his head drop back against the pillow, surrendering to her ministrations. Instead of taking the blunt head of his erection into her mouth, as he clearly expected, she touched her tongue to the heavy sac below.

He shuddered. "Jesus, Sidney—"

"Don't you like it?"

He didn't say no, so she did it again, lapping at him like a kitten until he moaned, thrusting his fingers into her hair and bringing her head up. With his other hand, he gripped the base of his shaft and brushed the swollen tip across her parted lips.

Indulging him, she opened her mouth and took him deep.

"Oh God," he gasped, his hand following the motions of her head as she moved up and down. She knew he was surprised by her shamelessness, but she couldn't resist pleasuring him, and herself, in the most explicit of ways. "Sidney, please, stop before I—"

His stomach muscles clenched and he grabbed fistfuls of the sheet at his sides, but the valiant effort was all for naught. The sound of his harsh cry filled her ears as the salty taste of him flooded her mouth. Tears sprang into her eyes once again, her love for him threatening to burst from her chest.

After a moment, she stretched out on top of him, laying her head over his thundering heart, feeling it beat against her cheek as he threaded his fingers through her hair.

"I love you," she whispered.

Beneath hers, his body tensed.

A jumble of images flashed through her mind, attacking her senses. He was thinking about another woman. A woman who had serviced him the same way. A woman he'd loved. A woman who had put her head against his chest just like this, just last night.

Crystal Dunn.

"You son a bitch," she yelled, jumping to her feet.

His eyes flicked over her, but he said nothing.

"You said you were working!"

He rubbed a hand over his tired, handsome face. "I was."

"With your ex-girlfriend?"

"I saw her," he admitted, rising from the bed. Unfazed by his nudity, he strode out of the room, as if the discussion were over.

Trembling with hostility, she followed him down the stairs and into the hallway, where he began to calmly transfer clothing from the washer to the dryer. Only the hard set of his jaw betrayed his anger.

"Don't you have anything to explain to me?" she asked, hands planted firmly on her hips.

His gaze rose from her bare breasts, which were quivering with indignation. "You expect me to answer to you because you said you loved me? Or is that what the porn-star quality blow job was for?"

Her hand itched to slap his arrogant face. "Get out," she said.

"Not until my clothes dry."

Realizing he'd be gone already if that wasn't the case, tears blurred her vision. "Fine," she said, heading toward the door. "I'll leave." Never mind that she was wearing only a very brief pair of panties.

She was almost outside by the time he caught up with her. Grabbing her around the waist, he yanked her back against him and held her there while she struggled. "I love you, too," he said in her ear. "But if you think I'll stay because of it, you're wrong."

"I never asked you to stay," she said, trying to break free from his grasp. "You're incapable of constancy."

That made him mad, she could tell. It also made him hard. She stopped wiggling abruptly, aware she was grinding her scantily clad bottom against his naked groin.

"I went to Crystal's last night," he began, "because someone left photos of us taped to my garage door. I assumed it was her. It wasn't."

"Photos of us doing what?"

"Having sex. In your truck."

She held herself very still.

"I wasn't thinking about her because I prefer her to you. Far from it. I was thinking about her because she's the last woman who told me she loved me, and I…didn't handle it very well." As her chest rose and fell with pent-up emotion, the undersides of her breasts rested heavily against his forearm. Despite the tension of the situation, or perhaps because of it, she felt herself responding to the way his body fit against hers. Her nipples peaked in arousal and a renewed heat pulsed between her thighs.

"I'm committing professional suicide by being here with you,

Sidney," he continued hoarsely, "but I can't stay away. Every time I look at you, I want you. Even when I close my eyes, I see you. I smell you." His breath was warm on her nape, his erection hot against her bottom. "I taste you," he said, pushing her onto the couch in front of him.

He stripped her panties down her hips and she gasped, bracing herself to be taken from behind. Instead of the heavy thrust of his penis, she felt his hands caressing her thighs, squeezing her buttocks. Panting with excitement, she looked over her shoulder, covering her breasts with her fingertips.

Making a strangled, urgent sound, he moved his hot, open mouth from the base of her spine to the back of her neck. Biting her there tenderly, he slid the length of his shaft back and forth along the moist lips of her sex until they were both slippery with desire.

"Please," she panted, gripping the back of the couch.

With a low, possessive growl, he filled her, driving all the way to the hilt in one smooth thrust. Almost sobbing aloud at the sheer pleasure of it, she began to rock against him, working herself forward and back.

"Sidney," he protested, tightening his hands on her hips to slow her.

"No," she said breathlessly. "Do it hard."

Groaning, he jerked her bottom against his lap, giving her what she wanted, hard and fast and deep, over and over again until she thought she might explode with ecstasy. He was huge and hot inside her, the slick friction so good it was almost unbearable.

He reached underneath her to cup her swaying breasts. "I don't know where I want to suck on you more," he rasped, pinching her stiff nipples gently. "Here—" he moved one hand down between her legs, delving into damp curls "—or here."

The mere suggestion of his mouth on her clitoris was enough to bring her to orgasm. Even before he touched her, she began to shudder and moan. As his fingers stroked the wet, throbbing flesh at the crest of her sex, she flew apart.

Burying himself deep inside her, he found his own release.

They stayed that way for a while, still connected, breathing heavily, hearts pounding. Finally he withdrew, tugging her panties back into place and drawing her into his lap. "I'm going to get you pregnant if I keep doing that," he murmured, his lips on her temple.

"I hope you do," she replied, lifting her mouth to his. He kissed her with passion, twining his tongue with hers, making her heart swell with hope.

"Why?" he asked when he raised his head.

Sidney grappled for an explanation. As far back as she could remember, she'd been alone, isolated by her strangeness, stranded by circumstance, emotionally abandoned by those who should have cared the most. Even her own mother couldn't come to terms with Sidney's affliction. So many times, she'd cried herself to sleep, aching to give her love to someone who would accept her for who she was.

How she longed to stroke a baby's cheek! To touch unselfconsciously, to love unconditionally.

"I adore my nieces, but Samantha doesn't bring them to visit often," she began, afraid to reveal the depth of her need. "My parents and I don't get along. If I had a baby of my own, I would cherish it."

He didn't ask where he fit into this rosy little picture, although his expression clearly stated that this was another one of her naïve fancies.

"I wouldn't expect anything from you," she clarified.

"Of course not," he muttered, pushing her off his lap. "I'm 'incapable of constancy.'"

She stared at him for a moment, a puzzle piece of his psyche clicking into place. He would feel obligated to marry her if she got pregnant. Maybe it was old-fashioned, in this day and age, but he wouldn't let his child be a bastard. Like he was.

"Oh," she said, her stomach sinking.

He jerked his head toward her. "You know, I really hate it when you do that. Instead of raping my brain, you could just ask me what I'm thinking."

"Right. You're such a great communicator."

"I've known you for a week," he defended, "and we're already talking about love and babies. This is not in my comfort zone, okay?"

"Then use a condom from now on, and we won't have to talk about it."

His dark gaze traveled over her breasts, still flushed from her orgasm, down to the V of her thighs. "Fine," he said, his face showing both anger and bewilderment, as if he couldn't fathom why he'd failed to use protection again. Then the dryer fell silent, signaling the end of the cycle, and he went into the hallway to get his clothes.

Sidney pulled on a robe and wandered into the kitchen to make breakfast, feeling shell-shocked. He'd said he loved her. That he wanted her.

And yet, the only promise he'd made was that he wouldn't stay.

Thanks to a Special Report by Crystal Dunn that aired over the weekend, women all over the city had been calling the homicide division to report uncommon canine behavior. After Detective Lacy narrowed the list down to single blondes with large breeds, she still had a dozen interviews to complete, and she couldn't do them by herself.

Although Chief Stokes had partnered Lacy with another officer, a rookie from beat, she'd asked Marc to help out on the grunt work for the case.

He wouldn't be able to stay at the kennel with Sidney.

A uniformed officer was posted on the street in front of Pacific Pet Hotel, but Marc was still reluctant to leave. "Do you have anything you use to control rowdy dogs?" he asked. "A stun gun or something?"

She looked at him like he was crazy.

"Pepper spray?"

Frowning, she rummaged through a drawer in her office and came up with a small yellow spray stick.

"Wear it on you. Clipped to your pants." She complied in dutiful silence. "I'll try to get back before closing," he murmured, taking her into his arms.

She accepted his embrace stiffly, and it occurred to him that not only was he jinxing himself by saying goodbye, but he was doing it in the mushiest, most sentimental way possible, as if he was afraid he'd never see her again. He let her go long before he was ready to, disturbed by the cold wash of fear that struck him at the thought of losing her.

The uneasy feeling nagged him the rest of the day.

By late afternoon, they'd completed all but the last interview. Annemarie Wilsey was a kindergarten teacher who frequently walked her dog, Greta, along an undeveloped section of land bordering Camp Pendleton. Like Candace Hegel, she lived alone in a neighborhood of tile-roofed tract homes with large bedrooms and small backyards.

"Greta was acting strange, you say?" Lacy prompted.

Annemarie gave a nervous smile, patting the Rottweiler mix on the top the head. "Yes. We'd just left the house, and she wasn't herself. She loves to go for walks, but that morning she was sluggish. Less than a block away, she just…collapsed."

"Did she have convulsions? Seizures?"

"Not that I could tell. The vet thought she might be epileptic, or even diabetic, of all things. He said if it happened again, he would try medication."

"But it didn't."

"No."

"And how did you get Greta to the vet? She must weigh as much as you do."

"A man came by and offered to help."

Marc's attention was piqued. "Go on," he said.

"He wanted to drive us there. Since I was so close to home, I just ran down the block to get my own car. He helped me lift her into the backseat." She blinked her guileless blue eyes a few times, looking back and forth between them. Then her pretty face went white. "Oh my God," she said, raising a hand to her trembling mouth. "Do you think that was *him?*"

"What did he look like?" Lacy asked.

She worried her lower lip. "Young. Dark-haired. Average-size, I guess."

"How young? Like Lieutenant Cruz?"

Annemarie studied him. "Yes. Or younger."

"Dark like him, too? His size?"

Her cheeks reddened. "Not quite as big. Darker hair. And his skin was more…pale."

"He was white?"

"Yes."

"Is there anything else you can remember about him? Anything unusual in his appearance?"

"No. He looked like a regular guy, I guess."

"What was he driving?"

She scrunched up her face. "Oh, I don't know. I was so worried about Greta, I'm surprised I can remember the man."

"A car or truck?" Lacy pressed her for details.

"Not a truck," she decided. "Just a basic car, I think, nothing flashy."

"Would you mind going to the station to work with our computer artist? You'd be amazed at what you can remember about a person's features with a little help."

"Of course," she said, patting Greta again with absent affection.

Marc wondered what Annemarie Wilsey had in common with the other victims besides the fact that she was small and blond and pretty. "Where did you get Greta?" he asked, shifting his attention to the dog at her side.

"At the pound. She's been a treasure."

Greta looked friendly, but Marc wasn't about to risk his hand by reaching out to pet her. Unlike a typical Rottweiler, she was pure black, with no tan markings. Her large head, stocky body, and cropped tail gave away her breed.

"Were you looking for a watchdog?"

"Yes," she admitted. "My garage was broken into last year. There wasn't much to steal, but it kind of scared me. A few days later, I got a phone call from a volunteer with the ASPCA. Greta needed a home. It seemed like a perfect fit."

Maybe too perfect, he thought. "Is she trained?"

"Not really. I think she's just naturally obedient."

On a hunch, he ordered the dog to lie down in German. Greta complied instantly, stretching out on her barreled chest. He told her to roll over, and she did that, too.

Annemarie Wilsey was astounded. "How did you get her to do that?"

"It's a gift," he lied, standing to leave. "If you can go down to the station right away," he began, and Greta stopped being obedient. She also stopped being friendly. Hackles raised in warning, she issued a low rumble from the back of her throat.

Marc froze.

"Greta!" Annemarie scolded, grabbing onto her nylon collar. "I'm sorry. She's never acted this way before."

"Don't worry about it," Lacy said, putting her body between the dog and Marc, saving him. "Lieutenant Cruz always has this effect on females."

In his car, Marc turned on the air conditioning full blast and rested his forehead against the steering wheel, trying to pull himself together. He could still hear growling, followed by the sickening crunch of Houdini's neck bones in his hands.

"You are such a head case, Marcos," Lacy complained affectionately. "Where'd you learn German?"

"I did a month there after Saudi."

"You picked up 'lay down' and 'roll over' in a month?"

He smiled weakly. "Oh, yes. They were essential phrases."

Instead of admonishing him, she regarded him with undisguised curiosity. "What were the women like?"

"They were...nice," he said after some hesitation, and they both laughed at his understatement. At nineteen, he hadn't been able to erase the disturbing images of war by scoring with sexy foreign girls, but he'd given the endeavor his absolute best.

Of course, all of them put together, and everyone since, couldn't compare to Sidney.

Chapter 18

Sidney spent a miserable day torn between worrying about Samantha and worrying about Marc. He called two minutes before closing time to tell her he'd be working late.

"Is there somewhere you can go tonight?" he asked. "I don't want you to be alone."

"I guess I can stay with my parents."

"Then drive straight there, and don't stop. The patrol car can't follow you."

"Whatever," she muttered.

"Do you promise?"

"Yes," she said in an exasperated voice. This time, it was she who hung up without saying goodbye.

Trudging outside, she took Blue out of his kennel to let him roam around while she performed the closing tasks. She was just about to leave when the phone rang again.

"Siddie?"

"Samantha," she gasped, both relieved and anxious, for her sister sounded scared. "Where are you?"

"At the Downs. Can you come get me? I've been thinking..." As she trailed off, Sidney could hear the clink of glass bottles and a bark of male laughter in the background.

"I'll be right there," she promised.

The San Luis Rey Downs Country Club was one of Samantha's old haunts. It was in Bonsall, close to the home where they grew up. On her way out the door, she considered calling Marc, but she was afraid he'd tell her not to go, and Samantha needed her.

Sidney didn't even pause to put Blue away, she just whistled for him to hop in the bed of the pickup and stepped on the gas. She was parked outside the bar next to Samantha's SUV a short time later.

At early evening, the place wasn't exactly hopping, but it was full of regulars, mostly good old boys from the golf course.

She didn't see Samantha.

Sidney checked the rest room, which was empty, before approaching the bartender. "Was there a woman here a few minutes ago? A pretty blonde?"

He steadied a tray of drinks on his shoulder, glancing at an unoccupied bar stool. "Yeah. She was right there."

"Did she leave with someone?"

He looked around the bar, perhaps wondering who was missing. "I didn't really notice," he admitted. When a man on the other side of the room let out a short whistle, indicating he was impatient for his drink, Sidney waved the bartender away.

Taking matters into her own hands, she ran her fingertips along the bar stool Samantha had been sitting on. The impression she got was vague and blurry, a wavering image of a dark-haired man. Frowning, because his face looked familiar, she moved on to the next chair. Touching it was like sticking her hand into decomposing flesh, and something clicked inside her head, like puzzle pieces falling into place.

The man who'd been sitting next to Samantha was none other than her childhood nemesis, schoolyard bully Kurtis Stalb.

At the public rest room near Guajome Lake, she'd been reminded of Kurtis, but because Sidney hadn't seen him in so long, she hadn't recognized his adult persona. The man in the mirror wasn't *like* Kurtis Stalb. He *was* Kurtis Stalb.

She couldn't believe she hadn't figured it out until now.

As an adolescent, Kurtis had lowered Lisa Pettigrew into an abandoned well and left her there for dead. He was the vandal who had eviscerated a helpless cat on top of Sidney's bed. He was responsible for the rape, torture and murder of Anika Groene and Candace Hegel.

And now, he would do to her sister what he'd done to the others.

Marc dropped off Lacy at the station and drove on in tense silence, cataloging details in his mind, searching for a break.

He thought about dogs. Greta was a German breed of questionable heritage, a watchdog Annemarie had picked up at the pound. Candace Hegel had adopted Blue, a similar mongrel, and Anika Groene's weird-looking mutt had also been a guest of the county at some point.

Could the killer have a connection to the dogs, if not the women?

A man who was familiar with the animals would have found them easier to handle. Easier to drug. Easier to manipulate.

Marc ventured a guess that all three dogs had been instructed to obey orders in German. Perhaps they'd all been to the same trainer, at some point, or even raised by the same breeder. Annemarie had said her garage had been broken into, an ordinary occurrence. He didn't know if the other victims had been burglarized, but if they had…

How difficult would it be for the killer to stage a break-in then turn one of his ugly hounds into the pound? Had he called Annemarie Wilsey, and all of the others, posing as an employee of the humane society?

As nefarious plans went, this one had a low probability for success, and it was premeditated to the extreme. Contrary to popular belief, most serial killers weren't masterminds. They attacked on impulse when an opportunity presented itself. Even so, Marc's heart was pumping double-time, telling him he was on the right track.

He called Lacy. "What are you doing?"

"Waiting for the composite sketch artist to come in."

"Can you run a search on dog trainers?"

"Been there, done that."

"What have you got?"

"Too many names to mention. I called Bill Vincent to see if he knew any of them."

"And what did the good doctor say?"

"He mentioned a breeder in Bonsall who does Schutzhund training. Some guy named Kurtis Stalb. He supposedly turns out mixed-pedigree watchdogs of 'dubitable nature.' And get this—he lives less than a mile from Derek DeWinter."

A chill raced down his spine. "What's the address?"

"It's 1431 Lilac. Do you want me to meet you there?"

"Yes," he said, and the instant he ended the call, his cell phone rang again.

It was Sidney.

"The killer," she said in a rush, "it's Kurtis Stalb."

All of his senses went on red alert. "Where is he?"

"With Samantha," she panted. "She just called me from the bar at San Luis Rey Downs. I think she left with him. No, I know she did. I know she did!"

He accepted her words without question. "Where did he take her?"

"I don't know. His house, maybe. He lives by Derek."

The anxiety that had been riding him all day skyrocketed. "Don't go there," he warned. When she didn't answer, he felt his blood pressure go through the roof. Stepping on the gas, he calculated the number of minutes it would take him to get to Bonsall. "Sidney, you will *not* go there," he stressed, tightening his fingers around the cell phone.

The only sound was static as the call was dropped.

Sidney didn't listen to Marc.

Just minutes after his voice cut out, she was standing at the edge of Kurtis's property, pepper spray in hand, looking down into the shadowed valley below. She'd never been there before, but she knew it was the right place.

So did Blue.

Recognizing the scent, he lifted his head and let out a tortured howl.

The house was set away from the road, down an endless gravel driveway that wound along the banks of a tributary of the San Luis

Rey River. Behind the house, a large concrete enclosure was visible in the deepening gloom. A kennel, with at least twenty dog runs.

No wonder Blue had been pacing outside her fence line when she first saw him. He was looking for Candace, and after being drugged, escaping from Kurtis's property and traveling more than ten miles, he was understandably confused.

Sidney knew she should wait for Marc, but she couldn't shake the feeling that she didn't have a moment to lose. Samantha's life depended on her immediate arrival. An unbearable sense of urgency propelled her forward.

"You want to get him, boy?" she asked in a low voice, meeting the dog's fierce gray eyes.

Blue looked ready to rip out throats.

Sidney figured it was as good a plan as any. She'd go down there, surprise Kurtis during whatever torture he was inflicting upon Samantha and sic Blue on him. Then she'd pepper spray his sorry ass, for good measure. Picturing the scene, she felt a strange, cold sense of calm, almost as if she could bare her own teeth and sink them into the killer's flesh.

"By whatever means necessary," she whispered, heading down the dark hillside.

She couldn't sneak up behind the house, not with a dozen or more dogs who would surely alert him to her presence, so she made her way along the side, moving quick and staying low until she came to an open garage.

Inside, there was a small black truck, its cooling system still ticking. Next to the truck sat a beige Ford Taurus with a gaping hole where the passenger window should have been. Sidney could see that the vinyl interior was chewed and torn.

Blue had really done a number on it.

Pulse pounding with adrenaline, she studied the door leading from the garage to the interior of the house. Reaching down, she unclipped Blue's leash, needing one free hand to turn the knob, the other to spray with.

Sidney didn't allow herself time to hesitate, or to speculate on Samantha's condition. Her sister was still alive. She had to be alive. He liked them scared, and alive.

Motioning for Blue to follow, she crept around the vehicles, stepping forward cautiously. When she reached out to test the doorknob, it turned easily, and just like that, she was crossing the threshold from the garage into the house.

A dark blur was her only warning before a blunt, heavy object smashed into the left side of her head.

The next thing Sidney knew, she was on her hands and knees, gasping for air, black spots obscuring her vision. The pepper spray stick was no longer clenched in her fist. Somewhere in the background, Blue's ferocious growling was cut off with a yelp, then nothing.

Warm wetness flowed into her ear and coursed down her neck. Fat red drops splashed onto the floor between her braced hands. The pain was so immense she couldn't believe she was alive, let alone conscious. Struggling to stay that way, she swallowed her fear, fighting against an almost overwhelming urge to lie down on the floor and die.

"Didn't see that coming, did you, psychic bitch?"

"The police will be here any minute," she said between gasping breaths.

"I guess I better hurry then." Grabbing her by the arms, he dragged her across the linoleum. Not only was she helpless to stop him, but she couldn't summon the energy to kick her legs or fight in any way.

On the other side of the door, Blue's prone body lay in a crumpled heap.

Sidney moaned weakly.

"Is that all you've got?" he grunted, stretching her out on the floor next to Samantha. Her sister was alive, bound and gagged, her blue eyes glassy with panic.

Kurtis stood over Sidney, legs splayed wide apart, arms crossed over his chest. He was much the same as she remembered him: tall and wiry, no better than average-looking, his coarse black hair falling over his forehead into dark, soulless eyes.

A malicious smile spread across his pale face. "Now this is a dream come true. The Morrow sisters at my disposal. A slutty little blonde and a dark-haired tomboy. I don't know who I want to do first."

Beside her, Samantha whimpered.

Kurtis raised his dark brows. "You volunteering, Miz Parker?"

Black flashes danced behind Sidney's eyes, beckoning her to oblivion. "You don't have time," she promised hoarsely, her head spinning.

He must have believed her, because he left them lying there alone for a moment. When he returned, he brought the tarp.

Marc arrived at Kurtis Stalb's house less than twenty minutes after ending the phone call with Sidney. He was lucky the country roads were deserted, because his driving gave the term "reckless endangerment" new meaning.

When he saw Sidney's truck parked by the side of the road, he slammed his open palm against the steering wheel, furious with her for putting her life in danger.

He turned into the driveway, cut the engine a few hundred feet from the house and was out running, Glock in hand, before his car came to a complete stop. The only vehicle in the garage was an older model black Ford Ranger. Between it and the door leading from the garage into the house, there was a small yellow object, hauntingly familiar. Sidney's pepper spray. It didn't appear to have been used.

Fear gripped him, squeezing his heart with a sweaty fist.

Abandoning stealth in the interest of saving time, he kicked in the door, holding his Glock out in front of him with both hands. A hundred pounds of fur and muscle sailed through the air, right at his chest. As he fell back against the wall, he discharged a bullet into the ceiling. Plaster rained down on his head.

The first time he'd fired his weapon in the line of duty, and it was an accident.

Growling and whining, Blue sank his teeth into the front of his T-shirt and pulled, ripping cotton away from flesh. Face-to-face with the deranged mongrel, staring into his silver-gray eyes, Marc came to the understanding that the dog wasn't trying to kill him.

"Easy, Blue," he said, surveying his surroundings.

Underneath him, a slick trail of blood ran from the door to the kitchen, where a small pool had collected on the middle of the linoleum floor. At the sight of it, a black rage fell over him, darkening the edges of his vision. When Marc found Kurtis Stalb, he was going to tear him apart with his bare hands.

Drag marks and smeared footprints traversed the length of the hallway, as if Stalb had pulled something along behind him. A tarp-wrapped body, for instance.

With a mouthful of his T-shirt clamped between his impressive jaws, Blue continued to jerk him backward, toward the garage, his claws seeking purchase on the slippery linoleum.

"Halt!" he ordered in German, hoping Blue wouldn't take offense to the language, as Greta had. Not only was the dog ruining his crime scene, Marc needed to check the other rooms.

Making a pitiful sound, Blue sank to the floor, panting, more worn-out than he should have been after the brief tussle. Marc noted the blood on his muzzle and wondered if the dog had already gone a round with Stalb, and lost.

The rest of the house was empty. In the back, behind the only other locked door he encountered, there was a small, dark room. Digitally printed photos were spread out over a bare mattress. Annemarie Wilsey. Anika Groene. Candace Hegel.

And Sidney. With him, in the truck. On the beach. At the mission.

Some of the photos were landscapes. Guajome Lake Park. Agua Hedionda Lagoon. The most puzzling of these appeared to be a stone fountain, several feet deep. He stared at the image for a moment before he recognized the scene.

The photo had been taken in front of the San Luis Rey Mission.

He left at a dead run, calling for Blue to follow.

In the trunk of Kurtis Stalb's Taurus, Sidney woke up. The uneven gravel road had made the first few moments of the ride bone-jarringly painful. After one of the roughest jolts, she'd slumped into unconsciousness.

Now the road was smooth, and she had no idea where they were.

She could smell her own blood, feel it clotted in her left ear, matted in her hair, working like an adhesive to plaster the tarp to the side of her face. Her head throbbed, but her mind was clear and she felt more alert than before. If he came at her now, she'd be able to fight. Except that her hands and feet were bound together, the ropes so tight her swollen fingers tingled when she wiggled them experimentally.

Being hog-tied, trapped in a trunk, wrapped in heavy, constrictive plastic, was a claustrophobic nightmare. She forced herself to breath evenly, knowing she had very little oxygen left. If he didn't dump her off somewhere soon, she could very well suffocate before she got the chance to drown.

So much for her gallant rescue attempt.

Sidney knew that if she'd waited for Marc, Samantha would be in this truck instead of her, but that fact was cold comfort now that they both would die.

Her arms were tied at the wrist over her stomach. She inched her hands up toward her mouth, little by little, until she felt coarse rope bite into her lips. Like a starved animal, she gripped it with her teeth and tugged. She tore at the individual pieces of twine. She chewed until her mouth bled.

By the time the Taurus came to an abrupt stop, she'd succeeded in tightening the rope around her wrists to an agonizing degree.

When she felt herself being lifted out of the trunk, she was actually relieved. Until she landed with a harsh slap on the surface of water. Remembering how Kurtis had enjoyed the sight of the others struggling, she told herself to remain motionless as she slowly sank.

Let him think she was unconscious. Let him think she was already dead.

Cold water began to seep into the tarp, reviving her senses, renewing her chances of survival. With wet hands, she might be able to slip free of the binding. Tears of hope stung her eyes, and she heard a sound, peaceful and pleasant, like the melody of a bubbling brook, barely audible through the layers of tarp and water.

She turned her head slightly, trying to get her sticky ear away from the plastic, and a wet flood rushed in, soaking her clothing, her hair, her swollen hands. It tasted clean and smelled fresh. She was in a fountain!

Sidney forced herself to stay still even though water was pouring in at an alarming rate. Her body drifted lower then touched ground. Her heart leaped! Why had he not bothered to weigh her down?

The answer came with a solid block of concrete, hitting the middle of her stomach, robbing her of breath. Anchoring her deep.

Terror assailed her, and her mouth opened and closed like a fish out of water, trying to suck in oxygen. White lights fluttered before her eyes, and a low rumble, like an underground vibration, sounded in her ears.

He was driving away! The roar of the car's engine faded into the distance.

Surging with adrenaline, she shoved at the concrete block on her stomach with bound hands. When it gave, she felt a frightening weightlessness. Desperate to get her head above water, she kicked her legs furiously, trying to put her feet under her so she could push off the bottom of the fountain.

It wasn't as easy as she thought. She was so disoriented she couldn't tell up from down. Panicking, she flailed this way and that, going nowhere. She struggled against the ropes, but she had no room to maneuver. She had no fight left. No air. No energy. No hope.

Sidney felt her body go slack as life left her.

By the time Marc pulled up to the San Luis Rey Mission, he was soaked in sweat, sick with fury, paralyzed by fear.

He jerked his car to a stop in front of the main fountain and jumped out, praying to God it was the right one. Blue was out in a flash, barking excitedly at the fountain's edge, but the surface of the water was still as glass and dark as death.

Swallowing back his emotion and denying the obvious, Marc leaped over the edge, telling himself this was a rescue, not a recovery.

He waded around desperately, submerged to the middle of his chest, searching for any sign of her. When his shoe glanced off the edge of a cinder block, the same kind that had been in Agua Hedionda Lagoon with Candace Hegel, his stomach dropped. He dove underwater to find another limp, tarp-shrouded body.

He was too late.

Grabbing her around the waist, he brought her up in a wet heap, holding her to him very tightly, as if he could squeeze the life back into her. "No," he said fiercely, refusing to accept the truth. Hauling them both over the edge, he laid her out on the soft dark grass, unaware that he was praying until he felt his cold lips moving.

Padre nuestro…

With trembling hands, he found the tiny knife on his key chain and flipped it up, carefully cutting the tarp away from her face. It was Sidney. Her lips were dark and her eyes closed. She was beautiful, even in death.

"Te ruego," he yelled, coming to his knees. As Blue threw back his head and howled, Marc held his open palms up to the night sky. *"Te ruego,"* he repeated. I pray to you, or I beg you. In Spanish, the words were the same.

On the ground, Sidney coughed and sputtered.

He stared down at her, astounded.

Water dribbled from the corner of her mouth.

He turned her on her side quickly, letting her purge the liquid from her stomach while he patted her back. When she was finished, he drew her into his arms and held her there, afraid to ever let her go again. He rocked her back and forth, not sure if he was comforting her or himself. Hot moisture coursed down his cheeks, and he realized he was crying, something he hadn't done even when his father died. Or since.

"Samantha," she whispered, her voice ravaged by the near-drowning.

He took her face in his hands. "Where?"

"With him. Kurtis."

Marc searched the area with his eyes. A beige Ford Taurus was the only car in the parking lot. At the entrance to the graveyard, a heavy metal gate stood open.

"Don't go," she pleaded, even though she'd just asked him to.

"I have to."

"Untie my hands."

He did, using the small knife from his key chain, and kissed each swollen palm. "I love you," he said with reverence.

"Please," she whispered, tears filling her eyes.

He strode to the car, grabbing his Glock off the passenger seat. "Lacy will be here any minute," he said. "Stay," he added, meaning both her and Blue.

She put her arm around the dog's neck and closed her eyes, too weak to argue.

Marc moved swiftly through the mission's historical graveyard, thinking it was a poor place to rape, torture, or kill women. The grounds weren't patrolled, but they were well-lit, and Marc didn't doubt there were security cameras recording Kurtis Stalb's every move.

The man was no longer concerned with getting caught. His intention, in coming here, was probably to go out in a big, symbolic hurrah, and Marc was more than eager to send him straight to hell where he belonged.

Toward the rear of the graveyard there was a stone wall with an altar upon which parishioners placed religious offerings. A dozen or more tall, glass-encased candles lit the scene. Samantha lay beneath them like a nonvirgin sacrifice. Her hands and ankles were bound, a handkerchief gag bit into her mouth and her clothes hung in tatters on her mostly nude body. She was the antithesis of purity.

Stalb loomed over her, taking a wicked-looking knife from a sheath at his waist.

Marc trained his Glock on the back of the man's head, but Samantha didn't give him the chance to pull the trigger. As Stalb cut the ropes securing her ankles, she lifted her arms and groped for one of the heavy candles resting on the ledge above her. When he positioned himself between her legs, she brought it down hard on top of his dark head.

Marc ran forward, vaulting over headstones, gun poised to shoot.

Stalb collapsed against Samantha, his body slack. She pushed him off her, but she wasn't done with him yet. Wielding the glass-encased candle like a bludgeon, she bashed it into the back of his skull, again and again and again.

By the time Marc reached them, Kurtis Stalb was good and dead.

Samantha looked up at him, tears streaming down her pretty face, shards of glass and colored wax in her bloody hands.

Kneeling beside her, he cut the gag away from her trembling mouth.

"He killed my sister," she said, her blue eyes opaque with shock. Without another word, she fainted in his arms.

Chapter 19

When Samantha celebrated her thirtieth day of sobriety, Sidney threw her a party at the beach.

For Samantha, recovery didn't happen right away, and it didn't come easily. Between the divorce, the media attention and the police investigation of Kurtis Stalb's death, she had several relapses. In the end, the case was quietly closed, even though the medical examiner's findings regarding overkill didn't exactly match up with the witnesses' accounts of self-defense.

Marc wasn't fired because of his relationship with Sidney, but he was demoted from lieutenant to detective and ordered to take six weeks unpaid leave. After returning to work, he began six months of desk duty, a fate worse than death, to hear him tell it. When this penance was paid, he would be repartnered with Detective Lacy—as her subordinate officer.

Deputy Chief Stokes had really outdone herself creating an apropos punishment.

Looking at Marc now, laughing with Samantha and the girls, Sidney couldn't see any signs of discontent. His shoulders were relaxed, his hands thrust deep in his pockets, his white shirt and dark skin contrasting brilliantly against the blue October sky. He'd accepted his fate with equanimity, claiming he'd have done a lifetime of desk duty, or even traffic detail, in exchange for Sidney's safety.

Greg and his secretary broke up after the divorce papers were filed, much to Samantha's amusement. Although he wanted Samantha back, she was abstaining from relationships as well as drugs and alcohol.

Sidney couldn't have been happier for her sister, or more proud.

"Isn't it time for the cake, dear?" her mother asked, snapping her out of her reverie.

"Hmm," she said, making no move to get up. The sun was warm, the breeze was cool and the scenery was excellent. She'd never seen such a collection of fabulous-looking people. It was hard to believe that she and some of them were related.

"Why don't I take care of it?" her mother offered with a secretive little smile. "I think your young man wants to talk to you."

Over the past few months, Marc had charmed Aurelia Morrow with simple flattery and impeccable manners. Sidney found his gallantry disingenuous, but Aurelia ate it up with a spoon, proving herself no more immune to him than any other female. Sidney had also noticed him talking to her father this afternoon, some deep, manly conversation made up of stern eyebrows, gruff tones and firm handshakes.

Sidney placed a hand over her lower abdomen. Did he know?

At that very moment, his eyes met hers, with that same spark of electricity she'd felt the first time she saw him. As his gaze traveled down her body, to the hand resting on her belly, the smile fell off his face.

He did know.

"Maybe you're right," she said with apprehension, rising from her chair to stand on rubbery legs. She tugged on the hem of her knee-length yellow sundress, wondering what had possessed her to buy it. It was a whimsical, feminine creation she'd worn to please her sister. Now she felt awkward, barefoot and silly, like a little girl playing dress-up.

Marc approached her leisurely, his hands still buried in his pockets, his expression guarded. "Want to go for a walk?"

Behind his back, her sister winked and made an okay sign, as if she thought they were wandering off for a quickie and she approved of the idea.

"Sure," Sidney said, smoothing her skirt again.

A few yards down the beach, he took her hand in his, a gesture that never failed to tug at her heartstrings. Blinking back the hot sting of tears, she looked out at the setting sun over the Pacific, its last rays casting brilliant golden light across that infinite expanse.

"I was going to tell you," she said in a nervous rush, "but everything's been going so well and I didn't want to ruin it."

"Tell me what?" he asked, pulling her toward him.

She stared at him without speaking, too anxious to be articulate.

"Why don't you tell me later," he murmured, brushing his lips across hers.

She wrapped her arms around him and buried her face in his neck, gripping fistfuls of his shirt, wishing she could hold onto him forever.

"Hey," he said softly. "What's wrong?"

"I'm pregnant," she whispered.

He jerked his head back to look at her. "You're what?" Any notion that he'd already guessed was dispelled by his wide-eyed, slack-jawed expression. "You're what?"

She couldn't make herself repeat it.

"You said you weren't."

"I wasn't. Now I am."

"We haven't even…"

"Yes we have."

His gaze dropped to her mouth, then her breasts, then her belly. She knew without asking that he was remembering the only time they'd failed to use protection since that first tempestuous week together.

About a month ago, they'd spent a steamy afternoon in bed. He kissed every inch of her body, worshipping her with his tongue, rousing her to a fever pitch. Instead of bringing her to climax, he begged her to do it herself while he watched, and she complied shyly, enthralled by his interest. After having lost the last of her inhibitions, she'd wanted him all over her, between her legs, between her breasts, in her mouth.

He'd obliged her thoroughly, dipping his engorged shaft inside her, pushing her breasts together and pleasuring himself there, plumbing the depths of her mouth. At last, he'd brought her to another orgasm with a series of slow, deep thrusts, before he withdrew, spilling himself on her quivering stomach.

The memory of that interlude was enough to make her body flush with embarrassment and arousal, even now.

"I pulled out," he said unnecessarily.

She smiled. "This may come as a surprise to you, but medical professionals don't consider that method particularly reliable."

Her humor was lost on him, perhaps because he was staring at her breasts intently, as if trying to find some visual evidence of her condition. Against the apex of her thighs, another physical change was developing, pressing hard into her.

"Marc," she protested, squirming in his arms. He was getting her all hot and bothered, but at sunset, the beach was far from deserted.

"I have to see you," he said roughly, doing a quick survey of their surroundings. Taking her hand, he pulled her toward an empty lifeguard tower about a hundred feet from them. It wasn't exactly private, but it would conceal them from all but the most prying eyes.

Blushing, she ascended the ladder ahead of him. The instant they reached the top, he fell to his knees in front of her and pushed her dress up to the waist, exposing her flat tummy.

"I can't tell," he said, moistening his lips.

"I'm only a few weeks along."

He traced her navel with his fingertip then brushed his knuckles back and forth over her lower abdomen.

She sucked in a sharp breath.

"Does it hurt?"

"No."

"Have you been sick?"

"Not yet."

"Knowing you, you will be."

She couldn't laugh or cry or even breathe comfortably, so she leaned her head back against the tower wall and closed her eyes.

He reached up to slip the straps of her dress off her shoulders, lowering the stretchy cotton bodice. She wasn't wearing anything underneath.

Cupping one breast gently, he said, "Your nipples are darker."

"Yes," she agreed, thinking she might die if he stopped touching her.

"It's barely noticeable, but now that I know..." He circled her swollen areola slowly. "Are you sensitive?"

"Yes." The tips of her breasts were tight and aching, pouting for his attention. When he laved each one with his tongue, she gasped, thrusting her fingers into his hair.

Murmuring something unintelligible, he slid his hand up her inner thigh until he reached her panties. Stroking her through the fabric, he asked, "What about here?"

"Yes," she moaned.

"I mean, are you sensitive here, too?"

"No more than usual."

"So as long as I'm gentle, I can still touch you like this?" He slid his fingers into her panties, parting the damp petals of her sex and caressing her gingerly. "And like this?"

"If you don't stop being gentle," she panted, "I'm going to kill you."

He stripped her panties away and released the buttons on his fly, freeing his erection. Straddling his thighs, she impaled herself on him, digging her fingernails into the fabric of his shirt and biting down on her lower lip to hold back her cry.

His breath was heavy on her neck, his hands hot on her bare bottom. Beneath her fingertips, his shoulders trembled. "You feel so—"

"Yes." She arched up, pushing against the floor with her bare feet and sliding back down along the length of his shaft.

Groaning, he braced one hand behind her and lifted his hips, pressing her back against the wall, thrusting hard, driving deep.

"More," she urged, tightening her legs around him. "More."

Giving her what she wanted, what she needed, he drove into her harder, faster, deeper. He loved her fiercely and filled her completely, giving everything, holding nothing back. When he stiffened, she exploded in pleasure, throwing her head back and crying out his name as he buried himself in her one last time.

When she caught her breath a moment later, he was sprawled underneath her, their bodies entwined in a tangled heap on the whitewashed floor. Now that the blood was returning to his brain, he probably didn't find her pregnancy half as sexy as before. In her limited experience, a man with a hard-on had a lot of stupid ideas.

Crawling off him, she righted her clothing in silence.

"My mother will be delighted," he said finally.

"What about you? How do you feel?"

"I don't know," he groaned, refastening his pants and straightening. "I never had any brothers or sisters. I've never been around a—" he swallowed "—baby."

Her mood plummeted. "This sounds remarkably like your argument for disliking dogs."

"I'm getting along with Blue now, aren't I?"

He had adopted the dog, with an exaggerated display of reluctance. Sidney knew the pair had forged some kind of bond, even though Marc didn't coddle him or really even pet him from what she could see. In return, Blue tolerated Marc with stoic apathy. It was a strange, if peaceful, coexistence.

God forbid she and Marc circle around each other the same way. "I don't want you to 'get along' with it. I want you to want it."

"I want you," he said, giving her honesty instead of promises. He reached out to clasp her hand. "Marry me."

She jerked away. "No."

"No?"

"You heard me."

He gaped at her incredulously. "Why?"

Instead of answering, she scrambled down the ladder, desperate to put some space between them before she fell apart. She jogged down the beach, her bare feet finding uneasy purchase on the shifting sand, tears blurring her vision.

"Why?" he repeated when he caught up with her. Wrapping his fingers around her upper arms, he asked again, his voice low with desperation. "Why?"

"I don't want to be your burden," she said, trying to stifle a sob. "Your obligation."

"You could never be that. I love you."

"You only want to marry me so our child won't be a b—" She stuttered over the ugly word, then blurted it out, "a bastard."

He released her immediately, a cold glint in his eyes. "Then why do I have this?" From his pocket, he pulled out a black velvet box and shoved it at her. With that, he left her standing on the sand, her mouth hanging open in shock.

She opened the box with shaking hands. A square-cut diamond sparkled from an elegant setting on a simple platinum band.

"Oh," she gasped, clapping it shut. "Oh, no."

She ran after him, her heart threatening to burst from her chest. "I'm sorry," she said, biting her lip to keep from giggling. Nowadays especially, humor struck her at odd times. "But you said you wouldn't stay, and I believed you."

He stopped to look at her. "I didn't mean it."

"Yes, you did."

"No," he protested. "Even then, I knew I could never leave you, but I was afraid to let myself…need you."

She put her arms around him, tears looming close behind her eyes once again. "I need you," she whispered, stroking her fingers through his hair. "I love you," she added, kissing his tense mouth. "And I would be honored to marry you."

He took her hand in his. "Are you sure?"

She met his eyes, whiskey-brown in the light of the setting sun. "Are you?"

He placed her palm over the center of his chest. "You tell me."

His heartbeat thumped beneath her hand, fast and strong and true. Any misgivings he had weren't about her, or the baby, but himself.

"I can't promise I'll be good at this," he warned. "I work all the time. I never had a family. I never really had a father."

Love welled up inside her, washing away her hesitation. "Don't promise anything," she whispered. "Just stay."

Falling to his knees before her, he wrapped his arms around her waist and pressed his face into her stomach. When he inhaled a shuddering breath, the tears she'd been fighting spilled over onto her cheeks, and she slid her hands into his hair, holding him to her.

He didn't say he would love her forever, but she knew it by the way he brushed a reverent kiss against her belly, saw it in his trembling shoulders and felt it in the strength of his embrace.

In the end, the promise he made remained unspoken, but she heard it all the same.

* * * * *

Dear Reader,

Dangerous to Touch is my first published book, and I'm thrilled to be sharing this experience with you, my first readers! I hope you enjoy getting to know my characters as much as I enjoyed creating them.

With Sidney Morrow, I really connected to the idea of her being an outcast. I think we've all had trouble fitting in at some point or another, and as a rebellious, bookish adolescent, I felt especially out of place. Immersing myself in the world of romance, where I was always welcome, made for a great escape.

Here's hoping that *Dangerous to Touch* provides a warm welcome and great escape for those who need it as much as I did.

Best wishes,

Jill Sorenson

The editors at Harlequin Blaze have never been afraid to push the limits—tempting readers with the forbidden, whetting their appetites with a wide variety of story lines. But now we're breaking the final barrier—the time barrier.

In July, watch for BOUND TO PLEASE by fan favorite Hope Tarr, Harlequin Blaze's first ever *historical romance—a story that's truly Blaze-worthy in every sense.*

Here's a sneak peek...

BRIANNA stretched out beside Ewan, languid as a cat, and promptly fell asleep. Midday sunshine streamed into the chamber, bathing her lovely, long-limbed body in golden light, the sea-scented breeze wafting inside to dry the damp red-gold tendrils curling about her flushed face. Propping himself up on one elbow, Ewan slid his gaze over her. She looked beautiful and whole, satisfied and sated, and altogether happier than he had so far seen her. A slight smile curved her beautiful lips as though she must be in the midst of a lovely dream. She'd molded her lush, lovely body to his and laid her head in the curve of his shoulder and settled in to sleep beside him. For the longest while he lay there turned toward her, content to watch her sleep, at near perfect peace.

Not wholly perfect, for she had yet to answer his marriage proposal. Still, she wanted to make a baby with him, and Ewan no longer viewed her plan as the travesty he once had. He wanted children—sons to carry on after him, though a bonny little daughter with flame-colored hair would be nice, too. But he also wanted more than to simply plant his seed and be on his way. He wanted to lie beside

Brianna night upon night as she increased, rub soothing unguents into the swell of her belly, knead the ache from her back and make slow, gentle love to her. He wanted to hold his newly born child in his arms and look down into Brianna's tired but radiant face and blot the perspiration from her brow and be a husband to her in every way.

He gave her a gentle nudge. "Brie?"

"Hmmm?"

She rolled onto her side and he captured her against his chest. One arm wrapped about her waist, he bent to her ear and asked, "Do you think we might have just made a baby?"

Her eyes remained closed, but he felt her tense against him. "I don't know. We'll have to wait and see."

He stroked his hand over the flat plane of her belly. "You're so small and tight it's hard to imagine you increasing."

"All women increase no matter how large or small they start out. I may not grow big as a croft, but I'll be big enough, though I have hopes I may not waddle like a duck, at least not too badly."

The reference to his fair-day teasing was not lost on him. He grinned. "Brianna MacLeod grown so large she must sit still for once in her life. I'll need the proof of my own eyes to believe it."

Despite their banter, he felt his spirits dip. Assuming they were so blessed, he wouldn't have the chance to see her thus. By then he would be long gone, restored to his clan according to the sad bargain they'd struck. He opened his mouth to ask her to marry him again and then clamped it closed, not wanting to spoil the moment, but the unspoken words weighed like a millstone on his heart.

The damnable bargain they'd struck was proving to be a devil's pact indeed.

* * * * *

Will these two star-crossed lovers find their sexily-ever-after?
Find out in BOUND TO PLEASE by Hope Tarr,
available in July wherever Harlequin® Blaze™ books are sold.

COMING NEXT MONTH

#1519 A SOLDIER'S HOMECOMING—Rachel Lee
Conard County: The Next Generation
When he learns the truth about his father, military man Ethan Parish is determined to reunite with his long-lost family in Wyoming. On his way into town, he clashes with policewoman Connie Halloran, whose captivating beauty entices him. Together, they confront the dangers inherent in family secrets.

#1520 KILLER PASSION—Sheri WhiteFeather
Seduction Summer
Racked with guilt over his wife's murder, Agent Griffin Malone tries to get his life back on track. Enter Alicia Greco, an attractive and accomplished analyst for a travel company. The two meet and find passion, which is exactly what puts them into a serial killer's sights. Will they escape the island's curse on lovers?

#1521 SNOWBOUND WITH THE BODYGUARD—Carla Cassidy
Wild West Bodyguards
Single mom Janette Black needs to protect her baby from repeated threats by the girl's father. Fleeing for their lives, she knows bodyguard Dalton West is the only man who can help. After taking them in, they brave a snowstorm and discover a sense of home. This time, can Janette trust that she's found the perfect sanctuary...and lasting love?

#1522 DUTY TO PROTECT—Beth Cornelison
Crisis counselor Ginny West is trapped in an office fire when firefighter Riley Sinclair walks into her life. A bond forms between the two, especially when he keeps saving her from a menacing client. As danger still looms, one defining moment forces the pair to reassess their combustible relationship.

SRSCNM0608